Advance Praise for *On Grace*

"A moving and vibrant debut that packs a sweet emotional punch. You'll laugh and cry along with Grace as she treads the complicated waters of marriage, motherhood, an unexpected betrayal, and a revelation that changes everything. Susie Orman Schnall is a fresh new voice in fiction."
–Kristin Harmel, internationally bestselling author of *The Sweetness of Forgetting*

"Grace is an imperfect woman with a less-than-perfect life, but readers will find themselves drawn to her authenticity and grit."
–Colleen Oakes, bestselling author of *Elly in Bloom*

"A telling, touching exploration of modern marriage, fidelity, and friendship, Susie Orman Schnall's debut is riddled with the little truths that make up the texture of women's daily lives. Fans of Emily Giffin will relate to this engaging read."
–Beatriz Williams, internationally bestselling author of *A Hundred Summers*

"An authentic portrayal of the intricacies inherent in modern relationships. Susie Orman Schnall's debut is relatable, honest, and insightful. I look forward to seeing what's next from her."
–Emily Liebert, bestselling author of *You Knew Me When*

ON GRACE

a novel by

SUSIE ORMAN SCHNALL

SparkPress, a BookSparks imprint
A division cf SparkPoint Studio, LLC

Published by SparkPress, a BookSparks imprint,
A division of SparkPoint Studio, LLC
Tempe, Arizona, USA, 85281
www.sparkpointstudio.com

First Edition 2013
Second Edition 2014

Printed in the United States of America.

ISBN: 978-1-940716-13-8 (pbk)
ISBN: 978-1-940716-12-1 (ebk)

Cover design © Julie Metz, Ltd./metzdesign.com
Cover photo © plainpicture/Fancy Images
Formatting by Polagrus Studio

For Rick, Jason, William, and Judson

chapter one

I am not planning on waking up tomorrow and feeling *completely different*. But I'm certainly not planning to feel the same as I do today and every other day. Tomorrow when I wake up, brilliant sunlight streaming through my windows, I'll feel as if nothing can go wrong. It will be a momentous day. Sure, momentous is a big word, usually saved for things like fiftieth wedding anniversaries and retirements that come with gold watches, but I've decided that I'm going to use that word and own it. Momentous. I like the way it sounds.

Today is the last day before I start the rest of my life, because tomorrow is the first day that both of my boys will be in school all day, every day. It's been eight years since I've had my days to myself all day, every day. Eight years since I've taken my own wants and needs and put them first. I'm not one of those coddling, helicopter moms, but even us good-enough moms can't really put our own wants and needs first. At least not all day, every day.

So as I prepare for momentous, I'm getting all the last-day-of-summer stuff out of the way. Today is haircuts, prepping backpacks, and the last day of collecting colorful summer bugs in glass jars. We'll take one last carefree bike ride in flip-flops and celebrate with a final late-afternoon trip to Longford's for ice cream where we'll probably see lots of other moms who can't wait for tomorrow and lots of other kids who can.

But for now, the boys are out back playing baseball with some neighborhood friends, and I'm standing in front of the open fridge, trying to figure out what the hell to make for dinner. When my phone rings, I check the caller ID and answer excitedly.

"Hey Cam!" I practically sing into the phone.

"Hey, Grace! How's it going?"

"Going great. I really can't wait for tomorrow. I know I'm going to feel so free, and joyful, and in control of my own life," I say.

"Wow, that sounds promising! Good girl," Cameron says enthusiastically.

"One more day and then I can start getting my life back in gear."

"What exactly is out of gear?" Cameron asks.

"Well, my marriage, my stalled career, my lack of any sort of fitness, and other miscellaneous things," I tell her. "Not necessarily, but possibly, in order of importance. I kind of have a little plan formulating in the back of my mind."

"How much of this is because you're freaked out about turning forty in a few months?" Cameron asks.

"I've told you, I'm not that freaked out about forty."

"You know, Grace, you're allowed to not be excited about it."

"But I *am* excited. I see forty as more of an opportunity to regain control of my life. Sort of like New Year's Eve. But with much less champagne."

"Well, I'll toast to that," Cameron says. "And while we're toasting . . . ," she adds with an unmistakable lilt.

"What? No! What?"

"Yes!"

"Yes?"

"Seven and a half weeks officially today."

"Oh, Cameron. Congratulations! And here I was rambling on and on about me, and you had such good news."

"Grace, it's fine. Really. I called as much to tell you about me as I did to find out how your day before the big day is going."

"Well, I'm so happy for you."

"I know. Sorry I didn't tell you right away. But you know with my history and all, I just really wanted to make sure. And today is a day longer than I've ever been pregnant before. Not that I wouldn't have told you if I had miscarried again. I just had some sort of weird superstition thing going on."

"No need to apologize. I completely understand. But to make amends, will you meet me for dinner tonight for a proper celebration? Tengda at 7:30?" I ask.

"Don't you have to be home with the boys tonight? Last day of summer and all?"

"I'm taking them on a long bike ride this afternoon so they'll be tired. And they'll think it's more special anyway if Darren is in charge of bedtime. So Tengda?"

"Raw fish."

"Right, raw fish. Méli-Mélo then?"

"It's a date. And you can tell me more about your so-called plan," Cameron says.

"I will. See you later. And Cam, I'm really so happy for you. Give my love to Jack."

And with that, I do a little jig for my best friend who has been trying to get pregnant for five years. I boot up my laptop to email

Darren the good news and the heads-up that I'll be going out tonight.

As I wash the lunch dishes, I think about the part-time job I'm starting on Monday. I'm going to be the new "Family Life" columnist for the *Westchester Weekly*, our county's glossy and hip-enough attempt at *New York* magazine. Each week, I'll file a 500-word article on something new and noteworthy in the county that's perfect for families, and I can't wait to start. It's nowhere near my old salary, but it's something. Plus, this job is more about the opportunity to rediscover the woman who's been deeply buried under the labels of "wife" and "mother" for the past eight years.

I met the *Weekly*'s owner/publisher, Matthew O'Donnell, in June at a friend's beach club. He and his wife, Monique, had just moved to our neighborhood in Rye (a leafy suburb of New York City where you would be confident no one would steal your car while you leave it running to dart into the post office, but you never *would* leave it running because people would be all over you about the toxic fumes released from idling). When I told him I had been an editor at two different fitness magazines before I had my kids (when I was still, well, fit), he asked about my writing and why I wasn't still working.

I wasn't sure what was the more pleasant surprise: the fact that I was actually having a meaningful conversation with a man other than my husband (something that doesn't usually happen at these beach club gatherings where the men all gather around the bar to discuss the double S's—sports and stocks—and the women hover nearby in their strappy summer wedges to discuss the double N's—nannies and nips and tucks) or that I might have a connection at a publication I'd love to write for. And he was right, why wasn't I still working? Well, I had two really adorable answers, but they were starting school in a couple months.

So, I told him, "I put my career on hold, because I wanted to be home with my kids. But they'll both be in school full time this fall, and I'll be ready to focus on my work again."

"Grace has done an amazing job with the boys," Darren said to Matthew. "They're lucky she chose them over her career, but she's not one of those women who is going to be happy playing tennis every day while they're in school. She needs more than that."

I looked at Darren and smiled, feeling so fortunate that he was so supportive. We had talked that afternoon about how I was feeling apprehensive about getting a job. How I worried I would feel overwhelmed managing both a job and my family. I knew I would be no good at all that Superwoman stuff. But I also knew that I ached to be creative again. To use my brain for more than just organizing soccer practice carpool schedules and finding innovative ways to sneak green leafy vegetables into mini meat loaves.

Matthew and I talked for a while, and I told him I thought the magazine could use a section dedicated to things families could do together, besides just the events listings in the back. When he agreed with me and said that was something his editorial department had been considering, I boldly—with a little help from my Riesling—suggested that maybe *I* could be the one to write it. A few phone calls, emailed clips, meetings with the editor, and trial columns later, and I was hired as the "Family Life" columnist for the *Westchester Weekly*.

I hear my cell phone ring so I wipe my hands on a dish towel and rush to find my phone in my disorganized purse. I find it just as the call is about to go to voicemail, notice it's an unknown caller, and quickly touch the screen to answer.

"Hello?" I say, completely unprepared for what's about to come.

chapter two

"Is this Grace May?"

"Yes."

"Hi, Grace, this is Margaret White from the *Westchester Weekly*."

"Oh, hi," I say excitedly. "Did you receive the signed copy of my contract?" I had met with Margaret, the somewhat menacing but quite beautiful director of HR, once at the *Weekly*'s offices. I sit down at my desk in the kitchen and grab a pen to jot down any first-day info that I'll need for next week.

"I did. That's not why I'm calling," she says, sounding not quite so menacing.

"Oh?"

"Grace, I'm so sorry to have to tell you this, but the magazine is closing, which, of course, means we no longer have a job for you."

"Closing?" I ask, realizing that my voice has raised an octave in panic and that I'm repeatedly stabbing the notepad with my pen. "Why?"

"I've been instructed by our lawyers not to explain why. Let's just say there's been a change in ownership, and the new owner has decided to cease operation of the *Weekly*."

And with that, she abruptly ends the conversation. And my nascent career.

What the hell?

I wake up my laptop and quickly type in the URL for the *Westchester Weekly*.

The site loads, but instead of the usual homepage, a tombstone of sorts announces, "We regret to inform you that despite fourteen successful years as a trusted resource for Westchester residents and businesses, we will no longer be publishing the *Westchester Weekly*. Our sincere thanks to our subscribers, advertisers, and friends who have supported us through the years. We will miss you."

Seriously? This is a moment when I would usually cry. I've never been one to hold my emotions in check successfully. I am seriously bummed. I had been envisioning that job as a kind of salvation for me. A huge hand lifting me out from underneath all that had been burying me, holding me up in the sky, proclaiming me a productive working woman once again.

My first thought is to find out why the magazine is closing so suddenly. All signs pointed to them doing well financially: Their last issue had closed with the highest number of ad pages in the publication's history, they had just hired me and an ad sales rep, and the publisher had just taken his senior executives on an expensive boondoggle at a fancy inn in the Hudson Valley. *Why would he sell?* It just doesn't make sense. I shoot a quick email to Darren with a "Check this out!" subject line and a quick rundown of what just happened along with a link to the *Weekly*'s site.

More pressing, however, is the fact that I am now jobless. True, and most importantly, no one will be going hungry at my house tonight or any other night because I have no job. And does it still count as losing my job if I had never started it in the first place? The concept of my being blessed that I don't *have* to work is absolutely not lost on me. I thank my lucky stars every day—well, almost every day, kind of like how I floss *every* day—that Darren does well enough that I don't have to work in order for us to make ends meet. Working is a choice I make to satisfy a need within myself, not to satisfy a mortgage payment.

Sometimes I feel guilty for not working outside the home, for not struggling when so many are. Cameron always says that's no reason for me not to enjoy my own life. That most of those women would trade places with me in a heartbeat. That, in a sense, I owe it to them to enjoy myself every day instead of feeling badly that I'm not them. And that my worrying about it doesn't change the lot for anyone else.

I'm crushed, but maybe this job loss is a sign. Maybe I'm supposed to be a stay-at-home mom after all. Maybe the "everything happens for a reason" adage holds true in this scenario. I'm just not so sure.

Later, after our bike ride and ice cream cones, more baseball, and an early dinner and baths for the boys, they watch *SpongeBob* in my bedroom while I finish getting ready for dinner with Cameron.

"Hey," Darren says as he walks in at 7:15, his voice unusually quiet.

"Hey, I'm off, I'm late. I have to be at Méli-Mélo at 7:30," I say, giving him a quick kiss before I stuff my phone in my purse, grab my sweater, and give him the hospital-nurses-changing-shifts download. "The boys already ate, and your dinner's in the fridge. They had ice cream this afternoon, so please don't give them a treat even if they beg, and please make sure they brush their teeth and that James puts on a Pull-Up before he goes to sleep. He wet his bed last night, so I just want to do the Pull-Ups for a few days."

"Okay, got it." He smiles without meeting my eyes.

"Oh, did you get my email that I lost my job?" I ask him, as I start to walk out of the room.

"Yeah, that's a bummer," he says, untying his tie. "I'm really sorry about that." He looks at me, "Sorry I didn't email you back. It was a crazy day."

"That's okay. I understand," I say. "Alright, love you, see you later."

"I love you, too. Tell Cam congrats," he says and finishes taking off his tie.

During the ten-minute drive to Greenwich, I sing along to P!nk and wonder if that was a strange interaction or if I'm just imagining it. I've been questioning a lot about our relationship lately. I've tried to analyze it from every perspective. It comes down to the simple fact that we're just not connecting.

I keep picturing a trapeze act. Darren and I are both up there swinging from our bars, acting as if the show is going according to plan. But every time I reach to grab his feet with my hands, I'm a second too late. I don't fall into the net, I just keep swinging, with a smile on my face and my sparkly leotard just so, waiting for the next opportunity to try and grab his feet again, so we can soar together. This image is totally at odds with how I've always known our marriage to be. We've got one of those marriages people gush over. Compared with a lot of our married friends, we actually still like each other as people. We hold hands in public because we want to. We drink wine in bed and giggle over *Curb Your Enthusiasm* repeats. We kiss before sex.

Darren and I met at Cameron and Jack's low-key-yet-elegant New York City wedding. I was a bridesmaid, and Darren was at the table for Jack's childhood friends that the other bridesmaids and I scoped out because all the ushers were married. Jenny Simms and I both called dibs on the handsome, tall guy with the dark hair and ridiculously blue eyes, but I brought her a lemon drop shot, and she let me have him. Turns out, she had her eyes on Jack's cousin anyway.

Darren noticed the shot-drinking at the bar and, with the perfect combination of confidence and shyness, approached us, asking if we were up for another. I caught my breath as I saw him up close. I was smitten. When the bartender presented a tray of tequila shots, I let out one of my deep, raspy laughs. Darren told me later, while we danced to a slow song and he stared at me with those gorgeous blue eyes, that he had never heard a woman with quite so sexy a laugh. And he was smitten, too. Neither of us had any interest in dating anyone else from that night forward, we got married a year and a half later, and we've had an excellent run of it ever since.

We've spent our marriage contentedly bonding over things we both love—Judd Apatow movies, authentic Chinatown dim sum, Coldplay, modernist architecture—and things we both hate—films with subtitles, pretentious restaurants, electronic music, the circus. He respects the things that *I* love—Nora Ephron movies, Jane Austen and Nicholas Sparks, red velvet cupcakes, Indigo Girls— and, in return, I tolerate the things that *he* loves—Coen brothers' movies, Stephen King and Michael Lewis, pork rinds (*pork rinds!*), Shania Twain. Now ten years, a suburban mortgage, two children, and countless deep, raspy laughs later, here we are. Disconnected. Over all the normal stuff.

I open the door to Méli-Mélo and see Cameron waiting for me at our favorite corner table at this unassuming Greenwich Avenue cafe. The Avenue, as it's referred to, is the long tree-lined thoroughfare in the heart of this chic town in lower Connecticut, right on the Westchester border, and home to a perfect combination of big stores (Saks and Apple), small boutiques, hip restaurants, and other town necessities such as banks, newsstands, and shoe repair shops. When Cameron sees me, she unfurls her long, athletic legs from under the table and stands to give me a huge hug.

chapter three

"You are glowing!" I say excitedly, admiring her rosy cheeks and bright golden eyes. Cameron has been glowing since the day I met her freshman year at the University of Pennsylvania. Our rooms were three doors apart in the Butcher-Speakman dorm in Penn's legendary and architecturally stunning quad. Unfortunately, our hall was known mostly for its abundance of rowdy football players (which turned out to be good) and architecturally challenged unrenovated rooms (which turned out to be not so bad).

Raised on a farm in Maine, Cameron arrived at our first hall meeting looking like a *Seventeen* magazine model. We became fast friends when we were the only two girls who voted for "cheese steaks and a movie" instead of "private tour of the university art museum" as the first hall activity. And as we got to know each other, I realized her looks were just an accessory to her brilliant mind and playful personality. She's always been a guy's girl, preferring sports bars over Sephora, *Die Hard* over *Dirty Dancing*, snowboarding over suntanning. But we connected that semester, and she's been Debbie Boone-ing my life ever since (note obscure reference to 1977 saccharine hit "You Light Up My Life").

"Why, thank you," she purrs, twisting her long, chestnut hair into a bun without using a ponytail holder.

"So, do you feel any differently?" I ask.

"My boobs kill. And that has never happened any of the other times I've been pregnant. And they're enormous. Too bad for Jack, though; I'm denying access because they hurt so much," she says with a smile.

The waitress brings our menus and without even glancing at them, we tell her we're ready to order: broccoli soup to start, chicken Caesar salad (no raw eggs in the dressing) for Cameron, and a prosciutto and mozzarella crepe for me. It is a Tuesday night, so Méli-Mélo isn't as crowded as it usually is during weekday lunches and weekend dinners. It's always been my and Cameron's favorite local spot as much for its delicious food, good prices, and energetic buzz as for the eye candy of the French chef Cedric presiding over the open kitchen.

"And how about emotionally?" I ask, putting my napkin on my lap and taking a sip of water.

"I really hope I can carry to term this time, Grace. I'm really scared. I want this baby more than absolutely anything in the world," she says with fierce desperation in her voice.

"I know you do. I feel good about it this time though, Cam. I think this is *the* baby. This time it's going to be different. And a year from now you'll be telling me your boobs hurt for an entirely different reason. And chances are, Jack won't want to go anywhere near those lactating beasts."

"Well, I'll toast to that." And with that, we clink water glasses and toast to placentas, nursing bras, and hemorrhoid pads, laughing hysterically and completely oblivious to the glaring eyes of nearby patrons.

After we finish our broccoli soup, Cameron turns the conversation to my plan.

"It just hit its first official snag," I say dejectedly.

"What happened?"

I tell her about the phone call from Margaret White and my realization that maybe this is all for the best.

"But," I say flip-flopping, "to be completely honest, I'm not sure that now my kids are in school I'll be happy being a stay-at-home mom anymore. I just feel buried. What is my identity? I'm a mom. I'm Darren's wife. I'm the smiling volunteer at school. And there's nothing wrong with those things. But I want to be more. I want to have a purpose that society respects and that comes with a paycheck."

"But you love being a mom. And it *is* respected by society. And why, for heaven's sake, on the brink of forty, do you still care what other people think of you?" Cameron asks in an exasperated voice as the waitress brings our entrees.

"I don't know why I do. I just do. I can't help it. And to answer your first question, of course I love being a mom. But that has nothing to do with it. I can't *just* be a mom anymore. It's time for more. I've been doing this mom thing for eight years. I miss the me I used to be."

"I wish you would just be more confident and not compare yourself to everyone else in the world. Just be who you want to be."

"I don't even know who that is anymore," I say. "As soon as I had kids, my entire identity as I'd known it disappeared."

"What do you mean?" Cameron asks.

"Do you remember the old me? The overachieving, confident, fashionably dressed, fit, extremely organized career woman who could write a brilliant 3,000-word article, run five miles, and throw a dinner party all in one day? Without getting frazzled? All with the caffeine equivalent of one green tea?"

"Yes, I remember her," Cameron laughs.

"Well, she's long gone. She's been replaced by someone who can barely write a shopping list, let alone an article. And I need at least three cups of coffee just to get through produce."

"You are way too hard on yourself, Grace. You do so much!" Cameron says.

"Did you read the 'Style' section of the *Times* last week?" I ask and continue without waiting for an answer. "They profiled women who are 'doing it all.' They had these women with three and four kids who have full-time jobs as management consultants or bond traders, and they also run charities and wear Prada. Size two Prada. Why can these women do it all, and I get overwhelmed organizing a cheese board?"

"First of all, the female editors profile these women to make *themselves* feel better, because *they* left their *own* kids home with a nanny. If they featured all the stay-at-home moms and how wonderful their children are turning out it would be cognitive dissonance for them. Plus, Grace, everything's edited to make it sound better. They clearly have left out the parts where the women miss their kids' birthdays because they are making 'very important presentations to very important clients,' where the women cry because it's just all too much, where the women get divorced because their husbands never get laid."

"True, true," I say, laughing. "I know the grass always seems greener. I have to realize it's probably not as rosy as the article professes it to be. But it would be nice to see women like myself represented respectfully sometimes. The only models of stay-at-home moms are in magazines about how to make the most ghoulish Halloween door wreath on the block."

"Fair enough. So let's assume you do want to find another job, does your plan have a provision for that?"

"Ha ha, no. But I'm just gonna keep my ears open. I'm planning on going on Craigslist, Mediabistro, and a couple other sites to see what kind of freelance writing jobs are out there," I say as I practically moan over how delicious my cheesy, gooey crepe is. "By the way, if any of your patients' parents let slip during an exam that they're looking to hire a writer, be sure to give them my name."

Cameron is a pediatrician. After we graduated from Penn, she continued on to Harvard Med and then to Boston Children's Hospital for her residency. Now in private practice on the Upper East Side of Manhattan—I've always liked the way that sounded—she is the most sought-out pediatrician of the Park Avenue mommy set. They love her bedside manner, they love that she has separate well- and sick-visit waiting rooms with BPA-free toys, and they love that despite her long hours she still manages to work in either Louboutins or Jimmy Choos. It makes them feel like she understands them better.

"Okay, Grace, but I can't really see that happening. 'Oh, Dr. Stevens,'" Cameron says in her best posh New York City lady voice, "'Tommy was up all night crying and complaining that his ears hurt. By the way, do you happen to know any talented writers? My law firm sure could use one.'"

"Point taken, Dr. Stevens," I laugh.

Then Cameron asks me what's going on with Darren. It's almost as upsetting to her as it is to me that there could be tension brewing in my marriage. Considering Jack and Darren have been friends since they were little and Cameron and I have been friends since college, the four of us are incredibly compatible and formed a tight bond soon after Darren and I began dating. We've spent holidays, vacations, and weekends together for years, and we all have strong relationships with each other. Cameron and Jack even moved up to Westchester shortly after we did, an unusual move for a couple with no kids and jobs in the city. I like to think they just missed us too much, but in reality, they had just had enough of city life and were ready to become homeowners. And parents.

"The good news is how bad can my marriage be if I still want to sleep in the same bed as him?" I ask, trying to add a little humor into a topic that has been making me anxious for weeks.

"I guess it depends on what you mean by *sleep*," she replies. "The kind punctuated by snores or by moans?"

"Snores," I say guiltily.

"Well, I guess there's some hope left if the thought of him in your bed doesn't repulse you. But it sure would help things along if you actually had sex once in a while, Grace."

"I do. We do. So I can't blame our state of blahness only on sex, because it's not like we never have it. Although we should have it more. But that's all part of the plan."

"Your plan stipulates sex?"

"Yes, but let me explain more before I get to that. So, I don't blame it on sex, or lack thereof, and I don't blame it on communication. If there's something we're good at, it's communicating. We don't have huge knockout fights. We still talk. It just seems like there's this foggy cloud between us, and the sun just can't break through. I know it's nothing we can't get over, but it's still upsetting," I explain as the waitress clears our plates and hands us dessert menus.

"We'll share a Nutella and banana crepe," we say at the same time, laughing.

"The first part of the marriage portion of the plan is all based on my sex-for-intimacy theory."

"Go on," Cameron says, tilting her head suspiciously.

"Men feel connected to women through sex. Women feel connected to men through talking. Cuddling and sex, too, yes. But for most women, the emotional connection is more important. Now, if I want Darren to give me the connection I want, it's only fair that I give him the connection he wants, right? Hence, my plan is to give it up more."

"Sounds simple, to the point, and, Grace, you might actually like it."

"I just might."

As we eat our dessert, Cameron and I discuss her job and the baby and how tragically ironic it is that she's been caring for so many children for so many years, yet has been unable to have a child of her own.

"The pangs I feel every time a new mother brings her baby in for his or her first visit are different now. I used to feel wistful and maybe a bit resentful, however horrible that sounds, but now I just feel excited," Cameron says as she snags the last bite of crepe.

"Speaking of pangs," I say in a seductive voice, jutting my left shoulder forward, "I have to go home and put the plan into action, if you know what I mean."

"Check, please!" we both say, erupting into laughter once again.

When I get home from Méli-Mélo, Darren is in bed watching a Yankees game. I give him a kiss hello, and he asks me how dinner was.

"Great," I tell him as I go into the bathroom to wash up and change into a little something-something that has been collecting dust in my underwear drawer. When I saunter back into the bedroom, with my best hitherto look and sexy strut, I find Darren sitting up, crying.

chapter four

"What is it?" I ask, alarmed. I get into bed and take hold of his hands. "Are the boys okay?"

"Yes, sorry, the boys are fine. I didn't mean to scare you. I just need to talk to you about something."

I have seen Darren cry just two times. The first was at our wedding. We wrote our own vows, and after he read his, beautiful words from a man who creates spreadsheets for a living, he started to cry, the emotion and love hitting him, he would tell me later, like a tidal wave. The second time was a week after our oldest son Henry was born when we found ourselves back in the hospital for three days while Henry received phototherapy treatment for jaundice. He was so tiny, and we were so scared. The enormity of that situation reduced Darren into a state I had never seen before. It moved me tremendously.

As Darren turns to me, holding my hands tightly, and my stomach begins to tighten, thoughts stream through my head. *Oh my God, this must be serious. Why is he being so serious? Is someone sick? Is it one of our parents? Did my dad have another heart attack?*

Are we moving to London? That's been a possibility. Maybe Darren found out today that we are.

"Gracie," Darren whispers, snapping me out of my thoughts by calling me a name he saves only for really, really good things or really, really bad things. Using the tears as a clue, I deduce it's the latter. "I don't know how to tell you this."

"What?" I mouth, the word getting caught in my throat.

He takes a deep breath and looks down at my hands, which are still holding his. "In July, when I was in Chicago for that telecom conference—"

And then I know. He cheated on me.

"I—"

"No," I say. "You did not." I drop his hands and forget to breathe.

"Gracie, I'm so sorry." He grabs my hands and looks at me pleadingly, his blue eyes glowing as the light from the television screen reflects off his tears. "I don't even know what to say. It's such a cliché. It didn't mean anything. I had too much to drink. I'm so sorry."

I loosen my hands from his grip and sit back on my pillows. I suddenly remember that I'm wearing lingerie, and I get under the covers self-consciously. I feel every emotion at once: anger, sadness, fear, humiliation, and shock. But instead of feeling them all distinctly, I just feel calm, like the colors of the rainbow mixing together to make white.

"Is she someone you work with?" I ask without emotion, ever the information-gatherer.

"No. She—" he turns his face and exhales loudly, and I know this is killing him. But I ask him to go on, because I don't really care how he feels. "She was a waitress at the hotel bar."

"A cocktail waitress?" I say, disgust in my voice. "And?"

"It meant nothing. I'm so sorry I did this to you. I wish more than anything I could take it back. I fucked up. I can't believe that I'm actually sitting here telling you I had an affair because it's not something I ever, *ever* thought I would be capable of doing."

Neither did I. "Go on. I need to know what happened."

He takes a deep breath and stares blankly at the television. He speaks quickly, as if the words are painful as they exit his mouth. "I was with John and Craig, and we had been at presentations all day, and we were drinking, and John kept ordering tequila shots and flirting with the waitress, so she was spending a lot of time talking with us." He stops and looks at me with an expression that means he's trying to figure out if I'm going to make him tell the whole story.

"And?"

"I kept doing the shots because it was the last day of the conference, and I just wanted to let off steam with my friends. Next thing I knew, she was coming up in the elevator with John and me. John had invited her to his room."

"What happened to Craig?"

"He'd gone upstairs already."

"I'm sure Elisabeth will be happy to hear that story one day," I say, thinking of Craig's pregnant wife. Darren has worked with John and Craig for years. They were all in each other's weddings. John and Amy got divorced last year. "And?" I say, allowing the torture to continue for both of us.

"John started to get all sweaty and said he was going to be sick and ran to his room. The woman—"

"What was her name?"

"Gracie." He looks at me, his eyes begging.

"What was her name?" I repeat, staring at him and trying to remember to breathe.

"Tina."

"Continue."

"We were laughing at John, and I put my key card in the slot and told her it was nice to meet her and good night. She pulled me toward her and kissed me, and then one thing led to another, and we were in my room." His voice is laced with shame. As it should be. He stares out the window in the blackness. The same blackness I feel in my heart, pounding. Pounding.

"Did you wear a condom?"

"Yes."

"You had a condom?"

"No, she did."

"Did she sleep in your room?"

"No. She left right after."

"Did you tell John and Craig?"

"No. I haven't told anyone."

I sit quietly for a few minutes, trying to think of anything else I need to know right now. My brain feels like a traffic jam—I hear lots of loud noises, but nothing is moving forward. I realize that I need to be alone; I need to think. The thought of him anywhere near me is repulsive. "I think you should sleep in the guest room." I mean to say that with conviction. It sounds more like resignation.

"Gracie, I'm so sorry. I love you so much. I realize that I've put our marriage, our family in jeopardy. Please forgive me. It meant nothing. You and the boys are everything to me. You are my entire life." He stands up, runs his hands through his hair, and wipes his eyes. He looks pathetic.

"I just can't have you near me right now," I say, as the tears finally start to flow.

"I know. I'm so sorry. I understand. But please, can we talk about this tomorrow? I'll stay home from work. I will do anything to make you understand that this was nothing."

"Don't stay home. I need to think. We'll talk tomorrow night. But I think you should leave for work before the boys and I get up." I turn to my side and bring the covers up to my face. Once Darren collects his clothes and toothbrush for the next day and I hear him shut the door to the guest room, I get out of bed and practically rip off the ridiculous getup I have on. I change into my most comfy pajamas, turn off the TV, grab a box of tissues, and get back into bed. My thoughts are racing, and I wonder if I will sleep at all. I try to remember the different calming breaths I had read about in a magazine once, but I can't stop the thoughts. They keep me up late into the night, but eventually the exhaustion of sorting out the rest of my life puts me to sleep.

The morning after my dad had his first heart attack, I remember waking up with a weird knot in my stomach. It took me a moment to figure out why I felt so strange, and then I remembered my dad was in the hospital. I have the same experience this morning as I wake up to my alarm, and then I remember. Darren cheated on me.

chapter five

I drag myself out of bed, feeling absolutely nothing like I'd planned to feel when today was still supposed to be the first day of the rest of my life. This is about as far from momentous as I can imagine. This is like if momentous were the North Pole, I'm hanging out with the emperor penguins in Antarctica.

I wash up, and walk down the hall toward the guest room. I'm relieved to see Darren is not there, and I'm surprised to see that, though it's not going to win any awards in an army barracks contest, the bed is made. Darren has never made a bed in the twelve years that I've known him.

I wake up the boys, trying to be cheerful about the first day of school, and then I make my way downstairs. I realize that I have to push all thoughts of last night aside and deal with getting the boys off to school. I will have plenty of time today to think.

"Please stop telling your brother that his scrambled eggs are dead baby chicks," I implore Henry, as I quickly spread butter and jelly on two pieces of toast.

"But they *are* dead baby chicks, Mom," Henry protests. "Last year on the field trip to the nature center, I saw the mother chickens pooping out the eggs in their nests. So the eggs are their babies, and when you cooked them you killed them, so now we're eating dead baby chicks," he says with all the authority of a precocious eight-year-old, pushing his gorgeous blond curls out of his eyes.

"They're not actually dead baby chicks, and they're not pooped out. They're laid. And they're not fertilized, so they were never going to become chickens," I say, trying to be patient.

"Well, they taste good, so let's eat them anyway," Henry says.

And with that, my two boys Henry and James (we just liked those names; it had nothing to do with any affinity toward a certain literary realist) dig into their scrambled eggs and whole-wheat toast with butter and jelly. *A nutritious enough first-day-of-school breakfast*, I think as I gulp my coffee, willing it to work. I cut up an apple and a banana, quickly arrange them on a plate, and slide it between the two vegans-in-training who are propped on the navy and white bistro barstools at our kitchen island.

"Good job with the shoes, James," I say to my little guy, noticing that he has put on his sneakers all by himself. *Wrong feet, but it's a start.* "Henry, remember what we talked about last night? That we're going to try to have better morning routines for school, to make getting out of the house easier this year? And how you'd put your shoes on *before* you sat down to breakfast?"

"I forgot. And you always say no shoes in the kitchen, so James is actually in trouble."

"He's not in trouble," I say, glancing at James who looks scared, his big blue eyes opened wide. I'm relieved that my voice is still calm despite the fact that we only have nine minutes left before we have to rush to the bus. "It's okay to break that rule in the morning, because I need you guys to be ready to go as soon as you finish breakfast."

"I'm so happy for school today, Mommy!" James says.

"I know, buddy. You are the kindergarten man!"

"Kindergarten's easy. It's for babies," Henry says, sneering at his little brother.

"It's not easy when you're the one in kindergarten," I say lightly. "And there are no babies in this house."

"No more babies!" the boys shout in unison, mimicking my familiar refrain whenever someone mentions we should have another baby. Two is just about all I can handle right now.

As the boys eat, I try to ignore the awful images of Darren's dalliance going through my brain. I implore myself to focus. *Just get them on the bus. Then you can collapse into a puddle.* I take a deep breath and lean the backpacks (camouflage for Henry, SpongeBob for James) against the door and check, for the third time, to make sure their necessary first-day-of-school forms are inside, including the health forms that I forgot to send before the deadline. All there. Ditto for the school supplies and mid-morning snack (packaged and nut-free). Relieved not to have to worry yet about jackets, mittens, and hats, I return to the kitchen to move things along.

"James's fish isn't dead yet, so you have to feed him, Mom," Henry reminds me.

"His *name* is Little Blue!" James insists, hands on hips and eyebrows scrunched, as I drop a few pellets into the tank. *Damn fish won't die.*

When the boys finish eating, Henry puts on his socks and shoes while I quickly brush James's teeth and load the dishwasher. I know what's coming next even as I try to brace myself and remain calm. I have ten months of school mornings until summer vacation, and I had pledged to make it through at least the first one without yelling.

"None of these socks feel good," Henry whines from the mudroom.

I feel the familiar knots starting in my stomach as a trickle of sweat makes its way down my back. I lower James from the step stool and stand in front of Henry. "But we tried on all these socks, Hen. You said you'd wear them."

"But they don't feee-eee-uhhll good," he replies, trying my patience.

"Well, you're just going to have to wear them," I say in a calm voice that surprises us all. The boys are no strangers to my frustrated urgency when it comes to getting out of the house on time. "We don't have time for this today. Just put them on and deal with it. Once you get your shoes on, you won't notice the socks anymore." This tactic has worked in the past, so I pray to the mothering gods that they won't disappoint.

"Fine."

Victory.

"Okay, now put your arms around each other. I need a first-day-of-school shot," I say, as I rally the boys and search for my phone in my purse. "Henry, don't make rabbit ears over James's head, please," I beg as the shutter clicks and captures Henry smirking and James looking behind his head to see what the hell's going on back there. It'll have to do. The bus is about to arrive. I sigh, "Come on guys, let's go."

The good thing about having my neighborhood's bus stop right in front of my house is that I have until the last possible moment before we have to rush out the door. And, on the days that I don't feel like engaging with the likes of Lorna Smithson et al., I can just send the boys on their way and wave from the house until the bus door closes. This being the first day, I brave the dewy grass in my slippers and join the other Central Casting suburban mothers and kids on my lawn.

Which brings me to the bad thing about having my neighborhood's bus stop right in front of my house: The likes of Lorna Smithson et al. feel some inalienable right to comment on the state of my grass, and I can always be sure that as the bus pulls away I will find sundry breakfast food wrappers from some of the neighborhood children littering my lawn, especially those for strawberry Pop-Tarts, which I know for a fact don't belong to Lorna Smithson's triplets, because I know for a fact she feeds them only steel-cut oats with organic blueberries and a kale shake. She just told me so. And how that woman gets those fifth graders to dress in identical outfits for the first day of school and actually have smiles on their faces, I will *never* know.

"Did you get a good first-day-of-school photo?" Lorna asks me, her monstrous Nikon hanging from her neck as her pink Prada scrunch ballet flats sink into the wet grass. She cornered me, despite my attempts not to make eye contact with anyone. *Just deal, Grace. A few more minutes.*

"Not so good. But good enough. I just like to capture the *essence* of the boys. I've always felt that the super-posed shots feel too forced," I tell her, crossing my arms in front of my chest so no one will be able to tell I'm not wearing a bra under my threadbare U2 *Joshua Tree* concert T-shirt. I'm convinced she can read in my eyes that my husband cheated on me.

"Mmmm."

Condescending bitch.

Lorna continues, "I actually have all our first-day-of-school photos framed in the hallway outside the triplets' rooms in shadow boxes with each year labeled and containing each child's photos from school, soccer, and Little League and/or hip hop. It's such a nice way of preserving the memories. You really should come over for coffee one day, Grace. You haven't been over since we finished the reno on the kitchen."

"I'd love to, Lorna," I lie, wondering how she has time in the morning to apply blush and her trademark red lipstick, put on a coordinated outfit including a belt, *and* prepare whole grains. Saved by the bus.

"Bye, guys," I say cheerfully to Henry and James, giving them big wet ones and giant hugs that swallow them whole. "You'll do great, James. I'll be right here after school. I love you!"

"Love you too, Mom," they say as they charge confidently onto the bus.

Love that. Love that they're independent and don't give a second thought to leaving me and going off into the world. Through the windows, I proudly watch Henry lead James into a seat and help him with his seatbelt.

"I thought the kindergarten moms were supposed to bring the kids into school on the first day?" Lorna asks accusingly, interrupting my thoughts.

"It's optional this year. Plus, James has been at the school so many times, and he has Henry with him on the bus and to walk him into school. He'll be fine."

"Oh. You must be so sad your youngest is starting kindergarten," she says in a baby voice. "I couldn't get Lisa Millerton off the phone last night. Poor thing was hysterical that Maddie was starting school."

When Henry started kindergarten, I walked him into school the first day, James on my hip, Henry's tiny clammy hand in mine. All the moms were swirling around, putting backpacks into cubbies, posing their kids for photos, greeting the teacher, the works. Like a seething tornado of attentive mothering. And most of the moms were crying. I tried. Honestly. I tried to cry. And considering I am ridiculously sentimental and cry at Harry Chapin songs and weight-loss reality television, I was surprised my eyes remained dry.

I wanted to feel what those other moms were feeling. That powerful sense of loss, of transition, of crossing that line from being in charge of the needs of your child 24/7 to relinquishing that responsibility to someone named Miss Marsha. But I just felt joy. Joy that I had raised my baby, that he was ready for this next step in life, that I was closer to regaining time for myself. Still, I felt sad that I couldn't cry. That I was denying myself a universal rite of motherhood. And, of course, me being me, I thought I was doing it wrong.

"No, I wouldn't call it sad. Maybe sentimental or nostalgic, but not sad. He's ready. And I'm certainly ready to have time for myself," I respond confidently to Lorna.

"That's great, Grace. I remember when the triplets started kindergarten, and it freed up my days. That's when I got involved in the hospital. Let me know if you're interested in working on the fall fundraiser. We need all the help we can get," Lorna says cheerfully.

"Thanks, I'll let you know," I say as the bus pulls away, and I pick up a few wrappers and go back into the house. I immediately start to cry as I release the intense tension I have been holding in all morning trying to act normally in front of the boys. Yesterday, when I thought of what that delicious moment would be like after the bus pulled away, I pictured myself skipping back into the house giggling, indulging in a bit of crazy dancing while singing George Michael's "Freedom," luxuriating in the feeling that I had no lunches to make, no appointments to get to, no mommy-and-me classes to slog through. I never pictured feeling the way I do now.

chapter six

I pour another cup of coffee and think about what I should do next. When I lived in the city, I would run around the reservoir several times a week. That is where I always got my best thinking done. I would come up with the perfect lead for an article I was writing, the perfect wording for a complicated email I needed to send my boss, the perfect idea for my and Darren's next travel adventure.

I decide to do a trail run at the preserve where Cameron and I hike every Saturday morning. My neighborhood is perfect for running, but I don't feel like having to stop and chat if my neighbors are outside. Even having to smile and wave would be too difficult for me right now. I'd heard your typical cautionary tales about the preserve and have never gone there alone, despite the fact that none of the stories had ever been proven. But I just don't care right now. I'm playing the odds. What are the chances I'll get raped the day after I find out my husband cheated on me? Plus, that preserve is my favorite place. Being in nature soothes me. I need soothing.

I'm happy to see the parking lot is crowded. There will be other people to hear me scream when the rapist attacks. That is, unless he gags me with a towel. These are the things that go through my mind. Constantly. Always the worst-case scenario. It happens when anyone I love gets on an airplane, when my kids go to a drop-off birthday party at one of those wretched indoor play spaces that I'm convinced hire child molesters, when the technician looks at me funny during a mammogram. And now it will happen whenever Darren goes on a business trip.

I hold my keys in my fist and keep one key sticking out between my fingers to use as a weapon should the need arise. I start running, my blonde ponytail bobbing purposefully, and the world seems to fall away. I'm left with my thoughts. My brain is not the shy, silent type. No, it's constantly churning, leading me to overanalyze, overspeculate, and overthink. At first, my thoughts are all swirling, and then I start to categorize them.

My first thoughts are purely about the physical contact he had with another woman; that disgusts me. I picture him kissing someone else, and my stomach clenches. In that picture, Tina, or as I've come to call her, The Chicago Husband Bandit, is in her late 20s and tall with long, brassy blonde hair, rust-colored lipstick, and eyebrows that she plucked too much and now draws in with a brown pencil. She's wearing a tight, black tank top with a plunging neckline that reveals her voluptuous breasts, a tight, black skirt, and heels that are sensible enough so she can work in them all night, but sexy enough to ensure good tips. I wonder if I really want to know what she looks like. I have a short fantasy about looking up the hotel name on Darren's corporate AmEx statement, flying to Chicago, and sitting in the bar to watch The Bandit in action. I'm not crazy enough to picture myself with a gun in that fantasy. I don't really blame her. I only blame Darren. He let this happen.

I start the first uphill part of the trail, and my heart starts beating hard. I haven't run in a while, and I'm not really in good-enough shape to do three miles. The anger fuels me, and I power ahead. I can't believe I've been so certain over the years that Darren would never cheat. That he would stick to his promise. Men cheat. It's what they do. I think of the politicians I've seen on TV over and over again: the man shamefully announcing his transgression into a microphone, the wife in her Chanel jacket even more shamefully standing off to the side wondering what her mother must be thinking, how her kids will get teased at school the next day, and how unbelievably fucking inadequate and humiliated she feels. I just never thought it would be Darren. I imagine most women think it will never happen to them. I can't imagine any woman thinking it *could* happen, or why would you marry the bastard in the first place?

But it's just so not Darren. So I wonder if I should blame myself. If things had been better between us lately, if we had been having more sex, if I had a better body, then would he still have been tempted by the big-boob Bandit? He said it didn't mean anything. I completely believe that. I have no doubt about that, actually. I do know that he regrets it. That he wishes more than anything that it didn't happen. But it did. I pass two women walking their dogs and realize the dogs can maul the rapist. I loosen my ersatz brass knuckles.

Then I start thinking that if it could happen once, it could happen again. Maybe this isn't even the first time. Maybe it's happened before, but for some reason the guilt finally got him and so he's admitting this one. Darren travels a lot for his job. He's had lots of opportunities. And he often travels with John. All of our

35

friends know that since John got divorced—because Amy cheated with her tennis instructor—he's been like a seventeen-year-old boy whose hormones just kicked in.

As I approach the next hill, I'm in a groove, and I resolve to start a regular running regimen again. It was part of my plan anyway, but I forgot how good the endorphins feel. Speaking of my plan, I realize this changes everything. All the energy I was planning on investing in reconnecting with Darren will now have to go into salvaging my marriage. Or not. At this point, I basically have two options. Option one is to get divorced and option two is not to.

There are loads of reasons why I should get a divorce. I tick them off in my mind: 1) How could I ever trust him again? 2) How much could he really love and respect me if he let something like this happen? 3) If he loved and respected me more, he wouldn't have allowed this to happen, right? 4) Will I ever be able to be intimate with him again?

On the flip side, there are loads of reasons why I shouldn't get divorced: 1) What we have (had?) is so solid. 2) I don't want to foist a divorce on my boys; I know they won't be the only kids in the world growing up with divorced parents, but having grown up that way myself, I know it's not ideal, and if I can avoid it, I'm going to try. 3) While I'm not defending his actions, I know that biologically, anthropologically, there's a difference between men and women when it comes to sexual needs. I did read *The Clan of the Cave Bear,* after all. I know that it is possible for a man to be unfaithful (I'm talking a one-time drunken sexual encounter, not a long-term emotional affair—completely different animals) and have it not mean anything. 4) I believe that Darren regrets this, loves me, and is hoping that I'll forgive him. At least I think I do.

I don't want to get divorced. I'm not convinced I want to be married to Darren right now, but I know I don't want to be divorced from him. I don't really know what I want. I'm still completely shocked that I am even in this situation. I can't believe it happened to me. How cliché am I?

I see the parking lot ahead, and I sprint, amazed at how much energy I have. I haven't done more than a mile on a treadmill in over a year. I know my quads will be paying for this burst of exuberance tomorrow, but I don't care. I don't really care about anything.

I mainly keep thinking that I don't know what I'm supposed to do next. Am I supposed to call my mom? Cameron? Am I supposed to call Darren and tell him off? Or tell him to come home? Or tell him never to come home again? Am I supposed to insist he sleep in the guest room? Or move out? Am I supposed to be consumed with anger? With sadness? With regret? Or am I not supposed to feel much of anything at all because I'm supposed to be in shock? Am I supposed to suggest counseling? Or is he? Am I supposed to make this hard for him in order to prove that he messed with the wrong woman? Am I supposed to make it not hard because he's my husband, and I love him for better or for worse? Or am I just not supposed to care what I'm supposed to do and just do what I want to do?

I get back to my car and feel like I'm going to throw up, mostly because of my run but partly because my confusion is manifesting itself in anxiety and that always goes straight to my gut. I stretch against my car as my breathing recovers and feel relieved that my worst fears for this run didn't come true. Then I check my email on my phone. Amidst the random ones from the PTA, Target, and various friends, there are three from Darren. They are apologies:

pleading, remorseful, groveling apologies. Our power balance has never been like this. It feels horrible.

"Was this the first time?" I text.

"Yes," comes the answer immediately.

I don't write back.

Later, after I've showered and answered emails and texts—all but Darren's—I email Cameron to see if she can have lunch with me in the city tomorrow. She can't always get away from the office for a proper lunch, so I hope that her schedule is light. I don't write that it's important in my email, because I don't want to alarm her. I want to tell her the story in person. Cameron is incredibly rational and able to be unemotional while dealing with stressful situations—handy traits for a doctor—and I need to discuss this with her.

She emails me back right away, says she's free, and asks me to meet her in front of her office at noon. I dock my iPhone, crank-up Cat Stevens, and spend the rest of the afternoon cleaning out my pantry. My pantry is like a vintage clothing store: There's way too much stuff crammed together, and a lot of it is way past its expiration date. The project is almost meditative—but not entirely. I can't turn off my brain, and I think back to when Darren and I first met.

We talked and danced all night at Cameron and Jack's wedding, much to the delight of Cameron and Jack. As we said goodbye, Darren whispered, "I can't wait to see you tomorrow" in my ear as he gave me a sweet kiss and said goodnight. I walked out of the wedding with a huge smile on my face, butterflies tangoing in my stomach, and the excited feeling that comes only when you've met a guy who is not insignificant.

The next morning at the post-wedding brunch, I could barely eat my omelet because every time he smiled at me, I felt—and blushed—like a thirteen-year-old girl with a wicked crush. In his fitted blue-and-white checked button-down and jeans, he was the perfect combination of conservative and sexy. I had to force myself not to stare. And when he asked me what I was doing the rest of the day, I decided my errands and laundry didn't hold a candle to this beautiful and exciting man.

We walked aimlessly through Central Park for hours, talking about our families (he grew up an only child in Atlanta; I come from a drama-laden family in L.A.'s San Fernando Valley), our jobs (he was on the rise at an investment bank downtown; I was an associate editor at a health and fitness magazine), our dreams (he wanted to give it all up someday and live on a Caribbean island surrounded by his kids, dogs, and palm trees; my dream had always been to be a dancer, but I took the safer route), and our bad habits (he often bought new clothes to avoid doing laundry; I read every issue of *People*, *Us*, and *The National Enquirer* cover to cover).

After a romantic late lunch at Isabella's on the Upper West Side, we walked toward my apartment at Columbus Circle while he held my hand and made me laugh. By this point it was early evening, and I invited Darren up to watch *60 Minutes*. We ended up talking on my couch for hours, sharing a bottle of pinot and a carton of Häagen-Dazs coffee chip, looking through my photo albums, and falling for each other. When our kissing turned to more, I told him that I didn't usually do this on the first date. He told me he usually didn't either, but he was willing to make an exception. And with that, we made and fell in love, all on our very first date.

I walk outside a few minutes earlier than the bus is scheduled to arrive, because I'm hoping to see Monique O'Donnell, whose husband Matthew is, rather *was*, the owner and publisher of the *Westchester Weekly*. I want to ask her what's going on. No luck. I see her nanny in the nanny huddle off to the side.

I approach the mom huddle and find Lorna talking to the Kelly-Ripa-esque Ellen Statler, whose newly purchased breasts— that are decidedly un-Kelly-Ripa-esque—are spilling out of her fitted V-neck. (My own tiny breasts twitch with envy.) Ellen and Monique are next-door neighbors, so I ask Ellen if she's heard anything about them moving away or Matthew switching jobs.

"Well, this is probably not news I should spread around, but I will tell you, Grace, because I know you don't gossip." At this point, I should pull her aside so that Lorna, who does gossip, won't hear, but Ellen is fully aware of that so I let her continue. "Monique's housekeeper told my housekeeper that they've been separated for a couple months. Apparently, Matthew had an affair and demanded a divorce from Monique."

"Wow. That's terrible," I say, trying not to stare at her breasts, which are abnormally spherical, while mentally adding the O'Donnells' to the growing list of affair-induced divorces among our friends and acquaintances.

"Why do you ask?" Ellen asks. *She's* harmless, but I don't want Lorna to know the details of my career, or lack thereof. So I fudge it.

"I went onto the *Weekly's* website today to check a restaurant review for a new Honduran place I heard about in Port Chester, and there's a notice on the homepage that the magazine is closing. I was surprised, and I wondered if they had sold the business." The divorce doesn't explain why the magazine closed.

"That's too bad," Lorna clucks, referring probably to the shuttering of the magazine, not the marriage. "And that Honduran place is fabulous."

As the bus comes to a stop, I search the windows for my boys and see James, his eyes closed and his cheek flattened against the window. When Henry shakes him awake, James catches my eye through the window, realizes where he is, and smiles that baby-tooth grin that slays me every time.

It must be noted that in many of the houses down the block and across the street, there are freshly baked cookies awaiting the kids, this being the first day of school. Lorna baked both chocolate-chip and heart-shaped frosted shortbread, and brought the overflow to the bus stop. She handed a paper plate filled with both varieties to the nannies to pass around their group, while she held court with the moms, distributing the cookies herself from a white basket-weave Tiffany platter. This from a woman who called the school board last year to complain that the cafeteria brownies were made with white flour.

At our house, we have something even more special. Just before the bus was to arrive, I realized I had forgotten to do the whole freshly baked cookies thing, so I scrambled and made a snacks platter out of all the cookies, crackers, and granola bars from their almost-empty boxes.

"Yummy!" cries Henry as he spots the colorful masterpiece of partially hydrogenated soybean oil-laden treats.

"I'm so glad you like it!" I say, happy that my boys have no clue that there is any domestication lacking in their mother. They settle into their stools, and I pour us each a glass of lemonade from the carton. "So?" I ask with anticipation. "How was the first day of school?"

"Good," they answer in unison.

"And?" I say, hoping for a tad more information.

"Just good," Henry answers. "Except my cubby has Megan on one side and Emily F. on the other. Not good."

"I thought Megan was your girlfriend?" James taunts.

"That was in kindergarten when I was a baby, dummy," Henry says, kicking his little brother under the counter while he stuffs another handful of unnaturally orange fish crackers in his mouth.

And let the games begin.

"C'mon guys. Henry, you know we don't say dummy in this house. I would appreciate it if you would be kinder to your brother." Trying to move the conversation onto happier subjects and bring back the brotherly love, I say, "So, Hen, did you walk James into class?"

"Yeah, and he has the same cubby I had when I was in kindergarten. Miss Marsha said she likes to do that for brothers. And she even let us write our names real small with marker way back inside the cubby. I did "James" for him because he can't write real tiny-like. It was cool."

"It was cool," James repeats, smiling adoringly at his big brother. This undying love for Henry allows James to focus less on the times Henry calls him names, gives him wedgies, spies on him, and splashes him in the bath. Instead, he focuses on the loving things Henry does which are plentiful as well, like generously doling out hugs, stories, and invitations to play baseball. And that's what makes it all bearable for James. And for me.

As they finish their snacks, we hear the garage door open.

"Daddy!" the boys shout, surprised and thrilled that their dad is home so early.

chapter seven

Being born with a name like Grace can put a lot of pressure on a girl. My mom, the oh-so-elegant Nina Roseman, always made a point to remind me that I should do my best to personify my name. She did not have such requirements or lofty expectations for my older sisters named Eva and Danielle. But I, Grace Julia Roseman, took the assignment seriously.

One of my first memories is from ballet class. I must have been four or five. I can picture us all lined up in head-to-toe ballet pink, hair in careful buns, standing at the barre waiting for Mrs. Murkowski, the ancient pianist, to begin. As Miss Natalya starts counting and telling us which positions to take, she says, "Remember, girls, be *graceful.*" Now, when you're four or five, you don't necessarily realize that word has any meaning outside of your one and only name. So when Miss Natalya, in her exotic Russian accent, entreated us to be graceful, I heard *be like Grace.*

I'd like to think that I was a little surprised that the teacher was asking all of the girls to be more like me. But I've seen the photographs from those days: they show a tiny little thing with her chin held high and her smile so proud. Modesty yet unlearned, I bet I believed that all of those little girls *were* being told to dance just like me.

My comfortable and sheltered upbringing allowed me to act with grace most of the time. Until I was fourteen, there was no darkness in my life. No opportunity to be less than graceful. True, my parents divorced when I was only three, but I was so young, I didn't know any differently. I have no memories of them married. Barely any photos of us all as a family. Having my mom and dad in separate houses with separate lives was always my normal. Their divorce didn't define me, and luckily, they acted in a civil way in front of my sisters and me. They spared us the unfair burden of having to choose who received more love.

Now, as my husband enters the kitchen, his transgression tainting my family's headquarters of warmth, tranquility, and love, I beseech myself to act with grace. I will do no less in front of my children.

"Hey, guys!" Darren says, kissing the boys. He glances at me to get a read. I am blank.

"Daddy, I get to be Star of the Week next week, the first one in the whole entire class!" James says proudly, the first I have heard of this. I imagine there's a note in his backpack listing all of the things I now have to do for this honor, including bringing in a nutritious snack for twenty-three kids and creating a poster of all his favorite things.

"That's so great, buddy. How was your day, Hen?"

"Good. We had science today and got to see all the new animals that Mr. Kellogg got over the summer. He got a tarantula, and it's so cool, and it's so ugly. And guess what? He said that over Christmas vacation we can volunteer to take one of the turtles or little snakes or hermit crabs home. Can we, Dad?" Henry asks, his eyes shining with excitement.

"Well, that's a long time from now. Mom and I will have to talk about it," Darren says, and he smiles at me.

I realize I can't do this. Not yet. "Guess what guys?" I say excitedly, staring into their innocent faces, putting my elbows on the counter and my chin in my hands. "Daddy came home early because he's taking you guys to the playground and then for pizza and ice cream!"

The boys cheer and look at Darren with their best you're-our-favorite-parent look while I busy myself with getting them ready. While he's not about to disappoint the boys after that announcement, Darren looks at me searchingly and asks me if we can talk tonight. I just nod and help get the boys into the car.

I figure they'll be gone for two and a half, maybe three hours, which only gets me till 6:30 or 7:00—too early to reasonably be sleeping when they get home. I feel guilty that this will be the second night in a row that I haven't put the boys to bed, but I know what I have to do. I send Darren an email.

> Thanks for taking them. I'm just not ready to deal. Would be great if you could tell the boys I'm not feeling well and that I went to sleep. Please sleep in the guest room again. I think I'll be ready to talk tomorrow night. Just trying to sort out how I feel. Thx, G.

I know I'm being kind, but it's just not me to be any other way. Even in a situation like this.

I doze off somewhere in the middle of the third rerun of *Real Housewives of wherever.* I awake to Darren coming quietly into our room. He gathers his stuff for work and turns off the TV. I pretend to sleep.

The next day, I take the 10:33 train from Rye, which gets to Grand Central at 11:12, leaving me enough time to walk the thirty blocks north to Cameron's office on East 74th Street, between Madison and Park. I don't miss living in the city, but being back always gives me a rush of energy. I love walking up Park, seeing whatever new sculptures have been installed in the medians, dodging tourists whose unmistakable pace is slower than a true New Yorker's, smelling the exotic scents emanating from the food carts. Yes, technically, I'm bridge-and-tunnel now (a condescending term used for those who don't actually live in Manhattan and have to enter the island via a bridge or a tunnel), but since I was a rent- and tax-paying citizen of Gotham for so many years, I feel I have an exemption. Plus, I walk fast.

I get to Cameron's office a few minutes early and wait outside. She rents space from a reputable art and antiques gallery, and the building reflects its dignified image: it's a beautiful old townhouse with distinctive iron handrails adorning the elegant front steps, window boxes displaying a colorful mix of blooms, and two potted topiaries guarding the handsome front door. As the door opens, Cameron walks out, a smile on her face and strappy crocodile sandals on her feet. She tells me she's starving and craving pancakes, so we make our way to EJ's Luncheonette on Third Avenue.

Though not the place I would have chosen for the moment I tell my best friend I've been cheated on, I'm not about to deny a pregnant woman her carbs. EJ's is packed when we walk in; it's mostly filled with moms and little kids, but there are pockets of businessmen and older people eating Reubens. On our way to a table in the back, Cameron is stopped by no fewer than five women who greet her with reverence. Turns out they're all parents of her patients. If they only knew how many times I've held the esteemed Dr. Stevens's hair while she's puked!

"This is a nice surprise," Cameron says, after we've placed our order for pancakes, buttermilk for her, multigrain for me. (I'm trying.) Her smile fades as she registers my expression.

"So," I start to cry, deciding to just blurt it out. "Darren cheated on me."

"What?" she reaches out and grabs my hand. "Oh, Grace. What happened?"

I manage to get the whole story out in between sobs while Cameron listens intently.

"Wow, I never would have suspected that Darren would ever do that to you," she says warmly, digging for more tissues in her purse since I've exhausted our table's napkin supply and there are no empty tables nearby to steal from.

I explain all the different thoughts that have been going through my head and tell her I'm just so confused, and I don't know what to do. Whenever I hear of women who had good marriages and then were cheated on once and proceed to get divorced, I always think that it's such a shame the couple couldn't work it out. That they've thrown away their entire family and history over one worthless night. But now, it has happened to me. And I understand. Rationally, it's easy to say that Darren's affair didn't mean anything, and the meaningful minutes, days, and years of our relationship that led up to that regrettable moment should stand for more than a quick orgasm. But the fact that that orgasm was in a vagina that isn't attached to my body clouds every rational thought. And that's where I'm stuck.

"I'm not trying to defend him, Grace, but you know Darren and you know that this is so uncharacteristic of him, and that has to stand for something. I abhor what he did. But I really hope you two can work it out," she says, putting her hand over mine.

I nod, crying, as the waitress sets down our pancakes. I wish I had ordered the chocolate-chip ones. With whipped cream.

Cameron continues carefully, "Would you consider counseling?"

"Yes. But not yet. I just want to sort through my feelings first before I let someone else pathologize them."

We spend the next hour talking through all of my feelings and coming to no conclusions. Outside the restaurant, Cameron tells me she'll support me no matter what I decide.

"Do you want me to tell Jack?" she asks.

"Not yet," I say, knowing how hard it will be for Cameron to keep a secret from Jack, but also knowing that she will.

"Thanks for your support, Cam. I just want to make sure you'll support me in whatever I decide. I don't really know what I'm going to do."

"You'll do what you have to do. Don't try to figure it all out right now. Don't worry about what you think you should do or what you think other people will expect you to do. Only think about what's right for you and your family."

We hug goodbye and she tells me not to fight the conflicting emotions, that I should explore and embrace them, that these emotions all serve a purpose in getting me where I need to be. She DVRs too much *Oprah,* but her words ease my mind a little. I take a deep breath and head toward Grand Central with just enough time to catch the train and meet the boys' bus on time.

Darren comes home that night with flowers. And even though the almost-wilted blooms scream end-of-day, train-station special, I realize he's trying. The boys eat their dessert—strawberries and chocolate chips—while Darren eats his dinner—reheated chicken parm—and I arrange the flowers in a crystal vase we got for our wedding.

We got married on a magnificent May day at The Ritz-Carlton, Marina del Rey in Los Angeles. Darren's family and many of our friends flew in from the East Coast for the weekend-long affair planned superbly with the help of my mom's good taste and my dad's checkbook. While not as low-key as Darren would have liked, it was warm, elegant, memorable, and a hell of a lot of fun. Each year on our anniversary, I recreate the meal we had that night—prime rib, herbed risotto, and roasted baby vegetables— and we eat in front of the TV while watching our wedding video. Darren always protests playfully, saying it's cruel and unusual punishment to force a man to watch a wedding video. But he's always the one who suggests we dress up, he's the one who insists we drink champagne while we watch, and he's the one who asks me to dance during Marc Cohn's "True Companion," our wedding song.

"Why did Daddy get you flowers, Mommy?" James asks, his teeth covered with chocolate.

"I'm not sure, James, let's ask Daddy, okay?" I say, handing him his glass of water. I don't trust myself not to start crying, so I focus on washing the dishes.

"Okay. Daddy, why did you get flowers for Mommy?"

Darren sets down his fork, and I can feel his eyes on me as I squirt more soap on the sponge. "Because I love Mommy very much. And sometimes daddies do things that aren't so nice to mommies and giving flowers is part of how we try to say we're sorry."

"What did you do?" Henry asks, and I imagine Darren regrets his second sentence. Saying things like that used to be okay when

Henry was little, but this stuff doesn't go over his head anymore. Thankfully, it still does for James.

"Something real dumb, Hen. I said something to Mommy that wasn't real nice." And here, he starts to cover his tracks so the boys don't have to think there's really something wrong. "I was really tired, and I got a little angry at Mommy for something that wasn't her fault. Mommy wasn't too mad because she knew I was just cranky, but I still feel really badly for hurting her feelings."

"Last year at my school, when you hurt someone's feelings you had to draw a picture for the person. Maybe you should draw a picture for Mommy," James sweetly suggests.

"Maybe I should," Darren says, kissing James. "But maybe what I should do is chase you boys up to bed because you are both silly heads," and he proceeds to make funny faces at them, tickle them, and then chase them up the stairs while they squeal in delight. He'll get them ready for bed while I finish in the kitchen. It was a good save. I'll give him that.

After I've finished cleaning up downstairs and checked that the oven's off, for the third time, I ready the backpacks for tomorrow. When I eventually get upstairs, Darren is in our bathroom washing up.

"Do you feel up to talking for a little while?" Darren asks carefully as he rinses his toothbrush and sets it back on the charger next to his sink.

"Sure," I say quietly. I pull my hair back in a ponytail and run my toothbrush under the sink. "Let me just wash up. I'll be in in a minute."

What a pleasant state of ignorant bliss I was in when I stood here just forty-eight hours ago about to find out my husband cheated on me. That calm-before-the-storm feeling. It's a shame not to have known the storm was coming so I could have better enjoyed the calm.

This happens to me sometimes when I'm driving. I'll be singing along to a great song on the radio, feeling the warm wind through the open windows, and I'll wonder if this is just a blissful moment before I'm about to get killed by some idiot driver not paying attention. I realize this is a horrible way to think, a horrible way to go through life always imagining the worst. But having a relatively blessed life means my number may come up soon. Maybe losing the prospect of a job and the security of a marriage on the same day will count. Maybe now I can relax in the car. Hopefully some force out there believes I've received my due.

I brush my teeth and wash my face. I even floss, and put on moisturizer and eye cream just to stall a bit. I'm still so utterly confused. I'm not sure I'm prepared to talk.

Darren is sitting on the bed, and the television is off. I know this is big for him because the Yankees are playing the Red Sox, a monumental event in the lives of sports-obsessed men up and down the Eastern Seaboard. As I get under the covers, hoping the warmth of the white, silky duvet will calm me, Darren looks at me and smiles cautiously.

"Do you want to start or do you want me to?" He's clearly tiptoeing here, uncertain of where I stand, and wanting to be respectful of how I want this to go.

"You," I say, unsure of where I'd even begin. I flash back to a conversation that started exactly this way about nine years ago. Darren had taken me out to our favorite restaurant, Gramercy Tavern, and told me there was something important he needed to discuss. I suspected it was about our decision to have kids, or rather my decision that I wasn't ready yet. Darren had been tossing out not-so-subtle hints for months (gift certificates for pregnancy massages, a maternity clothes starter kit box set, and an entire library of *What to Expect*-type books), and I had been lovingly objecting to his suggestions that now would be a perfect time to start a family. I was scared of the enormity of having kids, the responsibility, the pregnancy, the impact on my career, the loss of identity.

That night, Darren ordered a fancy bottle of wine and got us a table near the fireplace. He even wore a suit (something most investment bankers hate to do on a Saturday night), determined as he was that I take him seriously and that he give the subject all the reverence it deserved. He told me he loved me so much and wanted to create something that would be part of us. Something that we could love and nurture together. His voice trembled and his eyes pled, and when I exhausted all of the reasons why I was hesitant—he had really good rebuttals for each—I told him yes. And I meant it. That might have been one of the more special nights we ever shared. When we got home, we ceremoniously dumped my birth control pills in the toilet, lit candles, and made love. While that wasn't "the night," it definitely cemented a deeper bond between us. We were embarking on a joint venture, one that would connect Darren and me forever.

"Okay." He takes a deep breath and clasps his hands. "I've been thinking a lot about all of this, as I have been since it happened. And I've been really trying to look at this all from your perspective. And I can only imagine how bad this all is, Grace. I'm not sure where you're at right now in terms of how you feel about me and all this. I've been frustrated because 'I'm sorry' and 'I love you' don't say exactly what I want to say. I need much stronger words to convey the absolute regret I feel for doing that to you. I know I've hurt you so much, and I can't believe I was capable of doing that."

"I'm having a lot of trouble," I start, looking into Darren's glassy eyes. "I'm not really sure what I'm supposed to do and what I'm supposed to feel." I speak slowly, calmly. "I never thought I'd be in this situation."

Darren's voice turns determined. "I promised you I would never cheat on you. And when I made that promise I meant it with every ounce of my being. And the fact that I've gone against that promise is killing me. I can't forgive myself for what I've done to you."

"I need to know something." My voice is angry, accusatory. I'm relieved in a way that I'm not calm about this anymore. "How could you have had sex with me *after* you had sex with her?" I continue. There are so many thoughts buzzing in my head, so many big, important issues. "I keep coming back to the worry that even though you wore a condom, or say that you did, you might have gotten some disease from that woman!"

"I did wear a condom. And trust me, Grace, that was one of the first things that went through my mind when I woke up the next day," Darren says firmly. My germaphobic husband is staying in character. "I went to Dr. Lambert as soon as I got back and got tested."

"What did you tell him?"

"I told him the truth because I wanted him to test me for everything. I was mortified, it was one of the most humiliating things I've ever had to do, but I needed to know. I couldn't make you pay for me being a complete idiot."

"And?"

"And what?"

"And, did the test results come back showing anything?"

"Seriously, Grace. Do you think I would have been with you if there were any chance that I was going to give you a disease?" he asks with a hint of annoyance in his voice.

"Don't get annoyed with me, Darren," I say angrily. "You have no right to get angry with me. I have every right in the world to ask you that. And you have no right, zero, to be anything but kind and patient with me as I try to figure this all out." I'm mad. I start to cry. I walk into the bathroom to get a tissue. I decide on the whole box instead.

"You're right. I'm sorry," he says softly. "I know this is all going to get worked out on your terms. I know I deserve every ounce of anger you're feeling toward me right now, Grace. And I know I deserve to feel frustrated that I have no control over what you decide. I just want you to know that I will do everything I can to show you that we belong together. I will be a better husband than I have ever been."

"If I am everything to you, how could you have let this happen?" I ask, hoping that there's an answer, although I know there can't possibly be one.

"I ask myself that question every day. It's so easy to blame it on alcohol, but it wasn't like I was unconscious. I was there. I participated. I have actually been thinking that maybe I should go talk to someone and try to figure it out. Any excuse I can even try to think of sounds stupid and like a cop-out."

"Was it something about me or our marriage that you weren't happy with?" I don't want to accept blame in this because I think that even if a marriage has problems, the answer is not straying, the answer is figuring it out, but I feel like I have to at least ask.

"No. Absolutely not," Darren says fiercely. "I've been going over everything in my head, over and over, and there's nothing about you or our marriage or our lives that was upsetting me. I know we're not perfect, Gracie, but we're pretty close."

"I know we don't have sex that often—"

"Stop," Darren cuts me off. "You're right. We don't have sex as often as I'd like. But this has nothing to do with anything missing in our relationship."

"I guess it explains why I feel like we've been disconnected over the past few months," I say, and I suddenly realize I'm tired. Incredibly tired. And then, "Why didn't you tell me right when it happened?"

"I just couldn't. At first, I was trying to go through it in my mind. I kept trying to figure out why I did it. And I didn't want to hurt you. I couldn't imagine putting you through that pain. This pain," he says, gesturing toward me and my spent tissues.

"Did you consider not telling me at all?"

"Yes. I did consider that it would be better for you if you didn't know. But I just couldn't lie to you anymore."

"I'm tired, Darren. I need to go to sleep. And I need to think more. I don't know how long it's going to take me to figure this out, but I just don't know whether I can ever trust you again. How could we ever be us again?" I was bone tired, but my words were sharp, my thoughts were clear.

"I don't know how to convince you of that. And that scares the hell out of me. That I could have done something that will take you and the boys away from me. I guess, if it's okay with you, I'd just like to ask you to give it some time and not make any quick decisions. Please give me a chance. I love you, Grace. I love you so much." I know he is sincere, but when he tries to give me a hug, I recoil. I'm not ready to touch him yet. He apologizes.

I ask Darren to sleep in the guest room. I think of the popular marriage advice *'Don't go to bed angry,'* and I decide the person who coined that phrase was probably never cheated on. I wonder if I will ever go to bed happy again.

chapter eight

The next day I decide to test out the widely held notion that yoga has the ability to center a person, clear the mind, and cure every affliction known to humankind.

As I get the boys ready for school, I realize I'm pretty good at acting like there are not a million things wrong. It's easy to act normally around children; they have no frame of reference to detect subtleties in their parents' moods. So when I'm a little quieter than normal while whisking pancake batter—another favorite in my short-order-cook repertoire—they don't even notice. Luckily, they are unable to see the sadness in my heart and the hollow pit in my stomach. To them I'm just Mommy, and that's the way I want it.

I pour the batter onto the griddle and feel the familiar tinge of guilt. Guilt for even bemoaning my situation. There are people in this world with real problems. People who walk miles each day to access fresh water, people in third-world countries who die from diseases that are preventable with vaccines that our country has in plentiful supply, people who can't express their beliefs for fear of being tortured, people who hold vigil in their children's hospital rooms as doctors frown and say there's nothing else to be done. Those are real problems. My dealing with my husband's one-time dalliance doesn't compare a lick. Still, in my reality, it is a problem, and I must give myself permission to feel upset. Just because other people's problems are much bigger, much weightier, the fact that I acknowledge that should entitle me to feel distraught over my little problem in my little corner of the world.

Once I've given loads of kisses and hugs and said "I love you" to my adorable boys who are such troopers getting on the bus every morning without a complaint, I run upstairs and look for something I can wear to yoga.

I've devoted myself to yoga two different times in my life. The first time lasted one class. The second time lasted an impressive three. Each time, I became discouraged because I was unfamiliar with the poses and unable to hold said sad-looking poses for any respectable length of time. Yoga seemed to have the opposite effect on me that it was supposed to. It completely stressed me out. But, I owe it to myself to give it another try.

I joined the Rye YMCA last year mostly so the boys could take after-school classes. But I convinced myself I should opt for the "family" membership because I thought it would encourage me to take advantage of their fitness classes, gym, and pool. No such luck. Until now. As a member, I have access to the purportedly wonderful and free-for-members yoga classes offered nearby at the Wainwright House Yoga Center, housed in an historic, renovated carriage house overlooking the Long Island Sound.

I throw on black leggings and a T-shirt, pull on my Uggs, drain my coffee, and head to the 9:30 class. The room is buzzing and filling up as I grab a mat, two blocks, and one of those colorful yoga blankets and create my own little India in the back right corner of the studio. I choose the right side because in my vast experience with yoga, I've noticed the instructors always do the poses facing left first. So, if I'm all the way to the right, I will get a good view of the pose on the first side.

"Hey, Grace!" I hear a friendly voice and turn to my left. I had been engrossed in folding the yoga blanket just so.

"Hey, Callie!" I say. Callie Monroe is a petite brunette I have known for five years. She has a kind smile and espresso-colored eyes surrounded by thick, long eyelashes. The kind of eyes that looks better without makeup. Callie's daughter Amelia and Henry were in the same pre-school class. She and I clicked the first time we met because we were the only two moms who thought a two-week separation program was overkill. But it was the school's policy so we trudged it out, even though both of our kids separated easily by the third day. We lost touch over the years because the kids go to different elementary schools, but whenever we run into each other, it's always warm.

"I don't think I've seen you here before."

"It's my first time in a very long time doing yoga. So don't laugh at me," I say with a smile. I'm relieved that I'm next to someone I like. The thought of doing yoga next to someone like Lorna, who would undoubtedly wear fuchsia Lululemon, have a perfect pedicure, and be able to effortlessly reach the floor in the forward-bend pose (my Sanskrit is dusty) is too taxing.

"I promise, I won't. And Willow is an amazing instructor. She comes around a lot to make adjustments, and she's great and patient with beginners."

On cue, Willow enters the room. She looks like a sixty-year-old woman who can pass for forty, but you can tell she's really sixty. Her black hair is long and curly and streaked with grey, and her blue eyes are shiny. She strikes me as the kind of woman who is proud, not ashamed, of the lines on her face. Over the next hour,

Willow leads us in a yoga routine, er, practice, that is tough but not impossible. She dispenses clear instructions and poignant nuggets of wisdom.

"Sometimes when things seem really hard, just breathe, give in to the struggle, and open your heart to the possibility that the hard parts can be overcome," Willow says in her soothing alto. She has a gift for making everything she says relate to both yoga poses and life. My life. I pay really close attention to her messages. I forget to breathe half the time, I feel nothing like a warrior despite all the poses done in a warrior's honor, and I can't "grow my tree," but I listen. And Callie's encouraging whispers throughout the class really make it the most pleasant experience I've ever had with yoga. I pledge to myself that I will do this every Friday.

After class, as we're rolling our mats and refolding our blankets, Callie asks if I would like to join her and her friends for coffee.

"We go to Le Pain Quotidien in town. It's a really nice group of women from this class. You should come. We can catch up."

"Sure, I'd love it," I say, before I can decide if I really want to. But I'm glad I blurted that out. It will be nice to get back in touch with Callie. Plus, I love Le Pain Quotidien, or LPQ in local parlance. It's an outpost of a trendy and healthy Belgian restaurant-slash-bakery. They have the most delicious chocolate hazelnut spread that I love to slather generously on their fresh baguettes, but I have a feeling that with this crowd I'll not be having any of that.

As the SUV parade leaves the Wainwright House parking lot, I realize I actually feel happy. It's reassuring to know that despite the stress I'm feeling about Darren, I have the capacity to feel happy. Hmmm, maybe the yoga works after all! During the end-of-class *savasana*, when I was supposed to be thinking about nothing, I thought about some of the things Darren said last night.

I appreciate how kind and honest he was. It doesn't change the fact that he did a really shitty thing, but he has said and done all the right things since he told me. I'm incredibly angry at what he did, although I'm not angry at the way he's handling it. But yogic chanting or not, I still have no idea if I can remain married to a man who has the capacity to do what he did. Or am I just making a bigger deal out of something that may have been nothing? Would a divorce be like killing an ant with a sledgehammer?

I find Callie and her friends at the restaurant right away. They're easy to spot by their hip after-yoga wear and glowing faces. Callie introduces me around and tells the group where I live, how old my kids are, and where they go to school—the standard mom CV. And by those three facts alone, these other women can surmise a hell of a lot about me. Or so they think.

After we place our orders, Callie asks about the boys and Darren and then fills me in on her kids, her husband, and her latest endeavor, which is designing and installing residential organic gardens. She's so excited about her fledgling business and proudly tells me about her first two clients. When she asks me if I'm thinking about going back to work (Callie and I spent hours when our kids were little talking about the whole stay-at-home vs. working-mom issue), I tell her about the column I had been hired to write for the *Westchester Weekly* and how I lost that job before it even started.

"I can't believe I didn't think of you!" Callie exclaims, turning away from me toward the other women at the table.

"Think of me for what?" I ask, startled by her outburst.

"Nicole," Callie says to the woman across the table and to her left. "Are you still looking for someone for that email job?"

Of all the women in the group, Nicole seemed the most genuinely happy to welcome a newbie to their coffee klatch. I remember seeing her in class and noticing her long, auburn hair and strong arms; she was in the front row and did the poses effortlessly and elegantly. I actually watched and copied what she did because Willow would often just call out the pose and walk around the class helping pathetic beginners like me. Now, Callie was getting up from her seat, saying something I couldn't hear to Nicole, and insisting that Nicole sit next to me.

"So, you're a writer?" Nicole asks me, exchanging steaming mugs of tea across the table with Callie.

"Well, I was one in my past life, but, yes, I guess, technically I am a writer." *Way to be confident, Grace,* I think. "What was Callie talking about?"

"I own an Internet company called *Well in Westchester*. It's an advertising-supported online magazine filled with health and wellness content, social networking, an events calendar, listings, etc. Our new venture is creating a weekly email blast of short-form health and wellness content, and I'm looking for a freelancer to spearhead the project." Nicole wraps her hands around her steaming mug and smiles at me. Nice people make me so happy.

"Wow, that sounds really interesting!" I say excitedly, taking a sip of my mint tea that's made with fresh mint leaves instead of a tea bag.

"I told these ladies about the job last Friday, hoping one of them might know someone. I've placed ads, but it's always nicer to hire someone through a personal recommendation. And I don't know if you just heard what Callie told me about you, but it was quite a recommendation!"

Nicole and I spend the next half hour discussing the job and my experience. She says the emails will be about things such as a new yoga studio in the county, holistic suggestions for the changing of seasons, farmer's market recipes, etc. The job really appeals to me as it brings me back to my roots in health and fitness media, it's part time but enough time, and it might even motivate me to get in better shape and take better care of myself.

"Why don't we do this," Nicole says. "Here's my card. Over the weekend email me your resume and some clips of your past work, and we'll take it from there. I have a couple other people I'm talking to, but I'm planning on making a decision by the end of next week."

Nicole hands me her card, shakes my hand, and gets up to leave, saying she's got to get to the office. She had told me that she always blocks out Friday mornings for yoga and a quick tea with this group before she heads to work. Sure sounds like the type of boss I'd like to have! I finish my tea and get up to leave, too.

"Bye, Grace," Callie says, coming over to give me a big hug. "How did that go with Nicole?" While Nicole and I were talking, I had seen Callie glancing at us like a protective father spying on his daughter's first date, not wanting to be caught staring too intently but ready to pounce at the first sign of trouble.

"Great! Thank you so much for making that connection. It could be a perfect opportunity for me. Hopefully, I'll see you next Friday at yoga. It was so good to catch up!" I say, giving her another hug and realizing I'd missed our friendship.

When I get home, I spend an hour on WellInWestchester.com. I'm impressed with the quality of the articles, the edgy graphic design, and the amount of activity in their social networking areas. In About Us, I learn that Nicole Winters had a long career as editor-in-chief of *Yoga Journal,* but decided to create her own business so she could spend more time with her family. I write Nicole an email and attach my resume and clips. I say a little prayer and click send.

I really hope this job works out. It seems to be exactly what I'm looking for. I just hope that Nicole isn't discouraged that my most recent writing experience has been about school sustainability efforts for the *Midland Elementary School Parent Teacher News*. I imagine the other people she is interviewing are young and eager, and haven't been out of the job market for the last eight-plus years. As I'm wallowing in self-doubt, my email inbox chimes.

> Grace, thanks for your email. It was nice talking with you this morning. Can you come to our office on Monday at ten o'clock to talk a bit more? I'm having all the applicants prepare a 300-word sample piece in line with the topics we discussed at LPQ. You can bring that with you on Monday. I look forward to seeing you again. Please confirm the time. Have a great weekend, Nicole Winters.

Okay, I think. That settles that. She is considering me. I let out a little yelp and write her back to let her know that Monday at ten is indeed a good time. I get into the shower and let the hot water soothe my aching muscles as I think about a topic for my article.

After I blow-dry my hair, I go down to the kitchen to prepare a quick lunch. The kitchen is the one room we redid when we moved in. Our home is a 1930s white clapboard Colonial with black shutters—the kind of house I always imagined New Englanders lived in when I was growing up among the split-levels and ranches in L.A. Darren and I fell in love with the house's mature plantings, original dark-stained hardwood floors, plaster walls, and charming sunroom. Luckily, the previous owners had expanded the master bathroom and updated all the plumbing, heating, and electrical so the house was pretty much in move-in condition, save for a fresh paint job. But I hated the kitchen. Its dark (peeling) cabinets, ugly (peeling) grey vinyl floors, and avocado appliances (all of them) had decidedly *not* been updated by the previous owners. Considering how tastefully decorated the rest of the house was, I could only assume they weren't the cooking types.

When we bought the house, Darren and I agreed that because we were stretching our budget, we'd live with the kitchen for a couple of years and redo it eventually. So you can imagine how excited I was when I opened up Darren's birthday present to me a few months later and found it was the business card of a kitchen consultant from Christopher Peacock, the high-end kitchen design company in Greenwich. Christopher Peacock is the Gucci of kitchens. I would have settled for the Gap. "Go nuts and have fun," his card read. And that I did.

I spent the next several months going absolutely nuts and having giddy fun as I selected white flat panel cabinets and drawers with chrome bin pulls, a white subway tile backsplash, hardwood floors to match the rest of the house, countertops of Calacatta Gold marble (which is white with grey and beige veins), and top-of-the-line stainless steel appliances. I almost slept in that temple of beauty the first night after the installation was complete. Instead, I slept with my husband. The kind of sleep punctuated by moans, not snores. Lots of moans. Practically one for every gorgeous chrome bin pull.

The phone rings as I make myself a pb&j and banana.

"Hi, Gracie," my mom says. I can tell she's on her cell, and I picture her driving down Santa Monica Boulevard in her gold convertible Beamer.

My mom and I talk a couple times a week, and I always look forward to catching up with her. She asks me about the boys and the first week of school. She is an amazing grandmother, and the boys adore her. They have a weekly Skype "date" on Sunday afternoons during which the boys do an art exhibit, showing her all the projects they made in camp, now school, that week. It's very sweet and I'm thrilled that they have a good relationship. Much better than they have with my dad or Darren's parents.

"So, get this. I lost my job at the *Westchester Weekly*, but I have an interview Monday for a new job," I tell my mom and proceed to fill her in on all that drama.

"That's great, Gracie. I just wish you'd give yourself a little break, though. You're finally getting time for yourself. Why don't you just relax a little? Take some cooking classes. Join a theater club and get into the city more often."

"I can't do nothing, I need to do something," I say.

"Those things aren't nothing. They're rewarding and fun."

"But they wouldn't be fulfilling for me. I need to accomplish something. I need to work at something productive."

"Okay, well, it was just a suggestion. But you were always so hard on yourself, so I guess I understand. The website job sounds great, Gracie. Right up your alley. You'll be fabulous." My mom really likes the word fabulous. As does my sister Eva. They probably use the word fabulous more often than a Beverly Hills wedding planner.

"I really hope it works out. I might not get it though. She's interviewing other candidates who probably have more recent experience than I do and are more on the pulse of this wellness stuff."

"Don't sell yourself short, darling. And don't assume that anyone has anything over you. You are fabulous, and you deserve that job. So stay confident and put it out into the universe that you want it, and it will be yours." I'm assuming the reason she's driving down Santa Monica Boulevard is because she's on her way to her guru's office. My mom employs practitioners in all of the "healing arts," as she likes to call them.

At this point, I debate whether to tell my mom about Darren. She is a BFOD—Big Fan of Darren—and she'll be devastated, but she always gives me great advice, and I know she'll pull through this time, as well. I'm just not sure if I want to get into it with her.

"How's Darren?" she asks, and I decide to go for it.

"Mom, I have to tell you something," I say, and I know it sounds ominous. I walk to the couch in our sunroom and sit down.

Dead silence.

"What, Gracie. What is it?" she asks, and I hear her voice quaver.

"Darren cheated on me." I start to cry—talking to my mom about emotional things has always reduced me to a puddle—and tell her the whole story. She doesn't interrupt me once.

"Oh, Gracie. I'm so sorry." She asks me all sorts of questions: When did it happen? When did he tell you? Was it the first time? And then she surprises me. "I know it's going to be hard to trust him for a while, but you two will work through it. What you have is too important to give up over one silly night."

"Seriously, Mom?" I ask in a sarcastic voice. "You think I should just forgive him and act like nothing ever happened? I don't know if I can do that."

"Of course you can forgive him, Gracie. I'm not saying that you should pretend it didn't happen. Go see someone together. Work it out. You can't do that to Henry and James."

"*I* can't do that?" I start sounding a bit hysterical. "Wouldn't it be Darren doing that? So now, he did what he did, and if I decide that I would have a problem being married to a man who goes around sleeping with cocktail waitresses, it would be my fault for screwing up Henry's and James's lives? Is that what you're saying?" I am feeling incredulous at this point.

"No, Gracie. Take a deep breath, darling. That's *not* what I'm saying. And it was only one cocktail waitress, right? I'm just saying that I don't want you to think there's anything wrong with taking him back. You don't need to feel ashamed about that. I'm sure loads of your friends out there have been in similar situations and you don't even know about it. Just take some time; let him win you back. And then let him back in, Gracie."

I hold the phone away from my ear and stare at it, shocked. This is Nina Roseman talking. Strong single mother. Feminist bra burner. Marcher extraordinaire. "I'm a little surprised that you're so gung ho about me just taking him back, Mom. I'm not saying that I'm rushing out to get a divorce or anything, but I can't say I've entirely ruled it out."

"I've seen these things happen for years to friends, Gracie. Men have different needs. These things always end up worse when the marriage ends. I have friends who have been in your situation, and when the marriage was good to start with and it was just an indiscretion, the marriage can recover. And the same can happen for you. Just consider it, darling. I wouldn't want to see the two of you unhappy."

Happy. There's that word again. Why all this pressure in our society to be happy all the time? "I just want you girls to be happy." my mom would constantly tell my sisters and me growing up. What does that even mean? Who is happy all the time? I guess my mom is, what with her convertible, tanned silver-haired lovers, private Pilates sessions, and "fabulous" life. I realize I'm starting to sound bitter. But I'm just blown away by my mom's staunch support of taking Darren back.

The first time Darren met my mom was a few months after Cameron and Jack's wedding. Darren and I were inseparable at that point, and I asked him to join me in California for the weekend for my mom's sixtieth birthday party. She was throwing herself a little ball of sorts at the Four Seasons in Beverly Hills. Not exactly understated. Very Nina Roseman. Very fabulous.

My mom and Darren hit it off right away. She took us for dinner that first night at The Grill, one of her haunts in Beverly Hills, where the maître d' kissed her on both cheeks. My mom was on fire, asking Darren questions, practically interviewing him. And Darren deftly returned every shot. He put all his charm, intelligence, and good looks on display that night. And Nina Roseman fell hook, line, and sinker. Had he not been with me, she would have claimed him for herself. She told me so after a few Kir Royales at her ball the next night.

I guess I shouldn't be surprised that my mom is lobbying for us to stay together. She knows it wasn't ideal for my sisters and me to grow up without a dad in the house, and it would be even worse (call me sexist, I don't care) for little boys. But I thought she'd at least be a little mad at him. And give me a little more sympathy.

"Gracie, I don't want you to think I'm not sorry about that happening." *Ah, she redeems herself.* "I just hope you two can find a way to get past this. That's all. Okay, I'm at my appointment, darling. I have to go. Will you all be around on Sunday for my Skype date with the boys?"

"Yes, 2:00 my time."

"I love you, Gracie."

I tell her I love her, too, and hang up the phone. Immediately, it begins to ring. The caller ID shows my mom's number. I wonder if she's changed her mind about what I should do.

chapter nine

"Hi. It's me again. I forgot to tell you something. I ran into Rosalie Reynolds in the produce aisle at Gelson's in the Palisades, and guess what, you'll never believe it, Scotty is engaged!" My mom lets out a squeal.

"Really? Wow, that's so great. Do we know the girl?" I look at the clock to see how much time I have left before the bus. About an hour.

"No, she's British. Her name is Abigail. She came to L.A. to go to USC film school, and he was one of her instructors. Rosalie is thrilled to finally have a daughter-in-law!"

"I'm so happy for him. I'll shoot him an email to congratulate him. Thanks for letting me know."

"Email? Pick up the phone, Gracie. You kids and your emails. Anyway, gotta run. Love you, darling. Goodbye."

Scotty Reynolds and I met in kindergarten when he looked exactly like Dennis the Menace. We lived on the same street and played together every day after school. We stayed best friends all through high school when he looked more like Ricky Schroder, but there was never anything romantic between us. He tried to kiss me once when I was home for winter break sophomore year from Penn. I couldn't help laughing and was relieved when he started laughing, too. That was the beginning and end of our romance, as I was seeing someone back in Philly and had zero interest in Scotty. We've lost touch due to all the normal reasons, but I send him our holiday card each year, and we check in on Facebook occasionally where he now looks more like Brad Pitt. I will always have a very soft spot in my heart for him.

I start to feel like it's Grand Central in my kitchen because no more than five minutes have passed when my phone rings again. It's my sister Eva.

"Hey, Ev," I say, as I take a bite of the sandwich I have been trying to eat for the last half hour.

"Gracie, Mom just told me. I'm so sorry," she says in the serious voice I recognize from hearing her talk to her celebrity clients about serious things like magazine cover airbrushing gone wrong. She's a publicist with Farrar and Frank Public Relations, and she takes her job and her clients' careers very seriously. Being as cynical as I am about the entire Hollywood entertainment industry—that's what growing up in L.A. will do to you—I think it's pretty hilarious. But I don't tell her that. I'm not surprised that my mom hung up with me and called Eva right away. News in our family travels quickly.

"Thanks, Eva. I really appreciate the call. It sucks, but I'm just trying to figure it all out. I'm having trouble making sense of all my feelings," I say, trying to chew quietly.

"I have an idea, and don't say no, because I know you're going to say no. Just don't say anything and promise me you'll think about it," she says in the sycophantic voice I recognize from hearing her try to convince her clients to do things like go on *Dancing with the Stars*.

"Okay, I won't say no. What's your brilliant idea?"

"I think you should come out to L.A. for a weekend. It will be fabulous. We can go shopping at Fred Segal, get massages at The Peninsula, and eat at fabulous restaurants. The works. Say yes, Gracie. It will be good for your soul, and it will give you some distance so you can sort out your feelings." I hear the phone in her office ringing in the background.

"Thanks, Eva. I do appreciate the offer. I just think now isn't a good time. But I'll think about it. You sound busy. Go work. I'll talk to you later. Thanks for being a good sister."

"I'm all you've got, so I'll just have to do," she says with a tinge of sadness. "Okay, I understand. Take care, Gracie. I love you."

I could barely say goodbye as her last few words register in my mind. Eva *is* all I've got in the sister department, and she has been since I was fourteen and she was seventeen. Our middle sister, Danielle, died when she was sixteen. Her boyfriend, Brad, was driving her home from a high school football game when their car was struck by a drunk driver who was going sixty in a thirty-mph zone and ran a stop sign. Brad sustained serious injuries but healed. At least his body did. He was never the same, and from what I hear from mutual friends, he still isn't. My sister was ejected through the front window, and she died instantly when her head landed on the curb.

I can still remember the doorbell ringing late in our house that night and hearing my mom scream "Oh my God!" when she saw the two policemen at the door. The next few days are a complete blur in my memory. All I can make out in my mind are a steady stream of people, the phone constantly ringing, people coming softly into my blue-flower-wallpapered bedroom where I had retreated, and the horrific sound of my mother wailing. Up to that point, I had only heard my mother cry. Wailing is a completely different sound. Like an animal mother in the jungle who has just lost her baby to prey.

Our family was always close, but there had been alliances. My mom and Eva had that oldest-daughter thing going for them. Plus, Eva was everything my fancy boutique-owning mother could crave in a daughter: she was girly and she lived for clothes. My dad and Danielle were tight because she loved to play poker and go to the horse races with him. I had a good relationship with both of my parents, but my older sisters had them first.

I was closest with Danielle. We had long conversations, first about how we should do Barbie's hair, then about who was our favorite on *Charlie's Angels*, then about boys, and everything in between. And she taught me a lot, too: from how to tie my shoes when I was five to more advanced things as we got older like how to practice kissing boys with a pillow and how to hug your friend and smoke a cigarette at the same time without burning said friend's long, 1980s, Aqua Net-saturated curly hair.

Danielle's death severely affected everyone in my family in different ways. I just became a very sad girl. I escaped into my friendships and alienated my parents when I probably needed them the most. They were just too clingy then. Now, as a mother, I realize they were trying not to lose me. But back then, I thought they just didn't understand me. I started smoking pot with some of my friends who were into that. But I never lost myself. I always did well in school, I kept up with my dance classes, I respected my parents' curfews and rules. I just had this foggy outer self that I turned to now and then when I didn't want to be safe Grace.

Everyone at school knew what had happened, and most kids were afraid to talk to me. Elise Connors, who was in all my honors classes but was more of an acquaintance, actually told me that she didn't want to bring up my sister because she didn't want to remind me of it. She didn't realize that I was reminded of it every minute of every day.

When I went to Penn and started to develop new relationships, I felt the need to tell close friends about Danielle. I didn't think people could truly know me unless they knew about her. Cameron was really supportive, asking to see photos of her, and saying all the right things when the tears and memories would start rushing in.

Now that I'm older and time has softened the acute pain, I mostly miss Danielle in times like this. Times of crisis when I know her advice would have been better than my mom's and Eva's. I realize I can't really know that, because she was only a teenager when she died. But a profound relationship with a sister is like no other relationship, and we just knew each other so well. Sure, my mom and Eva know me, but they can be a little "on" for my taste sometimes.

I check the time, wash my plate, and head outside to greet the bus. Lorna calls to me as I make my way to the corner.

"Grace, I'm so glad I saw you. I feel like I haven't seen you the last couple days. Anyhoo, how is school going for the boys so far?" she asks. I know she's genuine, but there's just something too damn perfect about her that drives me nuts. She's like overly tasteful monogrammed powder room hand towels ironed just so. An impeccably matched outfit with no stains. A proper dinner party where nothing goes wrong.

"It's been going great, thanks so much for asking. How about for the triplets?" I ask.

"Stupendo! It's their last year in the elementary school, and they're starting to act a little tween-y if you know what I mean," she says, buttoning up her pale yellow cashmere cardigan. It's eighty-one degrees outside.

I *don't* know what she means, but I decide not to engage.

"So, Grace, as you know, I'm chairing the winter book fair this year, and I thought you would be interested in taking on a leadership role now that you have all this time on your hands."

I didn't. I'm not. I hopefully won't.

"I think you would be just perfect as the third-grade class chair! It's not too much work, just weekly meetings, frequent communication with the third-grade parents, and then working the three full days that we have the book fair in the gym, plus setup the day before and breakdown the day after," she says, leaning into me as if we're on the same team.

Act with grace.

"Oh, Lorna, it's so nice of you to think of me, but I'm so sorry. I'm not going to be able to."

"Oh?"

"Yes, I'm flattered you asked, but I'm actually going back to work part time, and I just wouldn't be able to give the book fair the time it requires or deserves. I'm so sorry." *Victory!*

"You're working? That's great, Grace," she says, pinching her lips. "What do you do?"

"It's not confirmed yet, so I'd rather not say, but it's a writing job. I'll let you know just as soon as it's all straightened out," I tell her, as I crane my neck to see if the bus is coming.

"You know, I'm a writer, too. I've written a darling children's book. Someday I'm going to have it published. Harvey is friends with a fellow from one of the big publishing houses in the city, and he says it won't be a problem at all."

"That's great, Lorna. Good luck with that," I say kindly as the bus pulls up. "I'd love to read it someday."

"Oh, that's nice of you, Grace. But I'm keeping it secret until it's published."

You do that.

"Hey, boys," I say to Henry and James, and we walk across the grass into our home.

"Hooray, woo hoo, it's Friday!" Henry shouts. "Screens!"

"Screens!" James shouts along.

Darren and I decided that we needed to limit our kids' screen time (computer, Nintendo DS, TV) or we'd end up with those kids they refer to on the news when they announce the latest obesity statistics and how it's all related to kids spending more time in front of screens rather than outside in the great outdoors—where they can be abducted. So we decided that the kids can only use screens from Friday afternoon when they got home from school to Sunday evening. Yes, I let them watch TV once in a while on weekdays when I have to get dinner ready or something like that. But they know the rules and don't push me too hard for TV time during the week. Come Friday afternoon, though, and it's a mad rush for the screens.

Next thing I know, the two boys are sitting on the family room floor side by side, backs against the wall, staring at their screens while their little fingers move nimbly on the arrow keys. Whenever I see them in a "brotherly love pose," as I like to call it, I get a *whoosh* in my stomach—a feeling of contentment. That I'm doing okay at this mom thing.

With the boys happily engaged in mind-numbing entertainment, I start working on dinner. As I assemble the ingredients for burgers, salad, and oven-baked potato wedges, I think about Lorna's offer. Not from the standpoint of even considering accepting it, but more because of what it represents in the mom world.

As I chop lettuce, I fantasize about the stay-at-home moms going on strike. Picketing all the school book fairs, hospital benefits, and canned-food drives that, if it weren't for their unpaid labor, would never happen.

"Movie night," Darren belts out as he walks in from the garage.

"Yay!" the boys shout in unison as they drop their DSs and run to give Darren a hug.

Every Friday night after dinner, we all change into our pajamas and cuddle on the couch to watch a movie and eat popcorn. The boys love it because they get to stay up late and eat in the family room. I love it because of the safe feeling I get when every member of my family is in the exact same place. It's comforting. And because I've been feeling unmoored by recent events, I'm looking forward to movie night to bring me home.

"Mom, we forgot to go to the library this week for our movie-night movie," James reminds me.

"I know. I totally forgot. Just choose one from the video case."

"Okay," they say and run off to the family room.

"How was your day?" Darren asks, trying to be normal, as he washes his hands in the sink.

"Good," I say, trying to be normal as well. If we're going to work on this thing we have to start somewhere. Plus, I don't want the boys to feel like anything's off. "I spoke to my mom. You'll be happy to hear that Nina Roseman is gung ho about us working it out."

"You told your mom?"

"Yes. Is that a problem?" I look at him, my fist reflexively going to my hip. I guess now's not the time to mention that I also told Cameron and my sister.

"I just thought that we would work it out without publicizing it first."

"*Publicizing* is a bit strong, don't you think?" I try not to sound too sarcastic and return to setting the table. "This is a pretty big deal in my life, Darren, and I need to discuss it with the people who know me best so they can help me get through it."

"Okay, Grace. That's fair. Do what you need to do. I guess I just don't want everyone to know."

"Everyone won't know. I have no desire to advertise this. I'm just as humiliated as you are."

He sheepishly comes near me and tries to hug me. I let him. My first instinct is not to let him touch me. But I also for a moment just want to be comforted by the person I love. It breaks my heart to think that that's the same person who is responsible for my needing to be comforted in the first place. He pulls away, and I see tears in his eyes.

"I'm so sorry, Grace."

"I know."

The boys run back into the kitchen and Henry is trying to pull a DVD out of James's hands while James shrieks.

"James wants to watch *Toy Story* which I've seen a million times, and it's just a stupid cartoon," Henry says emphatically.

"Hen, again with the stupid. Not in this house. And what do *you* want to watch?"

"*The Game Plan.*"

"Oooh, I love *The Game Plan.*" I never get bored of this movie that stars Dwayne "The Rock" Johnson as an NFL quarterback who is reunited with the eight-year-old daughter he never knew he had.

"I know, Mom, that's why I chose it," Henry says sweetly. I'm not quite sure if he really means that or if his little brain is clever enough to know that saying that might tip the scales in his favor.

"James, what do you think?" I ask, kneeling down and looking him in the eyes. "We haven't watched *The Game Plan* in a while. Does that sound good to you?"

"Fine," he says, crossing his arms and doing a little angry stomp that makes me laugh.

"Great. I like your cooperation. And you'll get to choose the movie at the library next week."

James smiles and bounds into Darren's arms, while I give Henry a kiss and thank him for being so thoughtful. Whether he was or not, I like to give him positive reinforcement as much as I can to counter the large amount of yelling I regrettably bestow upon the poor child when I lose my patience with him.

I tell the boys to wash up for dinner, while I open a bottle of sauvignon blanc and pour a glass for myself. As everyone sits down at the table, I announce, in my best chairman-of-the-board-commencing-a-meeting voice, that I have good news.

"As you all know, the job that I was really excited about at the *Westchester Weekly* fell through," I say lifting up my glass.

"Booo, *Westchester Weekly*!" shouts James.

"Thank you, James, for your support," I say. "Well, today, I met a woman after my yoga class. That's right, I said *yoga* class, and she has decided that I am clever and brilliant and may be perfectly suited for a writing job that she is interviewing me for on Monday morning!" I say excitedly. I've been open with the boys about my job situation. I think it's important for them (or me?) to know that I can work and find fulfillment in a career just like Darren can.

"That's great, Grace!" Darren says, smiling and clinking my glass.

As the boys discuss their favorite scenes from *The Game Plan* ("Fanny's Burgers make kids fat and give them gas," for Henry and "Thinnamon, I'm allehgic to thinnamon," for James), Darren asks me all about the job. Listening to the boys talk kindly to one another, drinking wine, and having a civil conversation with Darren is all a little too intoxicating, in more ways than one.

As I place the boys in between Darren and me on the couch, there is a warm feeling in our family room that night as four pairs of feet rest on the coffee table, and a family seems whole once again.

chapter ten

"Henry just caught me coming out of the guest room," Darren says, yawning as he comes into our bathroom the next morning while I'm brushing my teeth.

"He's up early. What did you say?"

"At first I tried to make it like I was just walking down the hall, but he looked in and saw that the bed was messed up. He asked me if I slept in there, and I said I did because I was coughing a lot last night and I didn't want to wake up Mommy."

"Nice."

"He bought it, but I guess we need to put the kibosh on the whole sleeping in the guest room thing," he says, looking at my reflection in the mirror.

"You're probably right," I say, going into my closet to put on my hiking clothes. Last night had been a sweet family moment, and I really tried to be normal with Darren. But I still didn't have it in me to let him sleep in our bed.

"Are you and Cam hiking?"

"Yep."

"Is Kimmy coming tonight?" Darren asks me, his arms outstretched against my closet door frame.

"Damn, I forgot to cancel her." Kimmy is our devoted and cherished Saturday night babysitter. Darren and I go out every Saturday night to dinner with friends or parties when we have one. When we don't have specific plans, we love to eat dinner at the bar in one of our favorite restaurants in Rye or have sushi and go to a movie. We don't have any plans tonight, and I would be perfectly happy staying home with the boys. But I always feel badly about canceling Kimmy because I know she depends on the money.

"Will you go on a date with me?" Darren asks sweetly. He sounds corny, but he looks so contrite I have to smile.

"Where are you taking me?" I say slyly, because I know he doesn't know.

"It's a surprise," he says, smiling back. This means that he has no idea yet but as soon as I leave the house he'll jump on OpenTable and make a reservation.

"Sure," I say, thinking a night out could do us some good.

Cameron is stretching against her car when I pull up for our hike. Ever the athlete, she's wearing such cool sports clothes she looks like she could model for Nike. Or run a marathon. She could probably do both, effortlessly.

"You ready, you pregnant goddess?" I ask as I get out of my car in head-to-toe Old Navy.

"Don't you want to stretch first, Grace?" Cameron asks, going into some deep side-squat maneuver. I tried that once. It was like a bad paint job—my color was off and there was a lot of cracking.

"No. I'm good. Let's go."

"So how are things going?" Cameron asks as we cross the parking lot to the trailhead. It's a beautiful morning and the sun is shining, but it's still cool enough for a sweatshirt.

"I want to talk about you first," I say cheerfully. "Let's talk baby."

"The good news, considering my profession and all, is that I can expertly burp a baby, change its diaper, and perform quality cord care, all at the same time. What I'm going to need help with, though, is shopping for all the gear." Cameron looks at me, and I see that lost look in her eyes. She sailed through medical school, reads lengthy nonfiction books about battles, and knows her way around a computer's motherboard, but the girl needs help when it comes to anything domestic. And while *I* think I'm just getting by in that category most of the time, Cameron thinks I'm a regular Martha Stewart.

"Well, then, consider me your official baby ambassador."

"Great," Cameron says, pointing out a leaf that has begun to turn gold. I love the fall and am ready for it to arrive. There are times when I miss the reliable and amazing Southern California weather, but I definitely prefer the seasons. There's something wonderful about changing the clothes you wear, the activities you do, the food you eat, and the way you feel every few months.

"Now," Cameron says as we get to the path near the river where we always skim stones (she reliably gets three or four skips; I get one, maybe), "fill me in on what's going on with Darren."

"Oh, where do I start?" I ask rhetorically. "It's all just so complicated. Half the time, I just think I'm overreacting, and I should just not make a big deal out of this. But the other half of the time, I realize it is a big deal, and I shouldn't be so hard on myself for not welcoming him back with open arms."

"I understand both of those sides, Grace," Cameron says. "But I think you're thinking too much. I know that's what you do, but I just think you should let things unfold, take it one day at a time, and not do your usual thing of coming to grand conclusions every few hours."

"Well, you are very lucky that you are not a drama girl when it comes to emotional stuff, but I just can't help it. It's all just too fresh. You'll be happy to know, I tried to act normally last night, and it was nice. And he's definitely trying. He's taking me on a date tonight."

"Well, that's good!"

"We'll see."

"I'm sure it will be a step in the right direction."

I stop and look at her with a puzzled look on my face. "What's it like to feel so confident about things?" I ask, completely without sarcasm.

"What do you mean?" Cameron asks.

"You're like one of those women they interview in magazines about what they can't live without. Those women seem so self-assured and confident about why that particular literary classic is their favorite book, or why that's the only perfume they'll wear, or that they'll only use this one type of elegant stationery hand engraved by a century-old, family-owned factory in Italy. And then there's me, with my stack of half-read chick-lit books, the little Jo Malone trial perfume set I got from the Duty Free in the airport, and the folded note cards I got in a charity solicitation that I decided to keep without making a donation. I just find myself feeling inadequate lately. Like I was supposed to develop into a fully formed real adult by now with convictions and tendencies and preferences, but instead I'm just trying to get by and put out fires."

"Grace, you are really way too hard on yourself. Think of what you have accomplished. So what if you don't use fancy stationery or don't have a favorite author. First of all, you're refreshing because you don't need to impress anyone with name brands. Second, you've got to stop putting so much stock in how people are portrayed in magazine articles. I am certain that if *Vanity Fair* magazine called you tomorrow to do a profile on you, you would come off sounding incredibly adult-like, and other women would feel inadequate compared to you. I'm not blowing smoke up your ass, Grace. And I know you're in a rut right now. But enough with the lame-plain-Jane game. You are magnificent, and you know it. Why else would I be your friend?" she asks and nudges me in the arm.

We start the uphill climb, and I tell Cameron about my job interview on Monday. She is very excited and thinks it sounds like a great opportunity.

"You'll never believe this one," I say to Cameron, stopping suddenly.

"What?" she asks, stopping and looking at me.

"I found a grey pubic hair this morning!"

"Grace!" Cameron exclaims a little disgustedly, but she is laughing.

"What? You're a doctor. Surely, I can discuss anatomical developments with you," I say, laughing along and starting to walk again.

"Well, you're almost forty so it's fitting. Speaking of which, have you figured out what you want to do for your birthday? You need to get on this. It's *only* five months away," Cameron says sarcastically.

"Ha ha," I say. She knows I like to plan far in advance. "I think my original idea of you, Jack, Darren, and I going on some indulgent Caribbean vacation is out of the running at this point."

"Why? Maybe it's just the thing you two need." I can tell Cameron and my mom are on the same page here. Cameron is also a BFOD. Maybe even president of the fan club.

"Maybe just a luncheon with friends," I say.

"A luncheon? What are you, eighty?"

"What's wrong with a luncheon?"

"How about just a 'lunch'? A luncheon is something that smells like moth balls and ends with Jell-O. It just sounds so old."

"Well, then, it's perfectly fitting."

"Oh come on, Grace. Forty is not old."

"You're right. As I mentioned to you the other night, I'm excited about forty. I think it's going to be the beginning of a new direction in my life." And then I add solemnly, "I just didn't think it might be without Darren."

"Okay, don't get all down on me. You and Darren are going to be fine. And I think a ladies' luncheon will be lovely." Cameron doesn't use words like "lovely." I know she threw it in there to emphasize her distaste for the word "luncheon."

"I hope you're right. On both accounts."

When I get home, there's a note from Darren saying he took the boys to the playground. A nice relaxing shower without my little Rugrats coming in to disturb me will be nice, and then I plan on working on my article for Nicole Winters.

After I've showered, had cereal, and made coffee, I open my laptop to start writing. First, I log on to Facebook to check in with Scotty.

I see I'm not the first to get to his wall to offer congratulations, and it's fun to see all of the people who have already posted. I don't keep up with many friends from high school, but apparently Scotty does, and here they all are. I rarely check my Facebook page because I end up spending so much time looking at people's pictures, reading what they've been up to. It's a time suck.

I look at Scotty's photos and am thrilled to see all the ones he's posted of Abigail, Abigail with him, more of Abigail alone. She's beautiful, and they look very happy. *Good for him.* I write something witty on his wall and then send him a longer, more personal private message. I'm about to click over to see if there's any activity on my page when a chat box pops up.

JakeDoyle: hey grace!

I giggle and type back right away.

GraceMay: Hey Jake! Why are you up so early?
JakeDoyle: about 2 go surfing
GraceMay: So why are you on Facebook?
JakeDoyle: you ask a lot of questions at 7am
GraceMay: I heard the good news about Scotty.
JakeDoyle: who says it's good news?
GraceMay: Why? Something wrong with Abigail?
JakeDoyle: yeah, she stole my wingman
GraceMay: Oh, I see.
JakeDoyle: guess I'll have 2 settle down now
GraceMay: You? Never!
JakeDoyle: can't-the good 1 got away

```
GraceMay: Who?
JakeDoyle: u
```

I spent the bulk of my high school years lusting after Jake Doyle. Free-spirited Jake played the guitar, was an artist and a surfer, and had an uncanny resemblance to Rob Lowe—pure high school rapture. We were in the same crowd but, unfortunately, Jake Doyle did not have eyes for me. I wasn't ugly, but I was no Stephanie Campbell, Jake's tall, blonde, blue-eyed (this was L.A. after all) girlfriend.

We lost touch after high school, but at our twenty-year high school reunion a couple years ago, Jake and I ended up next to each other at the bar. He looked at me, then down at my hideous yearbook photo name tag, and then again at my face and said, "Gracie Roseman. No way! I had the biggest crush on you in high school!"

```
GraceMay: You had your chance.
JakeDoyle: ouch!
```

And then I don't know what comes over me.

```
GraceMay: Marriage   isn't   all   it's
cracked up to be anyway.
JakeDoyle: say   it   isn't   so   gracie!
trouble in paradise?
GraceMay: No.
JakeDoyle: what did mr fancy investment
banker do?
```

Seriously, Grace? Why are you doing this?

```
GraceMay: Nothing.
```

Good girl.

```
JakeDoyle: that's convincing-need me 2
break his legs?
GraceMay: Of course not!
JakeDoyle: not going 2 try and read into
it but any guy who would do anything 2 u
is crazy
GraceMay: You think?
```

A little flattery never hurt anyone.

```
JakeDoyle: ur a catch gracie, i was
blind :-)
GraceMay: We were young.
JakeDoyle: ur still as pretty
GraceMay: Almost 40!
JakeDoyle: like a fine wine
JakeDoyle: gotta run but if things don't
work out with u and mr fancy call me
GraceMay: You got it.
```

Yeah right.

```
JakeDoyle: i'll catch up with u soon,
what's ur email address?
```

I give him my email address and say goodbye, giggling out loud. I'm surprised by all the tingling in my body. It feels like soda is rushing through my veins—all popping and bubbling. I feel like I'm sixteen again, when I used to wonder whether Jake would like me better in the blue oversize sweater with shoulder pads or the green one. Not that he ever noticed, but thoughts of him did go into my daily wardrobe selection. I wonder if flattery from thirty-nine-year-old Jake Doyle might even be better than attention from sixteen-year-old Jake Doyle.

I grab my coffee mug and see the photo of Darren and me on my desk. I return to reality and realize I might be guilty of Facebook Flirting, an epidemic sweeping the nation. Usual onset of the disease happens to thirty-eight-year-olds at their twenty-year high school reunions. The afflicted are often long past the honeymoon phase in their current relationship when everything was new and the sex was exciting, and most are not getting the adulation from their spouses that makes them feel attractive and desirable. Along comes the reunion and with it, fun encounters—usually accompanied by sexy outfits and tequila shots—with long-lost crushes who make said afflicted feel sixteen again. Upon returning home, the disease flares up when the afflicted become "friends" on Facebook and engage in flirty repartee. This can quickly lead to an outbreak of symptoms that include inappropriate emotional and often physical interactions. The natural progression of the disease results in ostracism, regret, and in severe cases, divorce. The only known treatment is Facebook abstinence.

That's so not what I'm doing, I think and log off of Facebook. *It was just a short, friendly, unsolicited exchange with Jake Doyle,* I convince myself. *So why are you blushing, Grace?* I can't help myself so I Google Jake to see if there are any recent photos of him floating around. His Facebook profile photo is of a surfboard. There are a few listings of articles from art journals about his latest opening, and a search result that leads to his own website, which I click on. I'm taken aback by photos of his art—beautiful, vibrant, large-scale canvases in the abstract expressionist style, which is my favorite. And I'm even more taken aback by the photo I find of him. He's standing on the beach, his dark hair is longish and blowing in the wind, and his face looks a bit weathered, but the unmistakable resemblance to Rob Lowe is still, most definitely, there.

The bottom line, though, is that Jake just gave me butterflies, and they feel really, really good. I haven't gotten that feeling from Darren in quite a while. It's not that I don't love him; it has nothing to do with that. It's just that butterflies fade as a relationship deepens. But what replaces that new-relationship glow is arguably even better: the patina of contentment, of safety, of knowing that the person you love is truly there for you physically, emotionally, forever.

I spend the afternoon working on my piece for Nicole. I decided to make it about starting a mindful meditation practice. The boys play DS, build Lego ships, and play baseball outside. Darren works for a while, and, later, joins the boys for batting practice. If someone like Lorna were watching us through binoculars, and I wouldn't put it past her, we'd look like the picture of family bliss. Just goes to show that you have no idea what's really going on inside anyone's marriage by appearances alone.

When I sit down at my makeup mirror to get ready for my date, I gasp in surprise. One of the boys has been playing at my vanity again and turned my mirror to the 10x magnification side. Once a woman hits thirty-five, it's rarely a good idea for her to look at her face magnified 10x—there's absolutely nothing to gain—unless she has to pluck her eyebrows or squeeze her blackheads. I could join the ranks of my peers booking Botox appointments, getting fillers injected into their frown lines, and opting for plastic surgery on their lips, chins, eyelids, eyebrows, and cheeks. But I don't really mind how I look. At least not yet. At regular magnification. I won't say I'll never call a plastic surgeon, but I hope that when I do start minding how I look, I will be old and wise enough to feel like the wrinkles give me a sort of street cred, that I'll not succumb to the trend of making fifty- and sixty-year-olds look like weird, molded twenty-year-olds. Or, for that matter, like the cast of *The Hills*.

I opt for a pair of flattering, dark-rinse jeans, an off-the-shoulder sheer black blouse with a black camisole underneath, and strappy black wedges. After going back and forth about it, I decide to wear the necklace Darren gave me for our ten-year anniversary: a sapphire heart rimmed in diamonds on a gold chain. I check myself out in the mirror. It had never crossed my mind before that Darren would consider a younger, sexier, skinnier version of me. But that's all changed. I know he loves me for who I am right now, but I can't help thinking that if my man strayed once, my man could stray again, and I may have to work a bit harder to keep that from happening. I wouldn't be the first woman to do so.

chapter eleven

Darren takes me to Moderne Barn in Armonk. The restaurant has a great New York City vibe and it's packed with a chic crowd. I love the decor of the dining room, which is lined with Roberto Dutesco's stunning and evocative, oversize, black-and-white photographs of wild horses. I'm happy I decided to accept Darren's invitation.

After we're seated and order drinks, a scotch for Darren and a glass of chardonnay for me, I excuse myself to the ladies' room.

"Hi, Grace," a woman says as I open the door.

I turn to see Margaret White, the HR Director who had so unceremoniously canned me from the *Westchester Weekly*, applying lip gloss.

"Hi, Margaret, how are you?" I ask. She's wearing a little, emphasis on *little*, black dress and black stilettos. She pulls them both off quite well. Her dark hair hangs pin-straight to her shoulders, and her legs are tanned and toned. She is as beautiful as I remember.

"I've been better," she says with a small smile. "I worked for the *Weekly* for nine years. It's hard being on the job market again." She turns back to her reflection and continues with the lip gloss.

"I'm so sorry. I still can't believe that Matthew sold the company. I thought it was doing so well."

Margaret looks under the bathroom stall doors, and when she confirms we're alone, she leans into me and says, "Can you keep a secret?"

"Yes," I say, leaning in with anticipation, despite the strong smell of alcohol on her breath.

"Matthew didn't sell the company," and here her voice gets sharp. "His ex-fucking wife, pardon my French, got her goddamn lawyer to take him for everything he had, including their house in Rye, their house in Aspen, and his magazine."

"So Monique owns the magazine?" I'm a little confused, and Margaret seems particularly emotional about this whole thing. But she did lose her job and all, so I guess that makes sense.

"For now, I guess. But the goddamn bitch will probably sell the name and the holdings. She won't even get that much money for it. She just closed the magazine out of spite because Matthew fell in love with someone else, and she couldn't handle the humiliation."

"Wow, I don't even know what to say." I guess Ellen Statler's account of the affair was true after all.

"Anyway, you didn't hear it from me. But it was good to see you, Grace. Good luck with everything. I better get back." She sticks her lip gloss in her clutch, takes one final glance in the mirror, and turns to leave.

"Thanks, Margaret. Good luck to you, too."

When I get back to the table, I tell Darren about what just went down in the bathroom.

"That's a coincidence. While you were in there, I was looking around, and I could have sworn I saw Matthew O'Donnell at the bar." Darren takes a sip of his scotch and gestures toward the enormous bar that lines the entire right side of the restaurant.

I follow his gaze and am shocked when I see Matthew sitting at the bar talking, and laughing, and, whoa, now kissing a woman with pin-straight dark hair and a little black dress.

"Well, that explains everything, I guess." I say this with a stilted laugh as I take a sip of my chardonnay.

"Cheers," Darren says. "I would like to make a toast."

I tilt my glass toward his and he continues.

"I know that I dropped a bomb on you Tuesday night."

"To say the least," I say.

"Okay, let's change that to an atomic bomb," Darren says regretfully.

"Let's."

"And I just want to thank you for being here with me tonight, for hearing me out, for being fair," he pauses, "and graceful." He smiles. "Thank you for realizing that I love you, and for giving me another chance." He clinks his glass against mine and starts to take a sip of his scotch.

"I will drink to all of that, except the part about giving you another chance. I haven't quite made up my mind on that one yet," I say seriously.

Tears well up again in Darren's eyes as he lifts his glass in the air again and says, "Well, then, let's toast to hope."

I decide that is a perfect thing to toast to, and I clink his glass and take a long, satisfying sip of my wine. I'm looking forward to it taking the edge off of what has been a stressful week.

When our waiter comes around, I order the Caesar salad and almond-crusted cod, and Darren orders the beet and goat cheese salad and hanger steak. Darren also orders a side of the rosemary sea salt fries because he knows I love them. Again, got to give the guy props for trying so hard.

"You look really pretty tonight," Darren says, staring into my eyes.

"Thanks," I say, a bit sarcastically.

"Why do you say it like that?" he asks, spreading butter on the bread the busboy just brought us.

"Because, you don't often tell me I look pretty, so when you do, I feel like you have an agenda."

"I do, too, tell you you look pretty."

"Not so much."

"Well, whether I say it or not, I always *think* you look pretty. I always have."

"Did you do it because of the butterflies?" I ask him, and I feel the warmth of the wine spreading through my body. It's a welcome feeling.

"What do you mean?" he asks, straightening up a bit.

"I mean, did you sleep with the cocktail waitress because being with someone new gave you the butterflies? Did she make you feel attractive in a way that doesn't happen anymore when you've been married for ten years?" It's a bold question, but it gets to the heart.

"I'm not sure. Maybe. I hadn't really thought about it like that before."

"Do you ever long for the excitement of a new relationship? The butterflies?"

"Do you?" he asks me as he creases his brow in a worried look.

"I asked you first." I take a bite of bread. I was going to try not to eat bread tonight, but the wine eliminated my willpower.

"No."

Good answer.

He continues, "When I met you, Grace, I was done with dating girls I didn't see a future with. I was looking for a lasting relationship. I'm not interested in someone new just to have that feeling that never lasts anyway. I like what we have. It's better."

"Do you remember the movie *It's Complicated?*" I ask, as the waiter brings our first course.

"Sure, with Meryl Streep and Billy Baldwin."

"Alec," I say laughing. "You never could get those Baldwin brothers straight."

He laughs and takes a bite of his salad, "Yum, you want a taste?"

"No, thank you. Anyway, Alec Baldwin leaves his wife and goes off for the hot, young thing and then realizes that he really misses the familiarity of his marriage and the maturity of his wife. He realizes that even though what he and Meryl had wasn't 'exciting' anymore," (I use my hands to make quotes in the air for emphasis), "what they had was even better. A lot of movies show men leaving their wives, but not too many show that the grass, though possibly better landscaped, is not always greener. Plus, what is new and exciting with the replacement woman will fade at some point anyway."

"Grace, I'm not interested in finding someone new. I'm interested in doing whatever I need to do to stay with you."

"I just wish you had thought of that before you seduced your cocktail waitress," I say, with the intention to sting.

"C'mon, that's not fair," Darren says sharply.

"Really, since when did fairness become part of this situation?"

"I thought you were trying here, Grace."

Seriously? Now I'm pissed.

"Darren, I'm sorry if you haven't noticed, but I'm trying really hard. I'm trying to sit here calmly when all I really want to do is punch you in the face. I'm trying not to tell the kids that their father fucked up, literally, and that now I have to forgive him or else they will grow up without a dad in their house. I'm trying to give you the benefit of the doubt because you keep telling me that you love me. And all the while I'm doing all this trying so that *you'll* be happy, I'm making myself absolutely crazy," I say, with obvious frustration in my voice.

"I know," he says.

"No, you don't know. Because you're not in my shoes right now. If you were, you'd know how damn much they hurt."

I flag down the waiter and order another glass of wine. Darren gets up to go to the bathroom, prompting a much-needed time-out. While he's gone, my wine comes, and I take a few big sips. I just want to get out of my head. I decide to back off and just get through the rest of dinner. When Darren returns, we talk more about us, calmly. We talk about my job. We talk about the kids. We share a tiramisu. We even laugh a little. And when we get home, we make love. My wine-impaired brain convinces me that being intimate will make me feel closer to him. Afterward, he holds me and tells me he loves me. But when that part is over and we separate to our own sides of the bed, I turn away from him and quietly cry myself to sleep.

The rest of the weekend passes uneventfully. We go to the movies with the boys on Sunday, and then Darren takes them to the market. Later, as Darren prepares his weekly Italian feast, the boys get their last fix of screens, and I put the finishing touches on my assignment. I'm not sure if it's going to get me the job, but I think it's pretty good. I've also made a list of ten ideas for additional articles. I print out the article, the idea list, and my resume and put them neatly in a folder and then into my purse. I take another quick glance at the website to make sure I'm well versed in the company, and then head downstairs where Darren is carefully layering his lasagna and belting out *The Barber of Seville.*

On Monday, I arrive at Nicole Winters's office ten minutes early. My heart is beating wildly, but I'm not sure if I'm nervous or excited. Probably both. After I apply lipstick and recheck that the folder is in my purse, I head into the office building. It's a small two-story building on one of Armonk's side streets, not far from the Moderne Barn. I fantasize about staff lunches and after-work drinks at the bar.

The lobby directory shows a mix of small businesses: an interior designer, a landscape architect, a speech therapist. I head to *Well in Westchester*'s office and knock on the door.

"Come in!"

I open the door slowly, and there's a forty-something woman with an ill-fitting suit and an out-of-date hairstyle standing in front of me.

"Grace May?" she asks curtly.

"Yes," I reply, wondering what I could have done in that one second to possibly offend her.

"Nicole said you'd be coming. She ran out to get a coffee. Why don't you sit right there? She'll be back in a minute." She gives me the once-over and gestures to a small conference table against the left wall of the large room.

"Thank you," I say politely and head over to the table to sit down.

The office is one big rectangular room with a few offices on the side across from the door I just entered through. In the main room, there are five desks. The nameless woman who rudely greeted me sits at a desk facing the right wall. The other four desks are grouped together in the center of the room. I see that two of them are filled. The people turn to me, smile, and return to their work. The glass door to one of the offices is shut and a nameplate says *Nicole Winters*. Another office appears to be a storage area, and I recognize all the same "stuff" that used to pile up at the fitness magazine I worked at: exercise bands and balls, skin-care products, packaged health food, books, etc. I try to crane my neck to see what's in the third room, and it looks like a little kitchen. The office is decorated in that hip modern look popular with web operations in New York City and San Francisco: simple white lacquer West Elm Parsons desks, ergonomic black chairs, raw wood floors, flat-screen computer monitors, exposed brick walls, and lots of natural light streaming through the many windows. It's a beautiful space.

The door opens, and Nicole walks in. She greets her staff and they respond cheerfully.

"Grace, hi. So sorry I made you wait."

"Not a problem," I say, smiling.

"Why don't you come with me?" she asks kindly, leading me into her office and gesturing to one of the white leather upholstered armchairs across from her desk. We sit down, she boots up her computer, takes a sip of her coffee, and turns to me.

We talk about some of the same things we discussed at LPQ, and then she gets into more specifics about her expectations for the job. She would like the email editor, as she calls the position, to come in three days a week; take part in the weekly Monday staff meeting; brainstorm topics with the editorial director; coordinate art for the weekly email; work with the tech guy to arrange the distribution of the email; work with the ad sales rep to develop a sales sheet so she can sell incremental space on the email; etc. She reveals the salary she is offering, and I'm thrilled to hear it's significantly more than I was going to make at the *Westchester Weekly*.

"It sounds like a perfect opportunity for me," I tell her, hoping to communicate that she should pick me, pick me.

"It's a small operation as you can see," she says, "so you may be asked sometimes to do something not exactly in your job description."

"That won't be a problem," I say.

"What is it about this job that appeals to you?" Nicole asks.

"Well, so many things, really. I've spent a lot of time on your site, and I'm very impressed by the content, the design, the user interface, the community aspect. I have a lot of experience in this space, and I'm excited to jump in and use that to help build your product. I have the energy and the motivation to exceed your expectations in this job," I say. And to top it all off, "I promise you won't be disappointed in my work," I say confidently, as I recross my legs and search her face to reveal what kind of impression I'm making.

"Speaking of work, did you bring in the assignment I asked you to do?"

I hand her the article and the idea list, and I watch her face as she reads my piece about meditation. I cited research about the benefits of meditation. I listed several meditation practices offered at yoga studios around the county. I highlighted two smartphone apps that provide guided meditation. And I gave tips on how to incorporate meditation into a busy lifestyle. All in 312 carefully selected words. When she finishes reading, I see a hint of a smile on her face that develops into a full smile as she looks at the second page and reads my ideas.

"Well, I have to say, you did a really nice job on this. It's on a relevant subject, it captures our voice, and you've tied it to the county nicely."

"Thank you," I say beaming. This is why I need to go back to work. I don't get this feeling at home. Not even when James sees a photo of Reese Witherspoon in *People* and asks me why I'm in a magazine.

"Do you have any other questions?" she asks.

I fear I'm opening a can of worms, but I can't avoid the one thing that I hope isn't a deal breaker. "What are the hours that you're expecting the email editor to work?"

"My staff typically works nine to five. I'm flexible when someone has an appointment or," she laughs, "a Friday yoga class, but that's usually what I aim for."

My heart sinks. The job at the *Weekly* would have allowed me to leave around 3:00 so that I would be able to get my kids off of the bus. If I get this job, I would have to arrange childcare three afternoons a week. I guess my face reveals what I'm thinking.

"Would those hours be a problem for you?" Nicole asks.

"I'm not sure," I say honestly. "I guess I had assumed that I would be able to leave around three so I could be home to get my kids off the bus and be with them in the afternoon." I'm hesitant to ask her for those hours because I haven't been offered the job, and I don't want to put my chances in jeopardy because I know she's still considering other applicants so I add quickly, "But I'm sure I could work something out." My heart sinks again.

"Great," she says and stands up. "It was nice talking to you, Grace. As I told you on Friday, I'm talking to a couple other people, but I plan on making my decision by Thursday afternoon. I'll call you then to let you know."

"Thank you for your time," I say also standing up. "I'm so glad Callie introduced us!"

We make small talk as she walks me out of the office. When the door shuts behind me, I pray that I didn't just screw that up.

When I get home, I write Nicole a thank-you note on one of my charity-solicitation note cards. Then I realize that I've been out of the interviewing game for so long that I don't know whether it's proper etiquette to send a thank-you via email or snail mail. So I do both.

I return Darren and Cameron's emails asking how the interview went. I tell them it was great, that I think she really liked my piece, that I think I came off sounding both qualified for and interested in the job, but that the hours might hurt my chances. I tell them she might sense that I'm not committed and can't put in the hours because of my kids. Or, if I get the job, I may need to turn it down because I hadn't planned on hiring an afternoon babysitter. Or, maybe I'll have to hire the sitter. Maybe, I realize, I'm kidding myself and I'm not even being seriously considered for the job, and she's just going through the motions for Callie. I guess the easiest thing would have been to ask her if she'd consider shorter hours for me as long as I'm able to get all my work done. I bang the heel of my hand against my forehead and realize this is exactly the type of overthinking Cameron is trying to get me to stop doing. *Turn off your brain, Grace.* It just doesn't stop.

My email chimes. It's Jake Doyle.

```
hey grace. don't know why but thinking
of you. crazy, right? just double
checking to make sure you don't need me
to break any legs. anyway ever since we
chatted i can't get you out of my mind.
```

sorry i'm probably not supposed to say things like that to a married woman. man i really messed up in high school didn't i? later, jake

What the hell? I think that email definitely qualifies as flirting. Maybe he's just lonely? And why can't he use capital letters? I stare at the email and reread it several times, distressed to find that the butterflies are coming back. I can't deny it feels good to be flirted with, even if that wasn't his intention. I write back.

Hey, Jake. It is crazy, but you've always been a little crazy, haven't you? Surely, wasting your precious high school years on Stephanie Campbell would qualify you. I don't know why you got any impression that *my* marriage was in trouble so no legs need breaking over here. But thanks for looking out for me. Not the first time. Do you remember that motorcycle ride you took me on after my sister died? For the first time in my life, I wasn't afraid of anything. Not sure if I ever properly thanked you. I was pretty much in a daze. So thank you. Grace

I wait.

i do remember that-you were so sad. i think you were afraid tho. your arms were wrapped around me so tight i could barely breathe but i also kinda liked it. i think thats when i started having a crush on you

The email exchange continues, one after the other.

Me: Why didn't you ever say anything?

Jake: because stephanie would have ripped my balls off. man she was a drama queen. plus you could have had any guy you wanted. especially all those guys who were 10 times smarter than me. didn't think you'd ever go for a surfer like me

Me: I hardly could have had any guy! Hilarious that that's what you think. Always fascinating to hear how other people perceive you. I went through high school desperate for a boyfriend. Oh how I swooned over you.

Jake: do you still?

Me: No. Sorry. Now I've got a husband to swoon over. You lost your chance.

Jake: and i will always regret it. what kind of work do you do?

Me: Funny you should ask, I had an interview today for a writing job for a health and wellness website. I really hope I get it. For the last eight years I've been taking care of my kids. Henry is 8 and James is 5. They're adorable.

Jake: sounds great, gracie. really does. your family is lucky to have you. i

always thought of you as kinda mature so
you must be a great mom

Mature? No wonder he didn't want to date me in high school.
What sixteen-year-old boy is going to choose mature over hot and
slutty? Two things I was never able to pull off.

Me: I think I am a great mom. Try to be.
But ready to go back to work to
challenge my "mature" mind again. How is
your art?

Jake: always struggling but i just
scored a show at a gallery in santa
monica that has hollywood clients so
that would be super rad if it all goes
well. i've been getting a lot of
interest from another gallery too so
things may be picking up-keep your
fingers crossed

Me: Fingers, toes, and eyeballs. Anyway,
gotta go. Nice talking to you. Take
care.

Jake: u2

I sit back in my chair and take a deep breath. I realize that I
have a huge, ridiculous smile plastered across my face. *Am I flirting,
too? Or just catching up with an old friend?* When I decide to delete
the entire conversation because I'd be mortified if Darren ever saw
it, I realize I'm doing the former. At least I think I am, and that's
all that really matters. I decide not to initiate any email

conversations with Jake. I don't decide what I'll do if he initiates. The thought brings the butterflies swarming.

chapter twelve

About two years ago, I was in the kitchen one Friday afternoon overseeing one of Henry's homemade science experiments that he used to conduct with club soda, baking soda, food coloring, and other household staples, when I heard the familiar email chime on my laptop. The email was from Darren and said, "Want to see if Kimmy can sleep over on Saturday so we can go to New York City for the night?"

I immediately wrote back, "Who is this and why have you stolen my husband's computer?"

He wrote back, "Hello? Who is this? This is Grace's romantic husband."

I wouldn't characterize Darren as a romantic. He is incredibly kind, thoughtful, and loving. But it doesn't come naturally for him to show it. I accept that about him and really don't hold it against him. But when little glimmers of romance present themselves, and they do once in a while, I get really excited.

Kimmy had nothing going on, so she agreed to come late morning on Saturday and stay for twenty-four hours. Darren booked a room at the The Standard, the über-cool boutique hotel in the Meatpacking District. We spent that day meandering around, checking out art galleries, and drinking wine during lunch at Pastis. We had nowhere to be, nothing to do except whatever we wanted.

Darren surprised me by insisting we go into Scoop so he could buy me something to wear that night to dinner. Now, I've heard of men taking their women into boutiques, helping them select dresses, and then sitting patiently outside the dressing room in between showings of each dress. But I never, ever, thought Darren would ever suggest such a thing. One of his co-workers must have suggested it to him.

And even though we could blame the wine at Pastis for putting us in a silly mood, this was still one of the most fun things we'd done in a long time. We went through the store choosing dresses that we both liked and dresses that were outrageous, and I tried them all on. He *ooh'd* and *aah'd* and even gaped. At the end of our fashion extravaganza, we both agreed on a slinky black sleeveless dress that had a deep V-neck, a belted waist, and a slim skirt. It was gorgeous and made me feel incredibly sexy.

After our shopping spree, we went back to the hotel and did what The Standard is famous for: having sex in front of the huge floor-to-ceiling windows in our room. It was still daylight so we wouldn't really qualify as exhibitionists; we'd both heard stories about people turning on their room lights at night and doing all sorts of things while voyeurs looked on. But the sex was hot and being out of the house made me feel so free. I did things to Darren that afternoon that I hadn't done in a while. And he to me. And when we'd finally had enough of each other, we went into the shower where it just started all over again. I'm amazed we made it out that night, but we did. We had sex twice more—once after dinner and again when we woke up the next morning—and we returned home happy and refreshed.

It's times like those that make me realize that although Darren isn't your standard flower-delivery, heavy-with-the-compliments, let-me-pull-the-chair-out-for-you romantic, I prefer his way a lot more. I imagine the lay-it-on-thick guys just get pretty annoying and predictable, something that Darren certainly is not.

So I chuckle to myself when he brings home another bouquet of flowers for me tonight, something he's done a few times since he sprung his news on me. It's as if Darren is pulling out all the tools in his romance toolbox to fix our marriage. It's sweet, and I do appreciate the efforts. But flowers do not a marriage mend. It's going to take less-tangible things than that, like time, regaining trust, and my ability to move on. I'm still trying to figure out if that's something I'm capable of doing.

That night at dinner, we play Thumbs Up, Thumbs Down, a game where everyone has to go around and say his or her best and worst parts of the day.

"My thumbs up is that I scored two goals at recess, and my thumbs down is that Janie sat next to me at lunch and told me I was cute," Henry says, scrunching up his nose in disgust.

"That's so sweet," I say. "She probably likes you."

"I know," says Henry with a self-assuredness I envy. "But she's not one of my girlfriends."

Suddenly I'm living with Hugh Hefner. "Okay, James, how about you?"

"My thumbs up is I don't know, and my thumbs down is I don't know," James says, returning to his chicken nuggets.

"Come on, buddy. There's got to be something," Darren says encouragingly.

"Hmmm. Well, nonebody at school wanted to play tag at recess so that was my thumbs down, and my thumbs up is that we have chicken nuggets for dinner."

"Excellent," I say, not wanting to correct his "nonebody" because I think it's so cute. I've never been one to correct my boys when they say words wrong, like how James says "inficial" for "official" and how Henry still says "the Eastern bunny." I know they'll grow out of it sooner or later, and it's just my way of holding on to their babyhood. I do correct grammar, however. That I can't help.

"Your turn, Dad," says Mr. Hefner.

"Let's see. My thumbs down is that a mean businessman decided not to do a deal with my company today, and my thumbs up is that I'm so happy I have such a wonderful family with such a pretty mommy and such great boys," Darren says, smiling at each of us.

"Okay, Mom, your turn," Henry says, looking at me.

"Well, my thumbs up is that I think my interview went really well today, and I'm very happy about that. And my thumbs down is, hmmm, can't think of one." *I can think of a big one, but I'm not going to share it.*

The phone rings. The caller ID shows Cameron and Jack's house number. Little do I realize, but I'm about to have my thumbs down.

"Hey, Cam," I say cheerfully.

She's barely able to say my name she's crying so hard.

"Are you okay?" I ask, panicked.

Still more crying.

"I'll be right there," I say and hang up the phone. I explain to Darren and rush out of the house. Cameron is not one to make something out of nothing. I can only imagine it's the baby.

Unfortunately, I'm right. When I get to Cameron's house, Jack opens the door with a solemn look on his face and tells me she's in the bedroom. I quickly walk upstairs and find her in bed, tears streaming down her face.

"What happened?" I ask, reaching for her hand.

"I lost the baby," she manages to get out between sobs.

"Oh, Cameron. I'm so sorry." I start to cry, too, and then I get into the bed with her, and we sit there for a while.

"Do you want to talk about it?"

She takes a deep breath and starts to talk, "I had some dull abdominal pain this morning, but I just wrote it off as a stomach ache because we had Mexican last night. Then the pain got stronger, and I felt wetness in my underwear. I went to the bathroom and—" she starts to cry again.

"Did you go to the doctor?"

"Yes," she says calmly. "The baby's gone." And then she starts crying heavily again.

Jack comes in the room, and I get up to hug him. "I'm so sorry, Jack," I say.

"Thanks, Grace. I am, too."

"I don't know what's wrong with me," Cameron says, angrily. "I really felt differently this time. I really thought this time I was going to be able to do it. What's wrong with me?" Cameron sinks down under the covers and buries her face in her pillow. Suddenly, she darts up. "All I know is I can't do this anymore. I can't. And I can't go back to that office and take care of all those babies."

"Take some time off, Cam. Your covering doctor can pick up some of the load for a while."

"I guess it's just not meant to be." Cameron says in a high voice, and she stares at Jack. "I'm so sorry, Jack."

He comes over to hug her, and I suddenly feel like I need to leave this very private situation to them. In fact, I realize I rushed over without really asking if she wanted me to. But that's what Cameron and I do. I stay a little while more, consoling my best friend who just lost the second-most-important thing in her life.

Jack walks me out, and as we stand at the doorway saying our goodbyes, he says, "Grace, about Darren. He told me what's going on. I'm really so sorry you guys are going through this."

"Yeah," I say. "It totally sucks, but we're trying to make our way through."

"I know it's not my place to tell you what to do, but I wouldn't forgive myself if I never shared this with you." He hesitates and runs his hands through his hair.

"What, Jack?"

"Cameron knows this, so it's no secret, but I was in a similar situation myself at a medical conference once. A woman was coming on to me pretty strongly. Luckily, I was just sober enough to stay away. But I see how it could happen, Grace. And I see it happen with colleagues all the time, guys who are crazy about their wives. So, I'm not trying to excuse what Darren did, I'm just trying to give you a different perspective from a guy. It never means anything, Grace. Just a weakness men have."

"But you held back, Jack. You weren't weak. Darren was."

"I was just lucky, and as I said, just sober enough."

I laugh bitterly and turn to leave.

"He's a mess, Grace. I spoke to him today. Please just give him the chance to show you how sorry he is."

"Thanks, Jack. I appreciate what you're trying to do. I feel like I'm standing on a stool in quicksand, and I'm petrified that someone's going to take my stool away."

"Hang in there, Grace."

"Thanks, Jack. You, too," I say and give him a hug.

When I get home, the boys are asleep and Darren is in bed, reading the newspaper and watching TV. I tell him what happened, and he is crushed. After I wash up, I walk down the upstairs hallway, which is lined with framed family photos, to make my nightly rounds. I go into Henry's room first and find him asleep with a *Harry Potter* book open on his chest, his reading light still on. I close the book and turn off the light. He makes a sound and rolls over, and I cover him with his blanket and give him a kiss. Then I go into James's room across the hall. My "baby" is asleep, covers completely off, hair matted to his forehead with sweat. I lie next to him and start to cry. Tears for the fierce love I have for these two boys, tears for the fear I have that my marriage might not make it, and tears for the intense pain I feel for my best friend.

The next day after I've gotten the boys off to school, bellies full with French toast and a strawberry-banana smoothie, I call Cameron to see if she wants to go for a walk.

"How are you feeling?" I ask her.

"Never better," Cameron says sarcastically.

"Sorry, Cam," I say, unsure for the first time in our friendship how to handle her. We've been through the highest highs, the lowest lows, and past miscarriages, but I sense we're treading on new ground.

"No, I'm sorry, Grace. I'm just a mess. I couldn't sleep last night. I had Marjorie cancel all my appointments today, which you know I've never done before. I think I'm going to have a hard time with this one."

"You're entitled to," I say. "Do you want to go for a walk? Maybe the fresh air will feel good."

"No, but thanks. I'm just going to hang out with my remote and Oprah all day. Jack went into the office, but he's going to come home after lunch so he'll be with me."

"Can I bring you anything? Hamburger soup?" Cameron's mother invented the recipe for this hearty and delicious soup—a panacea for all illnesses and emotional crises. Cameron introduced me to it in college when she made me a batch after I got a really (really) bad grade on an English exam. Now, we even have a dedicated hamburger soup pot—an orange Le Creuset—that we use. I think it's at my house from the time this past spring when my dad had his most recent heart attack and Cameron brought me a batch.

"No, I'm not hungry. And I have some stuff in the fridge. But thanks, Grace. Thanks for being a good friend."

We talk a bit more and then say goodbye. Although I want to suggest she go to the doctor and figure out her options, or maybe look into adoption, I know that Cameron will do that when *she's* ready to.

While on a quick power walk around my neighborhood, I decide to approach this Darren cheating situation the way I've approached every other difficult or unfamiliar situation in my life. I will research the hell out of it. After a quick shower and a bowl of instant oatmeal, I head to the local bastion of data, Barnes & Noble at the City Center in White Plains. At the last minute, I opt for the Yonkers store, which is farther away, because I'll be less likely to see anyone I know in the self-help aisle. All I need is to run into Lorna while I'm balancing an armload of *He Cheated, He Lied*-type books in the checkout line. There she'll be with the latest Jodi Picoult, telling me about how erudite the discussions in her book club are while she glances down at the spines of the books

I'm holding and later broadcasts it to everyone in carrier-pigeon distance that yes, indeed, Darren May cheated on his wife.

Before I had left the house, I searched Amazon for "infidelity" and got 1,692 results. When I narrowed that down to paperbacks in their health, mind & body section, there were 382 results. I'm hoping Barnes & Noble just shelves the most indispensable of the lot.

I walk into the store and smell the calming aroma of Starbucks. I decide to fortify myself for this uncomfortable mission. A tall, no-foam, extra-hot, vanilla latte in hand, I'm ready to face the music. I find the long self-help aisle—its length a true commentary on our society—and then the subsection of relationships. I'm a little surprised that there's even a sub-subsection called infidelity. I feel like they should have a special back room for shameful subjects, like porn at the video store. They should issue special Barnes & Noble paper bags that you wear over your head with two holes cut out for eyes so no one can see your face as you scan titles on a subject that you are hesitant to even discuss with your mother, let alone advertise to anyone who just happens to walk into the store.

But no such luck at this Barnes & Noble. My dirty laundry is hanging out to dry in full view of anyone who feels like coming into the self-help aisle, where the petite blonde woman is about to burst into tears as she fingers book spines with names like *Infidelity: A Survival Guide* and *The Myth of Monogamy*. I've spent hours of my life in Barnes & Noble stores, but never in aisles like this. Sure, they know me in literature & fiction, I have loads of buddies in children's & parenting, and I've even been spotted a few times in diet & health and home & garden. But the self-help aisle is a bit foreign to me, and if it weren't for The Bandit, I would still be a self-help virgin to this day.

I take a deep breath, a sip of my scalding coffee, and hunker down. I pass over the books that look scholarly and opt instead for the ones that look like they're designed for people who want to have a little fun while they're analyzing the possible disintegration of their marriage. The covers show couples who look like they're done with the tears and they've come to some harmonious resolution, when in reality, he gets off the hook for sleeping around, and she just ends up paying a therapist to deal with her shame and a personal trainer to deal with her muffin top.

I alternate crying, drinking, and leafing through books as a small pile collects near my feet.

"Hi," a woman with a Southern accent says.

"Oh, hi," I say to the familiar-looking woman I didn't even notice make her way down my aisle. I try to blink away the tears, and I tell her that some dust from the books must have gotten into my eyes.

"I'm Ainsley Covington, we met at the Midland School orientation?"

"Right, hi. Grace May. How does your little guy like kindergarten?"

"Yes, Grace. So nice to see you again," she sounds so genuine. "Cody's really happy, thanks for asking. And my daughter, Hutton, is in second grade. So far, they're both adjusting really well. How is your son doing?"

"James loves it so far. And my third grader, Henry, is doing great, too. You're new to the school, aren't you?" I ask, switching my weight from heel to heel nervously, hoping she doesn't notice *Love Affairs: Marriage and Infidelity,* which is basically right in front of her face. Unfortunately, because I have my coffee in my other hand, I can't inconspicuously make my reading selection less obvious. I pray she minds her Southern manners and doesn't look.

Ainsley tells me she moved to Rye from Dallas during the summer because she recently got remarried and her new husband was transferred to New York.

"So, here I am," she says with a happy trill. Ainsley is statuesque and pretty in that beauty-queen-from-the-South kind of way. She has honest-looking brown eyes and thick brown hair she wears to her shoulders. And, being from the South (this is a stereotype that most Southern women I've met who move up North fulfill), she's dressed to the nines with a fully made-up face and a substantial handbag that matches her expensive-looking, cognac leather pumps. Either Ainsley Covington has a wandering eye or her curiosity is too strong, because the next thing I know, she's looking at the book I'm holding and glancing down at the little book hill I've started to erect. I see her register the situation, as I start to cry anew.

"Oh, honey," she says consolingly, wrapping me up in a bear hug as I try not to spill my latte on her camel cashmere sweater.

"Oh, these?" I say dismissively. "No, not me!" I laugh, hoping I sound convincing. "But it's such a shame, my sister's husband cheated on her. She's a mess, holed herself up in her bedroom. I told her I'd get some books for her to read. I feel so badly for her, I just keep crying. We're really close," I nod, lips pursed, *tsk tsking*. I pray she buys it.

"Oh, well, tell your sister that there's light at the end of the tunnel. I'm living proof," she says, and I can tell she didn't buy my story at all. But, at least she's minding her manners. "I see you've got a coffee, but I was just about to get one. Do you want to join me?"

"Sure," I say with a smile. "I'm almost done with this one anyhow and a second couldn't hurt."

I stack up the books I've amassed and find one of those carry baskets to hold them in. I turn the top book cover-side-down, so in case I have any more encounters with Midland School moms, I can avoid spreading my lies even further. Even better, as we walk toward the Starbucks, I pluck a copy of the latest Jodi Picoult from an end display and put that on top of the pile. When we sit down, Ainsley tells me that she's a marriage and family therapist.

"Wow," I say, "I should tell my sister about you, if she decides she wants to talk to someone."

She hands me her card, and as I read it she mentions that her office is in Yonkers. She's still building up her client base and had some time between appointments so she came over to pick up a new book about communication in relationships by one of her colleagues.

I remember meeting Ainsley at the Midland kindergarten orientation the week before school started. She definitely stood out. In her Milly dress and high-heeled sandals, she towered over the blonde-bob Midland moms in their seven-inch J.Crew chino shorts and sherbet-colored Lacoste polos. She was standing close to the sandbox talking to a little boy, while most of the moms were milling around near the benches. Always one to make the newcomers feel welcome, I walked over to the sandbox, where James was also playing, and introduced myself. I could tell right away that, though she oozed confidence, Ainsley was relieved to have someone to talk to. We only had time to introduce ourselves though, because Evan Castleton threw sand in James's eyes and I had to take him to the bathroom to clean him up and calm him down. When we got back to the playground, I didn't see Ainsley.

Now, over coffee, our conversation flows easily. We talk about the school and our town, and she asks me for recommendations for bakeries and barbers, pediatricians and plumbers, tailors and toy stores. We never revisit my sister's misfortune. After about an hour that just flies by, we walk back to the self-help aisle where she locates her friend's new book and I resume my search. When we say goodbye, I tell her I'll email her so we can set up lunch or a playdate for the boys. I really enjoyed getting to know her, and I'll definitely follow up.

That little break had a way of taking the emotion out of my mission, and after a quick scan of the rest of the relevant titles, I winnow my collection to the five that look the most promising and head to the checkout. The checkout guy is a pimply, twenty-something who doesn't seem to care that my husband cheated on me. I'm glad I didn't get the checkout lady at the next register. In her sixties and wearing glasses on the edge of her nose, I know she would have taken one look at the titles, glanced at me, and made some sound that meant she wasn't surprised at all.

When I get home, I stash the books under my mattress. My boys love looking in my nightstand drawers, through my desk, everywhere that I have stuff in their constant pursuit of Scotch tape, gum, and pencils. To my knowledge, they haven't once looked under my mattress. Darren is on a business trip until Wednesday evening, so I'll have plenty of time after the boys go to bed tonight and tomorrow to peruse my latest selections from the Scorned Women's Literary Guild. And plenty of time to worry that he's decided to push his luck with another cocktail waitress. Like when you get a parking ticket and then leave your car in the spot to run a few more errands because you know you're not going to get another.

I check my emails and see one from Nicole Winters. My stomach drops as I wonder if she's made her decision.

chapter thirteen

Sadly, she has not. She was just responding to my "thoughtful" emailed thank-you note. I guess I'll just have to wait patiently until Thursday when she'll let me know. The more I think about this job, the more I realize how badly I want it. And I know it's because I want the *job*, not because I want to beat my competitors. This is not a *Bachelor* situation. On that show, the girls with their plastic bodies and trashy pageant clothes just don't want one of the other girls with more silicone and more sequins to win. By the end, how many of them even want to be with the bachelor? In this case, though, it truly *is* the bachelor I want. I want this job.

It's strange having nothing to do. I'm ignoring the list I have dutifully kept over the years entitled, "Things to do when I have nothing to do." It contains perennial favorites, such as "make albums from digital photos," "clean kids' closets and donate too-small clothes," "plant bulbs," and the evaded-for-years "write in kids' baby books." Truth is, when I have time to do those things, which I haven't had until now—they're the last things I want to do. I'm used to being busy, busy, busy. This down time is getting me just that, down.

I call Cam to check in and she tells me she's doing okay, that she's been thinking a lot, and that she's going to take a nap. I really ache for her. But I'm hoping that once her body heals a bit and she's had time to grieve, she'll consider other options. Cameron will be a great mom someday. I just hope that day comes soon.

I check my other emails and see one from Jake.

```
hey gracie: what do you think of flying
your pretty little self out here this
weekend? bunch of the old group
including your girls kiki and arden are
throwing scotty and abigail a little
engagement dinner sat nite and we
thought it would be fun if you joined.
your welcome to crash here if you want.
i'll be a gentleman, i promise
```

While reading, I force myself to overlook certain things like the fact that Jake, unlike my eight-year-old, has still not mastered the proper usage of your vs. you're, so that I can focus on the content of the email itself. And, by golly, it appears as if I've been invited to L.A. for the weekend to hang out with all my old friends. I picture myself at that dinner, laughing with Kiki and Arden, doing shots with Scotty and Jake, filling Abigail in on the parts of Scotty's history that only I know. I feel giddy. Of course, I'd stay with my mom. I would never even consider staying with Jake. That sure would be a cozy conversation with Darren, "Oh, honey, by the way, when I'm in L.A. for the weekend, I'm gonna stay at Jake Doyle's house. Can you pass the ketchup?"

But let's get real. I can't go to L.A. I'm in the middle of trying to fix my marriage. My best friend just had a miscarriage, and she might need me. I have children to care for. And, if I get this job offer on Thursday, there are 647 things I'm going to have to get in order, like hiring an after-school babysitter and buying a couple of office-suitable outfits, before I start working. Would have been fun. But not going to happen. I write back to Jake.

```
Thanks  so  much  for  the  invite.  Sounds
like  it  will  be  a  great  night.  I'm  so
sorry  to  miss  it.  There's  just  too  much
going  on  here  right  now.  But  thanks
again  for  thinking  of  me.
```

I decide not to address the offer of becoming his harlot roommate for the weekend.

That night, I feed the kids neon-orange mac and cheese, a delicacy reserved for those special nights when my husband is off boffing cocktail waitresses. I make myself a healthy salad, but, of course, end up eating the boys' leftovers and the remaining contents of the pot. I would admit that I actually scraped the caked-on cheesy bits from the side of the pot, but that would be pathetic.

I bring the boys upstairs and read them *Owl Babies*, by Martin Waddell, a book that is way too young for Henry and almost too young for James, but it was Henry's favorite for years and brings out the sweetness in him, which is something I need tonight. Plus, I love the way Waddell structures his prose and how the words roll off my tongue as if they're a song, "'Mommy!' they cried, and they flapped and they danced, and they bounced up and down on their branch." It's Shakespeare for children. I didn't choose this book tonight with an ulterior motive, but I could have. It's about three sibling owls who wake up one night to find their mother is gone. They wait patiently, assuming she's out hunting but eventually become upset that she might never come back. Sure enough, the mother owl returns, announcing, "'What's all the fuss? You knew I'd come back.'" Because mothers, human or owl, always do. There's no mention of a father.

After a couple rounds of tucking in and kissing, I get into bed with my new reading material. I look through the books, trying to find sections that relate specifically to what's going on in *my* marriage. I'm drawn to the case stories, recounts of people— clients, in the case of the books that were written by therapists— who are dealing with infidelity in some way or another. I quickly realize that though I'm in the same boat as these case study subjects, I'm wearing sunglasses and a bathing suit and checking out the view while they're donning lifejackets and grimaces and trying to bail out the water that threatens to sink them.

I have three main takeaways from reading the books. The first is that while my situation sucks big time in the context of Darren's and my relationship, most other people have it much worse. From the asshole husband who was doing the nanny for three years while the wife actually gave her extra vacation days so she could visit her sick "dad," to the asshole husband who admitted to his wife that he had regular affairs with his secretaries, these situations seemed much more harsh than mine. (There were disproportionately fewer asshole wives than asshole husbands in these books.) In other words, if there were an ER for infidelity, the triage nurse would keep me in the waiting room for hours, maybe even days, while the other patients received the urgent care they desperately needed.

The second takeaway is that despite the pages upon pages of advice, the bottom line is that I have to do what's "right" for my particular marriage, for my particular situation, with my particular asshole husband. There is no one-size-fits-all solution to infidelity. Different experts say different things, and I realize I'm not going to find the simple answer I was hoping for. It's similar to the frustration I felt when I was a brand-new mom, and I felt overwhelmed by all the parenting decisions I had to make: Let the baby cry it out? Or sleep with me? Feed the baby on demand? Or by a schedule? Every book had a different opinion. And my pediatrician had her own as well. Just like then, I'm left to trust my instincts and try to figure this one out on my own. And just like then, I have no experience I can use to make an informed decision.

Finally, the books also make me realize that every cheated-upon woman (or man) goes through the process differently, depending upon the level of stability of the marriage prior to the indiscretion, and depending on her own upbringing, life experiences, religion, disposition, attitudes toward monogamy, and other factors. Whereas I might sometimes feel sympathy for Darren for having suffered a moment of weakness that has such monumental consequences, other women might only feel anger or resentment toward their husbands and head straight for divorce. And I know there are loads of women who would never think of allowing something like a one-night stand to end their marriage because of a whole host of reasons, including fear of being alone, the financial implications of divorce, because they just don't think it's a big deal, or because it would blow the carefully constructed image they so desperately want other people to believe.

It's been almost a full week since Darren did a number on my heart, and I'm making my way through all the emotions. I feel each one at different times of the day: Sadness when I'm getting the boys ready for bed. Shock when I look at our wedding portrait framed in sterling silver on the mantle. Anger when I'm cooking dinner. Confusion when I decide whether to wear my wedding band. Fear when I'm trying to fall asleep. And disappointment pretty much all the rest of the time.

It was a luxury last Monday when my mind was filled with pleasant thoughts like school starting, my new job at the *Weekly*, or whether I should serve hamburgers or chili at our Labor Day party. It's only when I am experiencing some sort of heartache—my dad's heart attacks, Cameron's miscarriages, Darren's screwup—that I realize how much I took it for granted when my brain was free to ponder the insignificant.

On Wednesday morning, I make a double batch of hamburger soup and bring it to Cam at lunchtime. She doesn't seem to have moved much from when I saw her on Monday night. She tells me that one of the pediatricians she shares on-call weekends with is helping with her appointments that can't wait.

"I don't know if I can ever go back to work, Grace," Cameron says, her eyes staring blankly at the TV screen.

"Well, you don't have to make that decision right now," I say, opening up the drapes and cranking open a couple windows in her bedroom to get the air flowing. "Just concentrate on getting through this one week. You can take a few walks around your neighborhood, and we'll go hiking on Saturday. In fact, don't we have dinner plans with you guys on Saturday night?"

"Oh, meant to tell you. About Saturday. I'm going to Maine. It's my mother's birthday, and she's been trying to get me to come home for a while. When I told her what happened, she convinced me that this would be a perfect weekend to visit. And now that I'm talking about it, I guess I am a little excited to see my family. It's been a while."

"That's great, Cam, really. I think that could be the perfect thing. You always come back transformed when you go home. It's like the you in you gets rebooted," I say, collecting a brown banana peel and some empty mugs from her nightstand to bring down to the kitchen.

"Yeah, that's true," and she smiles as I head downstairs.

When I finish straightening up a bit, she tells me that she had the ability to be very clinical about her first few miscarriages, that she digested the loss from the perspective of a doctor. But, this time, she's coming at it more from the perspective of a mother-in-waiting, a woman desperate for a child.

"I've never before regretted dedicating myself to my career in my twenties and thirties," Cameron says, as she sits up in bed and wraps her arms around her bent knees. "I always thought women who left the workforce in their prime to go have babies were selling out. Sorry, not you, Grace." She looks at me to see if I'm offended. I'm not. She continues, "I love working. I love what I do. But now I think the joke's on me, and I was the one who did it the wrong way. Because now I'm old, my eggs are old, and the only kids I've got to show for myself all call me Dr. Stevens. I just want the type that call me Mom." She takes a deep breath, and I see her eyes watering up.

"Oh, Cam. I don't even know what to say. I'm so sorry," I say, sitting on the edge of the bed next to her.

"Thanks, Grace. I'm glad you're here," she gives me a smile, and I know, because I know her, that she wants me to change the subject so she doesn't start crying again.

"So, you'll never guess who's been emailing me," I say mysteriously, obeying her nonverbal request.

"That creepy stay-at-home dad from James's baby swim class?"

"No, thank God." I pause for emphasis. "Jake Doyle," I say, as a grin inadvertently creeps over my face.

"Rob Lowe Jake Doyle?" Cameron asks.

"The only," I say.

"Why are you blushing, Grace?"

"I'm not blushing. I'm just hot," I say, as I open the windows a little more. I tell her about Scotty's engagement, my Facebook chat with Jake, and his invitation to go to L.A. this weekend.

"Wow, Grace, is this all on the up-and-up or does Rob Lowe Jake Doyle have some other motive here?"

"He's just being himself. I think. I don't know. It is a little weird, but it never hurt a girl to be flirted with a little. Especially after she's been rejected by her husband." I sit in the white leather Barcelona chair across from Cameron's bed.

"Just don't be one of those flirty Facebook girls. Look what happened to Elizabeth Bonder," Cameron says, pointing at me and shooting me a warning look.

"I know. I'm not going there," I say convincingly. "I'm so far from there. You don't have to worry about me."

"What *is* going on with Darren?"

I tell her about our date, about all my conflicting emotions, about my crash course in Infidelity 101.

"I'm just going through the motions of marriage," I say. "I don't think I have any other choice right now. I feel like I'm on the guardrail of a mountain road. If I go one way, I fall down a steep, rocky cliff. If I go the other, I find myself on a really windy road with obstacles around every bend. But how long can I walk on this narrow guardrail?"

"Nice analogy, English major. I get it. I think you just have to try to keep your balance and stay on that guardrail as long as you can until the road clears up a little and you come to a straightaway."

"Nice continuation of the analogy, organic chemistry major," I say, laughing. "I think that's exactly what I'm going to have to do."

That afternoon, Darren calls me between his meetings.

"How's it going?" he asks.

"Fine," I say pleasantly. "I just spent the morning with Cameron. I feel so badly for her. She's kind of a mess."

"That sucks," he says. "I think maybe I'll send her flowers."

"You're becoming a regular florist!" I say, a bit sarcastically.

He lets it go. "Hey, what's on the schedule this weekend?"

"I don't think much," I say, opening my calendar on my laptop. "James has a birthday party on Saturday morning. The boys both have soccer practice on Saturday afternoon. We were supposed to have plans with Cam and Jack on Saturday night, but Cameron just told me she's going to Maine so we have nothing Saturday night. And then just another birthday party for James on Sunday."

"Okay." Pause. "So what do you think of me taking the boys to the Yankees game Saturday night?" Darren asks cautiously. I think he feels he has to walk on eggshells with me. "One of the lawyers we work with just offered me three tickets. I asked him for four, but he said he can only get three."

"That sounds great, actually. The boys will love it. There's a new Rachel McAdams movie I want to see anyway. I'll be fine." I will.

"Cool, thanks Grace. I think the boys will be really excited."

"You behaving yourself out there on that business trip of yours?" I can't help asking. I don't want to be that kind of woman, but I guess I am.

Darren pauses. "Yes."

"Good," I say. I am mad at myself for acting like this, but I'm even madder at him for putting me in the position that would lead me to have to act like this.

"I guess this is what we're gonna have to discuss every time I travel," he says contritely.

"I've been reading some books, and they all say that the hardest part of this whole thing is regaining trust. Deep inside I do trust you, Darren. But I trusted you before this happened and look where that got me. I just don't know how to not wonder and not worry."

"I know. It just sucks. Is there some way I can reassure you?"

"Can you pinch me and tell me this was just a bad dream?" I ask softly.

"Wish I could," Darren says. "I love you, Grace."

"I know," I say, unable to return the sentiment.

"Any word on the job?" he asks, sounding relieved to change the subject.

"No. She said Thursday. I'm trying to distract myself from thinking about it. What happens if she offers it to me and says I have to work full time those three days?"

"Well, then, we'll just figure something out. The boys will be fine with a babysitter for a few hours. You have to do what's right for you."

"I know. Thanks."

"No problem. Okay, gotta run. I'll be home around 6:30 tomorrow night. Wait for dinner for me?"

"Sure."

"Thanks. I'll call you guys tonight."

We hang up, and I type "Darren and boys Yankees" in my calendar for Saturday night. Then I go onto Fandango and check what time the movie I want to see is playing in Port Chester, and then it hits me. *Cameron is going to Maine. Darren and the boys are going to soccer and Yankee Stadium. Could Grace go to L.A.?* I sit back in my chair and work out the details in my mind. Then I go onto Travelocity and see how much a last-minute flight will run me. No bargain, but not too bad. Maybe this little trip is exactly what I need. I call my mom.

"Hey, Mom," I say, trying to make out the sounds in the background. "Where are you?"

"I'm getting my hair colored," she says loudly into the phone. I can just picture all the other ladies with foils in their hair turning to see why Nina Roseman is shouting.

"Are you around this weekend?" I ask.

"I think so, why?"

"Well, Kiki and Arden are throwing a small engagement dinner for Scotty Saturday night with just our old group, and they invited me, and I thought maybe I would come. Darren is busy with the boys all weekend with soccer and going to the Yankees game, so it kinda works out."

"Oh, Gracie!" she shouts. "That will be fabulous! Wait till I tell Eva. She told me she invited you out here, and I thought that was a fabulous idea. I will clear my calendar and be yours all weekend."

"Thanks, Mom," I say. "I have to finalize some things so it's not a hundred percent yet, but stand by. I'll let you know by the end of the day."

"How are things with Darren?" She lowers her voice a little, and I'm grateful that the entire salon won't know my business.

"We're working on things. No major decisions."

"Good. We'll talk all about it this weekend. Just remember what I said the other day. There is no reason to do anything crazy like divorce or any of that nonsense," she says.

"Okay, Mom. I'll call you later."

After we hang up, I call Kiki.

"Hey, Kiks," I say excitedly. Kiki and Arden were my two best friends in high school. We get in touch every few months, but whenever I talk to either of them, it feels like no time has gone by, the sign of a true old friend.

"Hey, girl!" she says. "*¿Cómo está?*"

"I'm great! So, I hear there's a little engagement dinner for Scotty on Saturday night."

"Yes! You better be coming. I saw Jake at the Brentwood Country Mart, and he said he had been emailing you so I told him to invite you." I know right now, Kiki is twisting her long black curls around her right index finger.

"So what do you guys have planned?"

"Not entirely sure. Arden is in charge of making the reservation. But that's no surprise. I think she was afraid of leaving it to me. Ha! She should be," she laughs. "But it will be so much fun, and you have to come. Say yes. Say yes. Say yes."

"Ninety-nine percent yes," I say.

"Yay!" Kiki shouts.

"I just have to finalize a few things, but I think I'm gonna make it happen. I'll email you and Arden later to let you know for sure. I hope it works out, though. It will be so great to hang out."

"Okay, I'll tell Arden to add two more to the reservation just in case."

"Just one. Darren is staying home with the boys. They have soccer, and birthday parties, and all that stuff."

"Even better. Not that I wouldn't love to see Darren. It's just that Arden and I decided not to bring Andy and Marco. We thought it would be more fun to just be the old crew again. Except for Abigail, of course, who seems stuck up when you first meet her with that fancy accent, but you will love her."

Kiki and I met in tenth grade. We were in the same homeroom. Rodriguez and Roseman. Kiki walked into that classroom on the first day of school like she was Naomi Campbell on a catwalk.

Without the snarl. Our school started in ninth grade, and she was new, but she acted like she'd been friends with all our fellow Rs since she was in diapers. Candelaria Luisa Alejandra Rodriguez (story goes that when she was born her older brothers wanted a kitten instead of a baby sister so they dubbed her KitKit which morphed into KiKi and stuck) had recently moved to Encino from East L.A. I found out later that her dad, Alberto Rodriguez, had just been named Entrepreneur of the Year by *Los Angeles* magazine. He had immigrated to L.A. from Mexico and started his career drying cars at a car wash in Hollywood. After years of working hard and moving up the ranks at a McDonald's in Westwood, he went out on his own and founded Rock O Taco, a popular rock-and-roll-themed chain of Mexican fast food. Alberto Rodriguez had just proudly moved his family out of their humble beginnings into a fancy house in the Encino hills with shiny marble floors in the foyer and a custom mosaic in the shape of a guitar on the bottom of the pool out back.

When I saw Kiki later that first day in my honors Spanish class, she sat down next to me and asked if I wanted to hang out after school. I had plans with Arden (who had been my best friend since fifth grade) to go to Du-par's, a hangout on Ventura Boulevard, so I invited Kiki along. The three of us bonded over Du-par's famous pancakes with boysenberry syrup and were inseparable from then on. Kiki made us laugh so hard that first afternoon with her hilarious and spot-on impersonations of all the kids she had met that day. And she's been entertaining us with her crazy antics and crazier outfits ever since. Kiki and I come from very different upbringings—she and Arden even more so—but that never seemed to matter. There were even times when I felt closer to Kiki's mother, Luisa, than to my own. Luisa was just so humble, so warm, so maternal. She always made me feel safe, especially after Danielle died.

Arden, on the other hand, is basically Hollywood royalty. Her dad is Dean Miller Standish, the brilliant director who revolutionized the way special effects and technology were used in movies. He's won five Best Director Oscars, more than any other director ever. Arden grew up around movie sets and has had dinner with everyone from Ryan O'Neal to Ryan Gosling, from Anne Bancroft to Anne Hathaway. But she was not affected the way you'd expect her to be. That was her normal. And her parents gave her no reason to believe she didn't have to behave like a typical high school kid. So she did.

I email Darren.

> Thinking of going to L.A. this weekend. I'd leave Friday morning after the boys go to school and come back Sunday night. Kiki, Arden, et al. throwing an engagement party for Scotty. And my mom and sister have been trying to get me out there anyway. I'll arrange playdates for the boys Friday after school. What do you think?

His response comes right away.

> Sounds great. Go for it. We'll miss you, but it's probably a good idea for you to have time on your own to think.

I feel like I've just gotten away with something huge, like winning the lottery off a ticket I found on the street. And I wonder if having "time to think," if that's what he wants to call it, is going to save my marriage or result in the complete opposite.

chapter fourteen

I spend the rest of the week making the final arrangements for my trip (car service to and from JFK, aisle seat, latest Emily Giffin novel, stocked fridge for Darren and the boys); deciding on my outfit for Saturday night (dark jeans, sexy black halter top, black heels); engaging in somewhat-flirty-but-not-inappropriate email conversations with Jake; and anticipating Nicole Winters's phone call, which I hope will come early on Thursday, rather than late. I can't wait any longer. I am surprised by how completely unprepared I am when the call actually comes, considering how much time I've spent thinking about all the different ways it could go. I have just returned from putting the boys on the bus Thursday morning and evading some question from Lorna about the neighborhood Halloween potluck party when I hear the phone ring. I feel my stomach do a swan dive when the caller ID reads "WELLINWESTCH."

"This is Grace," I say, knowing it's Nicole and trying to sound professional. My mom always says to channel who it is you want to become. And I really want to become (again) someone who sits in a cubicle and answers her phone by announcing her name.

"Grace. Nicole Winters," she says in a clipped voice that I immediately read into. If she were offering me the job she would sound happier. But maybe she is just trying to sound professional, considering she's going to be my boss. After all, when I met her at the post-yoga coffee, it was under friendlier, on-the-same-level circumstances, so maybe this is just her way of exerting authority. It's like predicting the meaning of a college acceptance based upon the thickness of the envelope. A thin envelope could have a one-page letter containing a rejection. Or a thin envelope could contain a one-page letter offering congratulations and announcing that the thick admissions packet will arrive by the end of the week. But the rejections are usually thinner. So in this split second of trying to interpret Nicole's intention from three words, I have not only assumed I have and don't have the job, but I've returned to those stressful days of college admissions. *Snap out of it, Grace. For God's sake, find out what the woman has to say.*

"Oh, hi Nicole," I say casually, trying not to sound as if I am dying to find out what the woman has to say.

"So," she says and then pauses. *Oh no, not good.* "I really am so glad Callie introduced us. It was great to meet you and hear your ideas for our new email product."

But.

"But, I'm so sorry I'm not going to be able to offer you the job," Nicole says apologetically.

"Oh." *Oh? Is that all you can say, Grace?*

"I'll just be straight with you. I think you're incredibly qualified, but the woman I hired has a deep and up-to-date network of health and wellness contacts in Westchester, and I just think she'll be a better fit for us. I'm really sorry."

Key words: up-to-date. Cameron was right. Those of us who leave the workforce to have babies are suckers. When we try to go back, no one wants us. We're damaged goods.

"I am, too," I say. *Act with grace.* "But thank you so much for giving me this opportunity. I think you have a wonderful company, and I hope the new email product is a huge success. I'll definitely subscribe to it. "

"Thank you, Grace. Again, I'm sorry it didn't work out, but I'll keep you in mind if anything else ever comes up here or if I hear of anyone looking for someone with your skill set." *Packing snacks, writing the descriptions for the school benefit silent auction items, dodging sketchy neighbors.*

"Thanks, Nicole. I really appreciate it."

I'm crestfallen. I've never had the opportunity to use that word in my life. But it's so fitting now. When I imagined getting this job, I pictured myself on a surfboard riding the crest of a wave that would lead me from the vast sea— the one that had swallowed up part of my identity—onto the shore of my "self." But instead, the wave has crashed into the shore prematurely, preventing me from proudly standing on my longboard, cruising onto the beach. Crestfallen.

I pour a cup of coffee and sit on the couch. I stare out the window at the leaves that are continuing to turn. A red bird alights next to its twin on a branch. They flutter off, busy to get to the next branch, then the next. *To everything there is a season.* I can't help myself from going to that place in my mind where I interpret Nicole's decision (the thinner envelope) as a sign that I am not meant to have a *real* job right now. On the other hand, it could be the universe trying to challenge me to not give up so easily. Two job rejections do not a failed career reentry make. But I am really disappointed. I had really gotten my hopes up on this one.

To be honest, I do feel some relief. Relief because I won't have to arrange sitters three afternoons a week. Relief because I can stop waking up in the middle of the night to maniacally scribble half-legible ideas for the emails on the pad beside my bed. And relief because now I don't have to worry about doing a good job and proving myself. Despite always having high expectations for myself and putting my all into every project I've ever done in my life, I am inherently lazy. The dichotomy doesn't make sense. I just force myself to be productive, to be really good at whatever it is I'm currently doing, because I would be so disappointed in myself if I didn't. But most of the time, I'd rather just sit on the couch, drink coffee, and watch cooking competition shows. (*Will they be able to move the ten-foot bridge made entirely out of candy from the prep kitchen to the judges' staging area without dropping it?*) This leads me to wonder what it is I really want in my life. And although I've had this conversation with myself a gazillion times, I don't know if I've been honest lately.

And since my plan had always been to go back to work once James started school, that plan just kind of took on a life of its own, first with the *Weekly* and then with *Well in Westchester*. I never really examined it carefully. It was just what I was going to do. But now that time is here and, maybe, instead of just being on autopilot I should think about why it's important to me to go back to work. *If* it's important to me.

Come to think of it, I've always run on autopilot, conformed to the norm: high school leads to college, college graduation leads to a job, serious boyfriend leads to marriage, marriage leads to babies. Never once did I picture myself taking a gap year after high school and traveling through Europe, moving to Colorado after college to teach skiing for a year, staying single, and choosing not to have children. Conforming is just what most mainstream girls do. I sometimes envy the frizzy-haired, hemp-wearing, child-free rebels sitting in their airy, light-filled outer-borough brownstones with their life partners leafing through photo albums of all the wonderful adventures they've embarked upon, stopping only to take a call from their agents letting them know that their debut novel has just topped the best-seller list.

Yes, there is a sense of fulfillment and identity I can only get by engaging in productive and stimulating work that is outside the realm of my children and their school. And there is something affirming about dressing in dry-clean-only clothes and sitting at a desk in an office that's not in my home. Something that I felt distinctly when I first graduated college and went off to work that first day in an Ann Taylor suit with the good leather work bag my sister bought me for graduation. Sure, after I exhausted the new wardrobe and all its iterations (white blouse with the navy skirt, white blouse with the khaki trousers, navy skirt with the grey blazer, ivory dress with the grey blazer) and I got comfortable with my job, that initial feeling faded and then I just became another drone trying to figure out if I'd already worn the navy skirt suit that week, packing myself into an already-packed subway car, trying to be happy with a paycheck that was in no way fair remuneration for all the hard work I did. But I felt important. And feeling important is magnificent.

I want to feel important again. Unfortunately, I don't know how many kids have the ability to make their mothers feel that way. Sure, my kids can make me feel proud, and loved, and needed in a way that prickles with pain and pure love at the exact same time. But they don't make me feel important.

Which leads me to wonder (overthinker at work) why it's so important for me to feel important. Is it the praise I covet? Is it the pat on the back from a person of authority when I do a good job?

Well, maybe partly. Mostly? Yes. If I could I would mainline praise. So maybe it's *not* the bachelor I want. Maybe I just want the bachelor to think I'm the prettiest, nicest, smartest, most desirable of all his suitors, and then have him go off with second-best and let *her* deal with all the crap that comes with getting chosen. And if I could muster enough of my self-esteem to realize I *already* am important, whether or not an eight-year-old or a highly respected boss tells me so out loud, then maybe I can finally let myself off the hook and relax for the first time in thirty-nine years. Maybe I can finally stop trying so hard to get everyone else to tell me I'm so damn special and just realize that I am.

"Do you want to hear the rap I wrote last night, Mom?" Henry asks me as he comes into the kitchen on Friday morning while I'm trying to bust out a few eggs-in-a-hole—the boys' favorite breakfast. I'm leaving for the airport the moment they get onto the bus, so I'm feeling a little rushed.

"Sure, buddy," I say. Henry has been into writing raps lately. There was the one about basketball (get it in the hoop/throw it for a loop/when you swoop) and the one about homework (math is tough/the carpet is rough/enough is enough). But I am not prepared for the masterpiece he is about to unleash. He opens with a beat-box intro.

"Oh fuck/you shuck a buck/and you got some good luck/some roses you pluck/oh fuck. . . ."

"Whoa! Whoa! Henry!" I say, and I can't help myself from cracking up. Here in the exact moment I should be stern and formidable, I am laughing so hard the pee is starting to leak out. "You can't say that," I say, trying to regain my composure as I frantically wave my spatula about.

Henry smiles. He knows exactly what he's doing. "What? I'm not gonna sing it at school."

"Seriously, Hen?" Again, I'm pleased I'm not losing my shit here. I'm handling this calmly, and he's actually listening. Or at least pretending to. "Why don't you write another rap about basketball or something? Or about Legos? You know if you sang that at school or told any of your friends about it, you would have gone straight to the principal's office, and I can't have you go to the principal's office today, because I'm going to be on an airplane, and I can't pick you up from school. So please, please, don't tell anyone at school about this." Then I bring on stern. "Plus, this is completely inappropriate. You may not use bad words in your raps or even out of your raps. It's not okay," I say, wondering if he's been sneaking a listen to the "explicit" songs on my iPod. I know I sound like one of those holier-than-thou parents who says, "My little Billy doesn't even know any bad words," but I honestly didn't know he knew the word fuck. Not a word Darren and I toss around. At least not in front of the boys. I guess that's what recess is for.

Disaster averted and little brother's ears thankfully not corrupted (James was still in the mudroom putting on his shoes during Eminem Jr.'s concert), I proceed with the breakfast prep and imagine Darren's face when I tell him. He'll laugh harder than I did. For some reason, fathers take it as a point of pride when their boys swear, perform arm farts, or burp the alphabet. Man training has begun.

"When are you coming home from California, Mommy?" James asks as he punctures the yolk with his fork and dips the crust in the ooze. He's not asking because he's sad. He likes to know what's coming next and when exactly that's going to be.

"I'll be home late Sunday night, but you'll be asleep, so I'll see you Monday morning. What should we have for breakfast on Monday?" I ask, trying to distract him from my impending absence.

"Chocolate-chip pancakes!" Henry shouts.

"Well, I'm in for the pancakes, but we'll see about the chocolate chips. Depends on how well you guys behave for Daddy this weekend." Who am I kidding? They're going to be angels. Kids save their best behavior for their dads. It's the moms who seem to always bear the brunt of their kids' disorderly conduct. Part of me hopes Darren has to deal with at least one meal refusal or a sock tantrum. I'll settle for a door slam. It's only fair.

As the boys collect their sweatshirts and backpacks, I don't tell them that I'll miss them or that I'll be so sad while I'm away. Because I don't think either will be true. I love my boys to the depths of my soul and beyond, but I can be away from them for a few days without self-combusting. I'm actually excited to be going away. It always makes the coming back so sweet and joyful. Like what working fathers get every single night they get home from work when their children rush the door and hang on them like they've been gone for a year fighting a war instead of in midtown Manhattan for twelve hours. I can't wait to feel that. That feeling of an unexpected gift, the first buds on my magnolia tree in April, the gold-sequined, top-hat finale of *A Chorus Line*.

"One more hug," I tell them both, squeezing them tight before they rush away to get on the bus. I inhale their little boy smells of laundry detergent, toothpaste, and sleep, and tell them that I love them. I wave till the bus is out of sight, then I rush inside, grab my bags, and get into the taxi that's waiting in my driveway to take me to the airport.

This is admittedly and embarrassingly lame, but when I get on the plane, in an effort to use my time wisely, I make a list of all the topics I want to ponder during the flight: Darren (with a subtopic of Jake Doyle), job, life goals, and how to help Cameron. True to form and order, once the plane is at cruising altitude, I get busy thinking about Darren. I'm big on attaching soundtracks to my life experiences, so I put on my "reflective" playlist which contains everything from "Fix You" by Coldplay (I cry when I think about how Chris Martin wrote that for Gwyneth when her dad died) to "Lovely Day" by Bill Withers (a guy I worked with eons ago turned me onto that soul-stirring classic), from "Unwritten" by Natasha Bedingfield (totally corny, but the words are inspiring) to "Superman" by Five for Fighting and "Superwoman" by Alicia Keys (both self-explanatory).

It's now been almost two weeks since the big revelation, and I realize that the emotion now making its debut in my limbic system is anger. Anger that takes over my body like I've freebased it. Over the last few days, I was strangely ambivalent about the whole thing, a position almost bordering on acquiescence. I just felt too tired to fight it. The basic facts are that he loves me, that we have a solid marriage and a great family, that he did something stupid, and that I should just move on. Simple. Done. Get on with my life.

I had moments of even forgetting the whole thing had ever happened. Like I'd be in a conversation with Darren and everything would be normal until I got some strange pang somewhere near where I imagine my gallbladder to be, and then I remembered that he did the dirty with another woman. But those blissfully blank moments around the pang made me realize that maybe the pangs are temporary, and when they go away, I'll only be left with the parts that don't ache. And then someday, memories of The Bandit will appear only once in a while, like when we're checking into a hotel on a family vacation and I glance over to the lobby bar or when we're away, just the two of us, and we come back to our hotel room after a few drinks, laughing in the hall, trying not to wake the conventioneers. Then as Darren slides the key card into the door, I'll imagine his expression when he brought her into his room instead of me.

But, here, 35,000 miles into the ether, the pangs have resurfaced, maybe even multiplied, and I'm angrier now than I have been since he told me. In a way it seems as if I've stepped out of myself and am viewing the situation as if it's happening to a friend. No longer is the affront personal, in varying shades of grey. Now, my friend is under attack, it's all black and white, and I'm pissed.

It is not okay that Darren had a momentary lapse and just happened to have sex with a stranger. Just like it wouldn't be okay if I did that. *So* not okay. And then his admission is supposed to lead smoothly to exoneration? Like a baby's smile leads to a mother's laugh, despite the projectile vomit all over the living room drapes? *Forgive me Grace, for I have sinned, but I wore a condom and it didn't mean anything and I feel really badly and I'm telling you so can you absolve me now?*

I'm not saying that the divorce attorney has made his way into my speed dial. I'm saying that the initial shock is over, and now I am mad. Plain old mad. Getting a notice for jury duty mad. Having to get root canal mad. And I don't know what to do with that feeling, except to let it fester for a while and then try to push it aside, so I can be grown up and try to figure out what the hell to do next.

I also feel like Darren's become a little complacent about the whole thing and is taking my ambivalence for granted. I'm not interested in receiving more flowers, more compliments, or more invitations to fancy restaurants. I'm interested in expressions of remorse, perhaps some groveling. Maybe some appreciation for my withholding severe bodily harm.

When Elton John's "Your Song" starts to play, I think of Jake. When Danielle died, somehow we all decided that would be her memorial anthem. I rarely hear that song on the radio, but when I do I immediately think of Danielle, and I smile, because I know she is with me. Now, I think of that motorcycle ride with Jake. My hair (at least the part sticking out from the helmet) blowing in the wind, my arms wrapped around a back I had longed to touch, my usually on-edge nerves completely numb, unafraid of the speed, unafraid of the true possibility that the sixteen-year-old boy who was operating this careening piece of steel could in any moment lose control and make my mother grieve and howl anew. The loss of two daughters in one week reducing her to absolute poignant nothingness.

Memories of my feelings for Jake rush back. I realize how trivial it is to even legitimize those feelings. I was a child. It was unrequited lust. There is nothing mature, meaningful, or lasting in those feelings. But here they are, camping out in my stomach, and I have a hunch they're going to hang out there for at least a few days. I didn't even realize I was missing that feeling of being adored until Darren started adoring me anew two weeks ago in the hopes of winning me back. And because it feels so forced with Darren, the recent genuine and, I believe, innocent (*am I naive?*) interactions with Jake make me feel young and unburdened. I am not a fool. I don't believe that Jake is trying to start something with me. He's just having a little fun, and so, goddamn it, am I.

These aren't emotions I'm proud of feeling when they're induced by another man. But I feel a bit entitled to them, especially because no one has to know about them, and I'm not going to act on them. Had Darren not cheated, I wouldn't even entertain the idea of allowing another man to make me feel like this. I have no interest in starting a relationship with Jake or any other man. The thought makes me shudder.

I am incapable of doing to my husband what he did to me. Incapable of doing that to my children. But I am capable of sticking my toe into the water, just to see how it feels because I know I'm able to pull it out and resist the temptation to do a full-on swan dive into the sparkly blue inviting pool. And possibly, if I get an ego boost from Jake, it might make me feel even with Darren; I might be more inclined to take him back. So I'm giving myself permission to flirt innocently with Jake this weekend, to smile and blush when he tells me I look pretty (he better tell me), and to feel a little dangerous—as if I'm back on that motorcycle again, but this time I've taken off my helmet.

When the pilot announces we'll be at LAX in thirty minutes, I wake with a start. I hadn't thought I'd sleep on this daytime flight, but the motion has a way of doing that to me. I regret not having had the time to address the other items on my list. At least I'll have things to talk about at lunch with my mom.

As I gather my bags and prepare to get off the plane, I'm struck by feelings of excitement (to see my old friends); calm (to be embraced by the care and love of my mom and sister, despite the fact that there will be a hefty amount of getting-on-nerves in the mix); freedom (to have an entire weekend of not having to discipline my children); and an intoxicating sense of anticipation at the thought of seeing Jake Doyle.

I check my phone as I make my way through the terminal. Emails from Darren and Cameron asking about the flight, an email from Eva with a tentative itinerary for our "fabulous" day tomorrow, and a text from my mom saying she's waiting for me at baggage claim. My phone vibrates as an email arrives from Jake.

chapter fifteen

i can't believe your actually coming. so
cool. 2morrow nite will be great. don't
look 2 pretty. that would be torture for
me.

I blush and smile as I follow the throng down the escalator. I notice people are looking all around. And that might be the main difference between L.A. and New York. In L.A., people are constantly giving themselves whiplash trying to spot a celebrity or see who's looking at them. In New York, people keep their heads down so they don't make eye contact with someone who could potentially get the wrong idea.

I make a pit stop, and as I wedge myself into the stall with all my stuff I try to figure out Jake's agenda. Knowing Jake, there is no grand master plan. He's all WYSIWYG, like the simplest 1980s computer: What You See Is What You Get. I'm not saying he's stupid. He's actually not. It's just that he's the type to operate on instinct. The caveman gene in Jake is still quite intact.

Do I think he wants a relationship with me? Well, if I weren't married, if I lived in L.A., if I liked to surf, and if I were really laid back, then I'm sure Jake would consider me. But I'm none of those things. It's simply that Jake is lonely, Jake had a crush on me a long time ago, Jake likes my Facebook photo, and Jake's just being Jake. I shouldn't read into anything, I shouldn't make assumptions, I shouldn't do all the things that come naturally to me when I analyze a situation. For once, I'm just going to try to be.

"Gracie!" I hear my mom shout and see her perfectly manicured hand waving to me.

"Hi, Mom!" I say. I'm really excited to see her. It's been a few months. When things are stable in my life, periodic phone conversations with my mom give me all the connection I need with her. But when things are unstable, like they are now, I regress, and being under my mom's care feels really comforting. As I make my way toward her, I am struck by how beautiful and healthy she looks. I'm sure the perfectly highlighted hair and gently tanned face have something to do with it. But she looks vibrant, and it makes me feel happy. And proud. She's wearing a bright yellow blouse and white capris. Her face is, of course, perfectly made up and her light pink lip gloss is glistening. This is another reason why women in L.A. look healthier than their counterparts in N.Y. They're not always in black.

I give my mom a big hug and she pulls back to take a look at me. And though I haven't touched up my lip gloss (in a few years), and I'm wearing sweats and sneakers, she gives me a big smile and tells me I look beautiful. Only a mother.

We don't have to wait for baggage because I carried on, so we make our way to her car and then to her condo. After I left for college, my mom pulled a George Jefferson. She sold the modest house in Encino and moved "over the hill" to Westwood, to a fancy, high-floor condo in a doorman building on Wilshire Boulevard. Her own deluxe apartment in the sky. I settle into her guest room and change into a sundress for lunch. It's strange that I don't have a childhood room anywhere. No place where my trophies, Judy Blume books, and Rob Lowe posters collect dust. Now, I sleep in a land of blue toile: blue toile on the bedspread, on the slipper chair, on the drapes, on the throw pillows. On the fucking tissue box holder. As if the award-winning Beverly Hills decorator ate a five-course blue toile dinner and puked it all over my mother's unsuspecting guest room.

When we get to Il Cielo, I realize that having lunch with my mom is like going to a high-society wedding: The crowd has been pre-screened for proper pedigrees, there are lots of air kisses, and you know you'll get a good meal. Il Cielo is one of my favorite restaurants in Beverly Hills. I love it for the food and the ambiance. My mom loves it because she knows all the right people will be there wearing all the right outfits giving her all the right respect. As we enter the restaurant, which looks like a beautiful home, my mom double-cheek kisses the maître d' who greets her by name and whisks us off to a table in the back garden, which is beautifully decorated with stunning flowers and pastel-dressed ladies. Usually L.A. women tend to show more thigh and cleavage than their New York sisters. But here at the rarefied Il Cielo, it feels very much like an ad from the Estée Lauder Beautiful campaign. Sans wedding dresses. And puppies.

"Hi, Guillaume," my mom says to the waiter as he approaches our table. "I'll have my usual please, darling." He smiles and writes something down. I think the only place I have "a usual" is at Starbucks, but the baristas never remember.

"May I please have the tomato soup and the vegetable risotto?"

"Very good," Guillaume says. We order two glasses of Riesling and a bottle of Pellegrino, and then Guillaume saunters off purposefully to take special care of the lovely Nina Roseman's lunch order. And that of her passable daughter. My mom waves to a well-coiffed woman dressed in cotton-candy pink on the far side of the patio.

"What's your usual?" I ask her.

"The tomato soup. It's divine. I'm so glad you remembered to order it, too, and the grilled calamari salad. It's fabulous." And a kiss is blown to a blonde in powder blue.

"So tell me, Gracie, how is Cameron?" my mom asks with concern as she adjusts the double-strand necklace of large amber stones that looks beautiful against her khaki Burberry trench dress. (She sometimes changes three, four times a day.)

"She's doing okay. I think. It's hard to tell sometimes with Cameron. She's got such a tough shell, but I know this miscarriage really destroyed her. I don't know what she's going to do. She's not even sure she wants to go back to work," I say as I start to take a sip of my wine and then stop. "I want to talk about Cameron, but first I'd like to propose a toast."

My mom picks up her glass and smiles at me.

I continue, "I'm so happy to be here, in L.A., in this beautiful garden, with you. I'm really so grateful that you are here for me, and I just want you to know I love you." We clink glasses and before I can take a sip, my mom stops me.

"And a toast to you, my beautiful Gracie. I would like to toast to your happiness and to only good things for you and Darren," she says as she clinks my glass again.

I wince, but she doesn't notice because she's smiling at a lady in cornflower blue who just walked by. I take a long sip of my wine and silently pray for an adequate supply of fortitude to last me the next forty-eight hours.

"As for Cameron," I say, "I just hope that she doesn't give up, that she looks into IVF or adoption or something."

"Well, she probably shouldn't have waited so long to have a baby," my mom says.

"Mom!" I say with a touch of anger.

"What? It's true. You girls, well not you Gracie, but a lot of my friends' daughters were so set on having a career that they missed their windows. It's very sad. My friend Melinda Waters has four children, and she's *still* waiting for a grandchild."

"It's not as simple as that, though. And it's people like you and Melinda Waters who told us to find a career that makes us happy, that we could do it all, that we could be mothers *and* working women."

"Well, maybe we were wrong," she says resignedly, fingering her bread and pushing it to the side of her plate wantingly.

"Maybe we were just meant to be barefoot and pregnant. It sure makes everything easier."

"What are you talking about?"

"I'm serious. I'm so conflicted about whether I'm supposed to have a job or whether I'm supposed to be home with the boys, volunteering at their school, learning mahjong. There are so many mixed messages about what women are supposed to do. It makes my head spin," I say, as I spread butter on my olive bread.

"Well, that's always been your problem, Gracie," she says with a dismissive wave of her hand.

"What?" I mumble, my mouth full of bread.

"You're concerned with what you're *supposed* to do, instead of doing what you *want* to do." She looks down at me. I feel like I'm seven. "Since you were a little girl, you worried about everything.

You tried to be the best ballet dancer because you thought that's what you were supposed to do, you tried to get the best grades because you thought that's what your father and I wanted you to do, you did everything to get into the best college because you thought you had to for some reason. We couldn't get you to just relax a bit and do what you *wanted* to do. Do you remember the pony farm?"

"No."

"You were about five. I had taken you girls to a pony farm in Canoga Park. Eva and Danielle both hated it. Eva didn't like getting dirty, and Danielle said it hurt. But you loved it. You said you liked the air in your hair. Your father asked you if you wanted to take lessons. You put your hands on your hips and said something like, 'pretty girls do ballet, they don't ride dusty ponies.' You were five, and you were already worrying about what you were supposed to do, when all you wanted to do was put on your jeans and ride. We tried to convince you to try a lesson or two, but you wouldn't give up your ballet. And you didn't even *like* ballet that much when you were little."

"I didn't?" I'm shocked. "I just remember doing ballet all the time."

"That was because Miss Natalya told us, told you, you had potential and that you were very graceful. You heard that and you asked to sign up for more classes. So we let you. You don't remember crying because you thought the leotards were scratchy and you got headaches from the tight hair buns?"

"No. Really?"

"Really. I probably should have pulled you out of that ballet school and pushed you to ride horses."

We sit for a moment, and I feel emotional. Raw. This woman knows me. Knows everything about me and all of the small moments that collectively conspired to make me the woman I am today. She was present for all the little decisions that informed the big decisions. And it makes me lightheaded (or is that the wine?) to think that my character was set so long ago. Or was it?

I realize that the character setting I put so much stock in was orchestrated by a five-year-old. And that five-year-old is still making the decisions, still telling me what I'm *supposed* to care about and what I'm *supposed* to do. I always justified my personality by saying "that's just who I am." But is it? If I had traded the ballet slippers and *pas de bourrées* for Levi's and riding lessons, would I be a different person today? Is the "me" I am just a fabrication? Just a construct of a child? I know I can't rewrite the past, but can I stop letting it inform my present and my future?

"Do you think it's possible for someone to drastically change the way they operate?" I ask my mom as Guillaume delivers our soup with a flourish.

"What do you mean?"

"I mean, I've been *this* person for so long," I say motioning around my whole body with waving hands. "This person who hungers for praise and recognition, who cares what other people think, who venerates the obligation over the desire, who analyzes everything in the hope that the overthinking might neutralize the fear and the uncertainty of doing the 'wrong' thing. Do you think that I can let go of all those hang-ups? Do you think I could just turn off the goddamn switch and start trusting my instincts more than my rationalizations? That I could finally lighten up a bit and stop having such high expectations for myself?" Before I can help it, I'm crying. My mom opens her Fendi, hands me a tissue, and smiles at me gently.

"Oh, Gracie. I think you could certainly try. But why don't you just practice it? Don't make a firm commitment to it or else you will make yourself crazy trying to be an overachiever at that, too. My healer likes to tell me to 'lean into things.' Why don't you try that, darling? I just want you to be happy."

"I know, Mom," I say as I shake it off, smile at her, and dive into my soup. As I suck down the velvety, tomato-y goodness, I'm struck by the thought that maybe I can stop blaming my character flaws on some set DNA. What if I go all *tabula rasa* and just start fresh? Just be comfortable in my own skin, confident with my decisions, and happy doing what feels good instead of what looks good. I am giddy with the possibility that I have just made a major breakthrough in my life, right here at Il Cielo.

We make small talk for a while about her latest interests: yogalates, labyrinth walking, wheatgrass, and then as our lunch plates are set down, again with a flourish, she asks me about Darren.

"So what's going on?"

I take a deep breath. "I'm not really sure, to tell you the honest truth. I go back and forth with my feelings about it. Sometimes I'm ambivalent, sometimes I'm really angry. Sometimes I'm sure we'll get past it, and sometimes I just can't imagine how I could ever trust this man again. And what's a marriage without trust?"

"Not a very good one," my mom says and looks down at her plate. "I'm not telling you to forgive him, Gracie. I just think forgiveness is overrated. I think you should somehow embrace the pain and let it propel you forward. Use it as energy."

"What exactly do you mean by that?" I'm all for spirituality, and I'm all for taking Cam's Oprah advice, but sometimes I think my mom gets a little far-fetched.

"I mean that you shouldn't be all high and mighty about a mistake that your husband made. Just think of it as a mistake. If he added an extra zero onto some deal at work and got fired, would you divorce him for making that mistake?"

"Mom, high and mighty? Come on, I'm not high and mighty. And I think you and I both know that's not really a good analogy. His pencil didn't slip. His penis did. He had sex with another woman," I say, slowly for emphasis. "He lied to me. He made me feel like shit."

"I know, darling."

"No, you don't know. You don't really know what this feels like at all because Dad never cheated on you. Has any man ever cheated on you?" I ask, getting angry. And maybe a little high and mighty.

"No, not that I know of," she says quietly.

"Well, then, I appreciate your concern about my marriage and what I'm going to do, but I just don't feel like it's fair for you to be so decisive about how I'm supposed to feel when you've never walked in my moccasins. Not that you would ever wear moccasins."

She laughs and reaches across the table for my hand. "You're right. I don't know exactly how you feel. I'm sorry for being hard on you. I just don't want your family to be broken up like ours was. I regret that deeply, Gracie. From the bottom of my heart, I don't want you to go through the same thing."

"I know, Mom. But you know I don't blame you for that. I know you always tell me not to, but I blame Dad."

"No, Gracie. This was not your father's decision." She pauses. "We came to that decision together. Things just weren't working," her voice trails off, and she looks away. I can tell the memory of their divorce is still painful for her. She loved my father. I think she still might.

158

"Well, I've never been a single mother and you have, so you've got some credibility there," I say, trying to lighten the mood. "I don't want to get a divorce. I don't want to be a single mother. I don't want to have to give up the boys every other weekend and have them go to Darren's fancy penthouse in the city where his twenty-five-year-old girlfriend named Britney who probably doesn't own any Spanx will make them the Mickey Mouse-shaped pancakes they're always asking for that I never have time to prepare. I don't want that. So I guess I'm just going to have to figure out how to make this work. But I also feel, for the first time, that I could be strong enough to do this on my own. That I don't need a man who made me feel so badly about myself around all the time to remind me of that. I don't know. I'm so confused."

"I know, darling. But you'll figure it out," she says and pats my hand.

We finish our lunch and talk about the plan for the rest of the weekend. After lunch, we'll go back to my mom's condo for a while. I'll read on her terrace or nap. Tonight, we're going to Eva's house for dinner. I'm really looking forward to seeing my nieces and Eva's adorable husband Sam. My mom decided not to join Eva and me tomorrow on our whirlwind day in L.A. She says she wants us to bond. It's always been one of her life goals to have Eva and me be best friends. It will not happen in *this* lifetime, but I am always willing to let my mom think it will.

"What is your plan for tomorrow night?" she asks me, taking a sip of her cappuccino.

"Kiki and Arden are picking me up at 7:00. We're meeting Scotty and Abigail and some other people at Koi at 7:30."

"Who are the other people?" My mom has always prided herself on knowing all of my friends.

"I think it's just Tommy Martin, Jake Doyle, and Sara Shaffer. I'm not sure who else. But I do know they wanted to keep this to just the old high school group. I guess there's some official engagement party in a couple weeks with all of Scotty and Abigail's grown-up friends."

"Oh, I remember that Jake Doyle. You had such a crush on him. What's he doing now?"

"I'm not really sure. I think he's an artist. I saw him at the reunion, but I haven't been in touch with him."

I don't want my mom to know about Jake. There is absolutely no reason for my mom to know about Jake.

"It sounds wonderful. Please tell Tommy to tell his mother hello from me. I see Sara once in a while. She's always pushing a carriage along San Vicente. Always seems to have a new baby."

"Yeah, I think she's up to four now," I say.

"I guess it's easier that your father's away this weekend," she says.

"I agree, it would've been hard to fit in a visit to see him, so it works out well. He's coming to New York next week, though, so we're meeting for dinner in the city one night."

My father, Reed Roseman, is a very powerful corporate attorney. He defended the Denihan case back in the 80s. When you tell anyone in L.A. that you were involved in the Denihan case, they nod deferentially. So my dad has been being deferred to for many years now. It defines him. He's a good man, and I love him very much, but I can't say he's been the greatest father in the world. Both of his parents died when he was a baby, and he was raised by a distant aunt, so when it comes to being a father, he's pretty clueless. He knows intellectually what he's supposed to do in the dad department, so he checks in with me and tells me he loves me, but he's never really been there emotionally. I think he's finding it easier to connect with me now that I'm an adult. I know I'm finding it easier to connect with him.

He's currently vacationing at his house in Kona, Hawaii, with his wife, Amanda. My dad and Amanda got married when I was ten. At that time, Amanda was a nubile twenty-six, twelve years younger than my dad. She had moved to L.A. from Nebraska a few years earlier to become an actress, but the furthest she got was holding a sandwich board in hot pants in front of the exotic car wash where my dad met her. Now she's fifty-five and a plastic-surgery addict because she's worried my dad will leave *her* for a younger woman. I think she's a vapid gold digger mostly because, well, she *is* a vapid gold digger. Eva tolerates Amanda better than I do. In fact, they go for mani pedis every few weeks because Amanda pays for them. And for the cappuccinos afterward.

The rest of the day is nice and relaxing. And dinner at my sister's is wonderful, though predictable. Eva only cooks from Ina Garten's *Barefoot Contessa* cookbooks because she believes they're the only recipes that turn out perfectly delicious time after time. And she's right. But Eva's menus don't vary much. It doesn't bother me because I am at her house so rarely, but her husband Sam calls her the Unfairfoot Opressa because he feels deprived of variety. I thoroughly enjoy our dinner of grilled tequila lime chicken, fresh corn salad, and herbed basmati rice, and it's nice to have someone else cook and clean for a change.

But I spend the entire night distracted. Jake Doyle is on my mind, in my mind, everywhere. It's something about being in L.A., about being back in the place where my childhood crushes and dreams blossomed. So, unfortunately, while my adorable nieces tell me about what they are going to be for Halloween (Hermione Granger and a ladybug), I imagine what Jake's expression will be when our eyes meet at Koi. While my sister is going over our plan for tomorrow, I am thinking about what it would be like to kiss him. My sweet brother-in-law busts out his guitar and starts playing Van Morrison—music we bonded over when he and Eva met because, like her cooking repertoire, her music repertoire is based upon one somewhat zaftig but extremely talented woman: Mariah Carey. But while I sit listening, trying to focus on his playing, I wonder if I *could* ever go where Darren went. If I could allow Jake to take me back to his place in Venice, to undress me, to caress me while we listen to the waves crash along the beach outside his window. To let the butterflies fly.

chapter sixteen

I wake up confused and jet-lagged on Saturday morning. It takes me a second to figure out where I am and another second to figure out how I feel. I remember that today's the day I'm seeing Jake, the culmination of all the interaction we've had over the last two weeks that I would be mortified if Darren ever knew about. I don't feel like I've been cheating on Darren, but I've been hiding stuff from him and that's the same as lying, and how far from cheating is that? I've gotten very good at justifying it all away, so that's what I do again right now. Plus, it's his fault I ever engaged with Jake in the first place.

Something changed in my brain at lunch yesterday. I feel a renewed strength, like maybe I can do this alone. Like how a toddler must feel the first time she takes a step and realizes her mother is not holding her up anymore. That feeling of pride and independence that she can do it on her own. Sure, the toddler usually falls. But if she keeps getting up and trying it, keeps standing on her own two feet, eventually she succeeds. And it's only a matter of time before she realizes she can run away.

My mom is still asleep, so I go for a jog. It's still cool, but the air feels perfect. As I run through the UCLA campus, I practice just being, not thinking. I pay attention to the feeling of my body as my heart beats faster and my legs work to keep the pace of the music on my "running" playlist. I look at the trees and marvel at the basic yet extraordinarily irrational concept of a thick piece of wood growing out of the ground and sprouting green. I observe the cloudless blue sky, scattered with acrobatic birds, and think about the force (I alternate between calling it God and The Universe) that has already decided what my future holds.

After my run, I stop at a cafe in Westwood Village and pick up breakfast for my mom and me: Greek yogurt parfaits, fruit salad, and two large cappuccinos. When I get back to the condo, my mom is on the terrace reading the paper.

"Did you get my note?" I ask, handing her a cappuccino.

"I did, thank you. And thank you for this fabulous breakfast," she says, clapping her hands, as I lay out the contents of the bag on the outside table. We eat quietly, lost in our own thoughts, staring at the trees, the sky, The Universe.

After breakfast, I get ready for my day with my sister and rejoin my mom outside.

"Anyone home?" Eva sings as she unlocks the door with her own key.

"We're out here!" my mom replies.

"Hi, Gracie! I'm so glad you're here," Eva says as she gives me a hug.

"Me, too."

"Ready?" Eva asks. She's all Kim Kardashian in a stylish grey tank top, a black scarf wrapped around her neck, white skinny jeans, lots of bracelets, and very high wedges. I am in an *unstylish* white Old Navy tank top, regular blue jeans, and flip flops. I am very me. And, I realize, I'm completely comfortable. I guess that's what nearing forty is doing for me. I no longer think my sister is right and I'm wrong. I think my sister is my sister, and I'm perfectly, happily, comfortably me.

Her red Audi convertible is parked outside, and I take a deep, anxious breath as I strap myself in. My sister is a horrible driver. She thinks she's Danica Patrick, completely in control. But she makes the mistake of always assuming what the other drivers are going to do. She leaves no room for chance. No room for the other driver to suddenly decide to change lanes while she speeds up behind and swerves around.

"Hey, Ev, mind if you go easy on the gas pedal and lane changing today?" I ask sweetly, trying not to nag and be all goody-goody.

"No problem," she says as the car lurches forward.

A white-knuckled fifteen minutes later and we're walking into Fred Segal in Santa Monica. I have loved Fred Segal since I found out what it was in middle school. Most people who've never been think it's one store, but actually it's a collection of amazing and unique boutiques. It's so nice to have the whole day ahead of us. We laugh and try things on, peeking into each other's dressing room the way sisters can, swapping clothes we know will look better on the other. I make my way through the handbags, jewelry, jeans, sunglasses, and casual clothes, happily collecting items that make me smile.

I'm not much of a shopper at home, so I give in to the experience and take advantage of the stylish and plentiful selection. Two hours later, we return to the parking lot overwhelmed by bags. I end up with a delicate gold necklace with horseshoe, starfish, and peace sign charms; a pair of J Brand skinny jeans (because I'm planning on getting skinny); a chunky cropped white sweater; and a pair of very high wedges (when in L.A.).

Eva had lobbied for The Ivy on Robertson for lunch, but whenever I'm in L.A., I have to go to Chin Chin, the California-ish Chinese cafe that's been around since 1983. I crave their Szechuan dumplings, pork bao, and Chinese chicken salad when I'm in New York, so goodbye Jennifer Aniston sightings at the Ivy, I'm going to Chin Chin. We head to Brentwood and pull into the parking lot of the strip mall where Chin Chin has been forever. I was such a fan growing up that I even worked in the Studio City location one summer just to get an employee discount.

After we place our order (Eva gets the chicken salad, too, but without the chicken), we settle in and talk about her job. She's worked in publicity since college, interning at the venerable Rogers & Cowan each summer she was home from UC Santa Barbara. And she is fully entrenched. Most people in the entertainment industry realize that their jobs, while vital to the economy and incredibly valuable to our culture, are not brain surgery. Eva does not. She believes that the world *will* stop if her client does not make it onto the cover of *Cosmo* the same month her new movie with Matt Damon comes out. That her client might *actually* die if there is no alkaline water available in the green room. It makes her a bit of a nut, but it also makes her a damn good publicist. Her corner office at Farrar and Frank and long list of A-list clients say so.

"Did you ever hear back from that website lady about the job?" Eva asks, sticking her fork in my steaming pork bao. She says she's a vegetarian, but that never stops her from eating meat.

"Yeah, I didn't get the job."

"Oh, Gracie, I'm sorry."

"Me, too. I had really convinced myself I was gonna get that job. But she hired someone who hasn't been out of the workforce for the last eight years."

"I understand why you want to work and all, but I don't know why you're putting so much pressure on yourself to get a job right away. I mean, *I* could never stay home, but you're so good at it."

"Seriously, Eva?" I say. "Why do you have to be so snarky?" And this is why Eva and I will never be the type of sisters who are best friends. She says everything that comes to her mind, as soon as it gets there, without filtering it. And then I go ahead and misinterpret it all.

"What do you mean? I just told you what a good mom I think you are," she says, taking a sip of her three-Splenda iced tea.

"Well, you say it like you could never do something so boring and meaningless as staying home with your kids all day. You've said that for years, how you could never stay home. It's such an insult. Like I'm simpler than you or you're so important."

"Hold on, Grace. If that's been upsetting you for years, why haven't you ever said anything? And, besides, that's entirely not what I mean. God! You always twist my words around."

I stare at her, wondering, once again, how we sprang from the same womb, and then I take a long sip of my Diet Coke. "I've never said anything because I never wanted to get into it with you. But I've decided to speak my mind more, and I'm practicing on you. How did I do?" I ask, smiling. That's the main difference between sisters and friends. Sisters can interrupt a fight to tell a joke. Friends just fight.

"You did fine," she says sarcastically, eyeing the plate of spareribs at the table next to ours.

"Thanks."

"But I don't mean it as an insult that I could never stay home," Eva says. "I just mean that I'm less patient with my kids, that I'm worse at being a mother than you are. I've always wished I could be as good with my kids as you are. I just get all frustrated and annoyed, and yell at them. I go to work so I don't have to spend as much time with them. There, I said it. Now it really proves I'm a bad mom," she says and crosses her arms across her chest.

"Well, I get frustrated and annoyed, too. And I would love to escape every day and work at an awesome job in a cool office, with real work friends and microwave popcorn at four o'clock, and come home every afternoon to get that same greeting that Darren does. But I just can't imagine leaving my kids with a nanny all day. At least you have Mom to be with the kids sometimes."

"First of all, Grace, Mom is rarely with my kids. She's very busy with her own life. Second of all, you could leave your kids with a nanny if you found the right one. And stop being so damn judgmental."

"I'm not being judgmental, I'm just being honest. Why is it that if my opinion is different from yours it means I'm judgmental? I hate that word." I thank the busboy as he takes our appetizer plates away.

"Damn, girl, you are just full of high and mighty ideas of how the world should operate, aren't you?"

"Have you and mom been talking about me behind my back and calling me high and mighty? Because she threw that out at our lunch yesterday. I am not high and mighty. I'm just a little high-strung. But there's a lot going on in my life. And I'm trying to figure it all out."

"I know, I'm sorry. And maybe we do call you high and mighty, but we say it with the deepest respect," she says and laughs. "Mom and I just wish you'd chill a little, stop taking things so seriously, stop thinking every decision you make is so important."

"I am chill," I protest.

Eva lets out a guttural laugh. The sparerib people stare.

"Seriously," I say. "You guys don't know me anymore. You see me a few times a year, you talk to me on the phone, but you don't see me in my life, every day, with my kids and my husband and my friends. I'm a lot more chill than you think. And high and mighty, I am not, thank you very much!"

The waiter brings our salads, and I close my eyes and inhale the delicious smell before I pick a few of the crunchy noodles up in my fingers and eat them contentedly.

"Anyway, back to the main point," I say, digging into my salad. "I would like to find a job, because I know that is what is going to fulfill me entirely. I love my boys, but that's not enough for me. And I'm so done with just being defined by being a stay-at-home mom. I would like to be proud of what I do."

"Okay, Grace. But I'll just say one more thing. You should be incredibly proud of being a stay-at-home mom. Just remember there are women like me who wish we could be stay-at-home moms. Some who can't for financial reasons. And some, like me, who can't because we just suck at it. So don't give it such a bad rap. Maybe you should just come at it a little differently and see it as a service you're providing society, bringing up two amazing citizens of the world."

"Hmmm," I say, as I digest all that she says. My heart stops as I look up and see Jake Doyle approach our table.

"What?" Eva asks as she sees the flushed panic on my face and then turns to see what I'm looking at.

"Hey, Grace!" Jake says, a huge smile on his ridiculously gorgeous face.

"Hey, Jake," I mumble as I try to chew the food in my mouth daintily while also smiling and trying to act very cool and relaxed. It's not working. My sister reaches over and pulls a piece of lettuce off of my cheek.

"I was in Brentwood doing some errands, and I called the number you gave me at your mom's place to see if you wanted to grab lunch or something. She told me you were here with your sister, so I just thought I'd stop in real quick and say hi," he says. He's wearing a grey hoodie and jeans with a knit hipster hat. His look, so different from Darren's, is arresting. I'm a mess.

"Oh, I didn't even know my mom knew we were here," I say. I have regained my composure and am clandestinely making fists with my hands under my napkin while at the same time yelling at myself inside my brain to just chill out. *Why am I acting like a love-struck little girl?*

"I texted her," my sister says, shrugging.

"Oh, sorry, Jake, this is my oldest sister, Eva. Eva, Jake." I still say *oldest* even though she's really my *older*. I often forget to reduce the set of my siblings to two and use the grammatically proper *older*. I still think of us as three. Jake doesn't know Eva because she was a senior in high school when we were freshmen.

"So, it's so good to see you!" Jake says as he awkwardly leans in for a kiss on the cheek. He grabs the chair from the empty table next to ours, turns it around, and sits down, legs spread wide. I am staring at him. Then I remember that my sister is here, and I turn to look at her. She gives me a look that means both, *What the fuck?*, and *who is this hot guy?* So I explain.

"Jake is an old friend from high school. He's best friends with Scotty. He's in the group that's going out tonight."

"Okay, got it," Eva says.

And that's why you're staring at him like you would like to sweep the soy sauce and sugar packets off the table next to you and let him have it right here in the middle of Chin Chin?

I am not!

You are, too!

"I don't want to interrupt your lunch," he says, putting his hands out like he's grasping an imaginary basketball. "Wow, you look great, Grace. I'll see you tonight." He pops up, pushes the chair back in, and gives me another kiss on the cheek.

Before I can think of something witty, yet non-incriminating to say that would at once be fittingly kind to Jake and convey that I am happy to see him, not give Eva any reason to believe that there is anything going on between Jake and me, *and* allow me to maintain my slowly retreating sense that I am not crossing a line, he takes off. As he saunters away, I see the muscular back I remember holding onto so many years ago.

"What the hell was that?" Eva asks me accusingly.

"*That* was Jake Doyle," I say, taking a bite of my salad so my mouth chews instead of smiles. Unfortunately, the blush slowly rising from my neck is giving me away.

"And why is it that Jake Doyle is making you blush like that, little sister?"

"Okay, fine." I decide to come clean with a story—more like a lie—just to get my sister off the trail. "I had a huge crush on him in high school. He found out I was coming tonight (lie), got my email address from Kiki (lie), and sent me an email. I emailed back and told him I was staying at Mom's and gave him the number in case he needed to contact me because he's arranging all the plans (lie). So I blush when I see him. Big deal. It's old news, Eva."

"Well, I can fully understand why you blush. He's smokin' hot."

"I know, right?" I ask, relieved to know she bought the lie.

As we finish our lunch, I ply Eva for sensational stories about her clients. She is good for loads of juicy tidbits. She's always dying to share these stories with someone, but she doesn't trust anyone in Hollywood not to run to a tabloid with the information. But she knows I won't, so she saves all the good stuff for me.

She tells me the long and scandalous story about one of her clients, a certain blonde starlet who shall remain nameless, who was discovered in the office of a particular A-list director making her case for a choice part that had already been offered to ScarJo. Said director's phone system was inadvertently turned to the mode where everything said in his office was broadcast on speaker through his assistant's phone, which happened to be located close to the office's cappuccino machine where other staffers had gathered. At some point, the blonde starlet's pleadings, in her unmistakable high voice, stopped and lots of moaning and slurping started. When she emerged from the director's office twenty minutes later, she noticed everyone staring and then suddenly turning away. She called Eva on the hunch that someone knew something and begged Eva to make sure the press didn't get wind of the story. So Eva immediately went on damage control: She called a press conference, had the starlet announce a hefty donation to a battered women's shelter, and effectively squashed all rumors of a casting plea gone wild.

After lunch, we decide to go back to her house and watch the girls swim. I fall asleep on her thickly cushioned, teak lounge chair as my mind swirls with images of Jake and Darren. I wake up sweaty and unsettled, and ask Eva to drive me back to the condo so I can get ready for dinner.

When I get back to my mom's, I sit on her terrace and scroll through my emails. There's one from Cameron checking in from Maine. She explains that it was a perfect idea for her to go there— she's being well taken care of. She has been on my mind constantly, and I'm so glad to know she's getting some peace and quiet.

I stop at an email from Darren with no subject and click it open. It's long. The longest email I've ever gotten from Darren. The longest thing Darren's probably written since his college application essays. I sit back, take a deep breath, and read.

```
Grace,

I hope you are having fun with your
family and your high school friends. I
think taking this time apart was
probably a good decision. The boys are
fine. They have been talking about you.
I think they really miss you. James
cried last night when he was going to
bed because he said he missed you. I let
him sleep with me. I missed you, too.
But I couldn't fall asleep. Besides the
fact that James was snoring, I just had
so much going on in my head. I came to
the conclusion that the hardest part of
all this is my deception. So, I've
decided to be completely honest with you
hoping that you will take this as an
effort to show you that I am so sorry
for what I did and that I can't stand
the idea of not being with you.
```

You asked me a while ago why I did it and I said I didn't know. I do know. I did it because it felt good. I know that sounds so stupid and horrible, but if I'm going to tell the truth, it's the truth. It felt good to have an attractive woman flirt with me and to have her want me. Add the alcohol and I wasn't strong enough to resist. I know that makes what I did horrible, but it doesn't make me a horrible person and that's what I need you to realize. I have tried to figure out how I feel about the whole thing and I came up with embarrassed, ashamed, sad, disappointed, and idiotic. I think a lot of guys do what I did and feel proud of it like they passed some man test. Grace, I don't feel like that at all. I know it's really hard for you to believe that I could have done what I did and have it not mean anything. It didn't mean anything, but I know that doesn't make you feel any better. I know you can't imagine how I didn't think about you when I did it. It's not that I don't love you and don't honor our marriage so I didn't think about you. It's more that I just wasn't thinking. I was an idiot and a stereotypical asshole man. I never thought I'd be like that. I guess I was wrong. I hope you know that woman and that night meant nothing to me. Unfortunately, I know they mean everything to you.

I'm not sure if I'm going about this apology thing the right way. You know I'm better with numbers than words. But I can't leave any stone unturned in my quest to make you understand how much I love you, how much I value our marriage and our family, and how sorry I am. I hope you can realize that what I did is not who I am and it will NEVER HAPPEN AGAIN! I beg you to keep letting the passage of time be on our side to allow this wound to heal. Please give me the chance to show you how much you mean to me. You don't need to write back. I just hope you think about what I said and that it helps a little. Knowing me and my writing, I hope I was able to convey what I feel, and I hope you realize that I love you very much.

With all my love, Darren

I start to cry somewhere around the part where he wrote that even though what he did was horrible, it doesn't make him a horrible person. That's really the crux of the whole thing. I am so thankful he wrote that to me. It's not difficult for Darren to let his feelings show, but it's difficult for him to actually put them into words. And I appreciate his effort.

I am suddenly exhausted. Tired of always trying to figure things out. Tired of the endless sorting out in my brain of what I *should* do, when I should do it. Should I work? Should I stay with Darren? Should I flirt with Jake? Should I even be nice to Darren and to Jake? Again, I admonish myself to just be. To stop the analysis for a while. Tonight will be a good opportunity to get out of my head. I'll be with my friends, and have a few drinks and a lot of laughs. And although I have softened a bit on Darren, I can't help the purely physiological reaction I have to Jake Doyle who I will be seeing in exactly one hour and twenty-eight minutes.

chapter seventeen

At 6:58, as I'm stuffing my money, ID, and phone into a small handbag, I hear the doorbell and then a lot of excited greetings. My mom hasn't seen Kiki or Arden in a couple years. My friends love my mom and they appreciate her for what she is. Kiki always said she wished her mom was less housecoat-wearing mamasita and more Gucci-wearing Nina Roseman. We all want what we don't (*can't?*) have.

I hurry to the front door, and the excited greetings start anew. We all hug, and Arden does one of her jumping-in-the-air side heel clicks—her trademark way of expressing glee. It's almost an optical illusion to look at thirty-nine-year-old women whom I've known since they were young. In my mind I see fifteen-year-olds. But if I squint a little and pretend these women are strangers passing me at the mall, they suddenly become the almost-forty-year-old women they are. And it's amazing for me to realize that we are as old as our mothers were when we were in high school. Our mothers looked old, like mothers. And they acted like they had their shit together.

Kiki is all decked out and gorgeous in a one-shoulder, white dress with a huge blue hibiscus on the torso that looks like something Carrie Bradshaw would wear. Arden's look is the antithesis in slacks (Who wears slacks? Arden wears slacks.) and a fitted cashmere sweater. Her straight blonde hairstyle hasn't changed since fifth grade. She's a classic beauty, all Clinique skin and Laura Mercier lips. She and Kiki are both lookers in completely different ways.

We pile into Kiki's Denali and make our way to Koi in West Hollywood. I've never been to this sexy, hip Japanese restaurant, but I've heard about it plenty from my sister and *Us* magazine. Kiki cranks up Madonna's *Like a Virgin* album to bring us back to 1984, right around when we all became best friends. So we're all singing our heads off to "Material Girl," windows down, driving up Santa Monica Boulevard toward La Cienega Boulevard, gossiping and laughing. My mind is a million miles from my marital problems and from my comfortable life in Rye, New York.

I feel like someone is kneading my stomach, like a baker with his dough, and I'm excited to see Jake. Tension has been building since that first Facebook chat a few weeks ago. And since I decided to actually make the trip, and since I told him I was coming, there's been a sense of anticipation I can't deny. However hard I try. It's probably good that I ran into him today at lunch; it's minimizing the anxiety a bit. Minimizing it enough.

I mentally go over my rules. I will allow myself to flirt, to feel pretty, to escape my life for one night. I will not allow myself to touch or be touched, to engage in any sort of Darren-bashing, to do anything that would make me feel embarrassed if Kiki or Arden saw. Just old friends hanging out. *Yeah, an old friend who I used to have a major crush on who still has some power over my heart and my nether regions. Act with grace, Grace. Act with grace.* It's not like I'm wearing special underwear or anything. And my long-overdue

178

bikini wax is more Botswanan than Brazilian. That proves I'm not interested in anything happening.

We pull up to the valet parking at 7:45 and make our way through the throng of paparazzi staked out to photograph whatever stars decide to dine tonight at Koi, a celeb hotspot. Kiki gives our name to the hostess who leads us to a banquette on the back patio. We get our paparazzi answer when we pass Leonardo DiCaprio at a table of beautiful women and Hollywood-agent-type guys. They're all laughing at a joke that we missed, but we still feel the punch line's transferred joy.

The restaurant is very cool, lots of wood and bamboo, lush greenery, and soft candlelight. Exactly the kind of ambience I was hoping for. I feel excited. The rest of our crew is already there, and there's lots of hooting and shrieking from the table when they see us approach. They all stand up to greet us. Scotty is on the end so he gets to me first and gives me a kiss on the cheek and a bear hug. Scotty is 6'1" and 200 pounds. There's nothing better than a Scotty hug. He pulls away, holds my hands, and scans me up and down.

"Gracie Roseman May, you look phenomenal!" he says, beaming at me.

"Why thank you Scotty Alden Reynolds, so do you," I say as I smile at him and give him another hug. There's something about being with old friends. There's something about being with Scotty. It's feety pajamas, a cold night with a fireplace, endless M&M's.

"I would like to introduce you to my beautiful and talented fiancée, Abigail Marlow. Abigail, this is Grace," Scotty says putting his arm around Abigail's shoulder.

"It's so nice to meet you," I say to Abigail, not knowing whether to shake her hand or give her a kiss. During that split second of indecision, she leans toward me and gives me a proper British two-cheek kiss.

"Grace, I've heard so much about you. Lovely to finally meet you," Abigail says warmly in her posh British accent.

She is a presence. As tall as Scotty, but with a lean, dancer's body, Abigail's auburn hair is cut in a pixie and she has Natalie Portman's face. Stunning, absolutely stunning. She looks at Scotty, and they smile and kiss. I feel a wave of love for my old friend. And happiness that he has found his wife.

"Stop hogging the import," Jake says as he bumps Scotty on the shoulder and maneuvers next to me.

"Hey, Jake," I say smiling, the baker in my belly getting a little frenzied.

"Hey, Gracie," he says, also smiling, and he gives me a kiss and a tight hug.

Just then, Tommy and Sara make their way over, and a new round of kisses and hugs begins.

Sara was the fourth in the Kiki/Arden/Grace group. But she was also the third in the Stacy/Samantha group (they liked to call themselves the SaSSy Sisters, even had off-the-shoulder T-shirts made—so lame, but this was the 80s!) so she and I were never as close as I was with Kiki and Arden. Sara is one of those girls who looks nothing like she did in high school. She went from Tracey Gold to Cameron Diaz. The tightly curled brown hair, unflattering nose, pimples, flat chest, and baby fat have been replaced with chemically straightened blonde hair, Cameron Diaz's nose (Kiki told me Sara brought a photo into her plastic surgeon's office and requested an exact replica), dermabrasioned skin, enhanced breasts, and toned arms. Girl looks good. A little fake. But this is L.A., and girl looks good.

After the greetings and compliments are exhausted, we slide into the U-shaped booth. On one end is Sara and the seating order next to her is Abigail, Scotty, me, Jake, Kiki, Tommy, and Arden. It's like the first day of school when the teacher assigns your seat that will be permanent for the rest of the semester. Your placement either sucks or guarantees you'll be next to the boy you think is cute or the girl you can cheat off of, wherever your priorities lie. I've scored big in the seating assignments tonight.

The booth is a little small for eight, so we're packed in close. My legs are pushed up against Scotty's on my right and Jake's on my left. But only my left is tingling a little. I pledged not to touch. But I have nowhere else to go.

We order a round of Koi saketinis and edamame. Kiki doesn't drink, which is why she's our designated driver. She orders a virgin Koi Chai Tea. The restaurant is loud, so it's hard to have a group table conversation. I start off on my right asking Scotty and Abigail about the wedding.

"We've decided to go to Hawaii, just the two of us, and get married in a tiny resort on Kauai," Scotty says.

"How romantic. How does Rosalie Reynolds feel about that?"

"Well," Scotty continues, "Rosalie Reynolds is none too excited because she wanted to throw the wedding of the century. But we're allowing her to have a small tasteful party for her friends when we get back. Unfortunately, small and tasteful in Rosalie Reynolds's world means 250 in black tie at The Beverly Hills Hotel. It's fine, though. Abigail's even a little excited about it, right, hon?" Scotty asks and turns to Abigail as he re-laces his fingers through hers.

Abigail leans over Scotty so I can hear her. "My mum died when I was little, and I adore Rosalie, so we're actually having fun with it. I'm the daughter she never had, and she's playing that mother-of-the-bride role for me. She's been lovely," Abigail says and smiles at Scotty.

"Well, I'm just really happy for the two of you," I say.

"Thanks, Gracie. There are only a handful of people who I would like to watch me get married, and you're definitely one of them," Scotty says, his eyes starting to tear up.

"Well, I'm honored to hear that. So just make sure you take lots of photos and email them to me."

"It's a deal," Scotty says.

Our drinks arrive, and Jake clinks a chopstick against his glass, proposing a toast to our guests of honor. He speaks loudly so we can all hear.

"I would like to take a moment to honor Scotty and Abigail. Scotty, you and I have been like brothers since we were just little dudes, hunting for babes, dreaming big dreams, desperately trying to speed up life so we could turn sixteen, get our licenses, and take off on a road trip that we never ended up taking. But you've taken an even better trip. A successful career and now a beautiful woman who you are about to marry. Abigail, I couldn't have chosen a more perfect, better-suited woman for my best friend. I wish you two all the happiness in the world. Cheers!"

"Cheers!" We all shout in unison, clinking glasses, laughing, delighting in our good fortune, our deep bonds, our warm feelings all around. I get caught in a man hug between Jake and Scotty. One of them smells really good, like Drakkar Noir, the cheesy adolescent cologne that gets me every time.

"That was really nice," I say to Jake as the smaller conversations around the table start up again. When he looks into my eyes, I feel my insides clench and the heat rise up my neck. *Don't blush, Grace. Hold it together.*

"Thanks. Didn't think I had it in me?" Jake asks, clinking my glass. We both take sips of our saketinis.

"It's not that. I guess I just don't think of you as the sentimental type, and that was really . . . thoughtful." I have to turn away from him and focus on the edamame because every time I look into his eyes I smile.

"Me? I am Mr. Sentimental!" Jake proclaims.

"Really? Well, I have to say that I don't really know you, or really most of the people at this table, as an adult. To me, everyone's still little sixteen-year-old Valley kids frozen in time but with crow's feet and more expensive watches," I say, popping some edamame out of their shell and tossing the empty pod into the bowl in the middle of the table.

"It's true." He laughs. "Sometimes I have to remind myself that we're not all going to meet up at a kegger at Jason Pontrose's house on Saturday night. Those days are long gone."

"Jason Pontrose," I say reminiscing. "Whatever happened to him?" I sneak a peek at Jake. He's looking at me. I smile.

"He lives in Tarzana and runs a smoothie shop."

"Nice."

"Yeah. I stop in whenever I'm in the Valley, and he gives me free smoothies. Talk about frozen in time, he still wears Op shorts and black-and-white checkerboard Vans."

"Wow." I take a sip of my drink and stare at the dancing fire in the votive candles. "I guess some people need to see the world and expand their horizons, and other people are quite content living their whole lives in the same place. I'm not saying one's better than the other, they're just different."

"Did someone say Jason Pontrose?" Sara asks.

"We were talking about the keggers he used to have all the time. Where the hell were his parents?" I ask, laughing.

"Sara, remember the time you passed out at his house and your parents filed a missing persons report because you never came home that night?" Kiki asks.

"Oh my God. I had completely blocked that out. That was horrible. The life of a teenager before cell phones. I remember waking up in Jason's bed, next to a completely nude Jason. I was completely dressed, of course," she says, "but I was so embarrassed. He swore nothing happened. Yuck."

We all laugh. I could talk about high-school memories for hours. I don't know if that makes me sentimental or pathetic. Probably a little of both. The waiter comes, and Jake orders a slew of appetizers for the table without even looking at the menu.

"Come here often?" I ask.

"Yeah, once in a while," he says modestly. "My agent's office is down the street, so she sets up a lot of lunch meetings here with potential clients."

"You're kind of surprising me," I say.

"Why? Because you still think of me as the clueless surfer dude who said 'stoked' all the time and skipped school when there were big swells at Zuma?" Jake asks, pushing his hair off his face. He's got that perfect hip casual look going on again tonight. He's wearing faded jeans, a white linen button down, and a cool silver necklace with some sort of Zen-looking charm around his neck. He's got a fresh glow on his face, like he spent the afternoon on the beach.

"Well, to be honest, I guess I kind of do."

"Well, then I'm going to have to change your perception of me." He smiles at me.

"Tell me about your art," I say, trying to steer us toward neutral subjects.

"I'm kind of transitioning my style. I do that every year or so as different things inspire me, like places I travel to, people I meet, challenges I overcome, social issues I become active in, music I listen to, books I read. When my perceptions change about things, and I open my eyes to new interpretations, it just seems to manifest itself in my art," he says. As he talks, his voice turns serious and he gestures meaningfully with his hands.

I'm so moved by what he just said that I realize I was holding my breath. Darren would never say something like that. He's just not evocative. Not the type of guy to read literature or have a favorite poem. Jake is so different from Darren. I feel the alcohol working, and I take off my sweater because I feel warm. I get a little stuck as I try to maneuver it off in the tiny space I've been allotted in the banquette.

"Here, let me help you with that," Jake says as my shoulder brushes across his chest. As it does, I catch his eye. He's smiling at me.

"Thanks," I say, turning away to get another edamame. I don't even like edamame. It's just giving my hands something to do.

"Jake, why are you monopolizing Grace?" Arden asks in her I've-had-one-drink-and-I'm-already-so-buzzed voice. Arden was the girl in high school who had one Bartles & Jaymes and was good for the night.

"Cuz she's just so damn pretty," Jake says in a fake cowboy voice.

"You really do look pretty." Tommy says. "I really screwed up when I let you go in eighth grade, didn't I?"

"You guys dated?" Abigail asks in a surprised voice.

"Oh, Abigail, you don't want to know about all the love drama that went down over the years between the people at this table," Kiki says, smiling at Tommy.

"Really? Well, even though it's ancient history, I'm sure it'll make me laugh so I think I do," Abigail says, giving us all searching looks as if she's trying to figure out who the guilty parties are.

"Okay, here we go, it's like this," tipsy Arden begins. "Everyone always thought Grace and Scotty had a thing because they were such good friends, but they never did until he kissed her once in college, but she had a boyfriend and that was the end of that," she clinks glasses with me and then Scotty. "Grace and Tommy had a little love connection in seventh or eighth grade, I can't remember which."

"Eighth," Tommy and I say in unison, laughing, and clinking glasses.

"Right, eighth," Arden says. "But Tommy dumped her at a bar mitzvah because Eliza Jandry had promised him a blow job in the bathroom."

"Doh!" Tommy says.

"Seriously?" I ask, turning to Tommy, my eyebrows raised.

"Guilty," Tommy says, shrugging his shoulders.

"That little slut!" I say and clink glasses again with Tommy.

"This is getting good," Abigail says.

"Then Kiki showed up at school, and she and Tommy were suddenly soul mates, making out all over school every day, and that lasted for a few years until they went to college and Kiki decided she didn't want anything holding her back."

Kiki and Tommy clink glasses.

"And Sara had that boring boyfriend Todd," Arden says.

"Todd!" a few of us say.

"He *was* boring," Sara says and laughs, clinking glasses with Abigail who is sitting right next to her and is a good enough stand-in for boring Todd.

"What about you Arden?" Abigail asks.

"Let's just say I had a series of suitors throughout my adolescence, but didn't find true love till I got to Berkeley. None of the boneheads at this table ever did it for me," Arden says.

"To boneheads!" the guys all shout and toast each other.

"Well, then, that just leaves you, Jake," Abigail says as we all turn to look at Jake.

"I wasted my high school years with a girl named Stephanie Campbell. She was nice, but I secretly lusted after our girl Gracie over here," Jake says turning to me. I feel my face turn red instantly.

"Really?" Kiki asks, with a sly tone to her voice. "I never knew that! I knew everything! How did I not know *that*?"

My guard is down so I continue, "To be fair, I had a massive crush on our boy Jake over here for years. But it was heartbreakingly unrequited, and I never knew the feeling was mutual. Didn't find out, actually, till our twentieth reunion last year."

"Well, just think how different high school could have been for the two of you," Tommy chimes in.

"Just think," Jake says, looking at me and raising his glass to mine.

"To Jake and Grace!" Arden shouts.

"To Jake and Grace!" everyone at the table shouts, clinking glasses all around.

By this point I am laughing and blushing, and feeling just fine. Jake and I clink glasses, look into each other's eyes, and finish off our drinks in a silent chugging pact. He kisses me on the cheek, and I feel like I'm going to vomit butterflies all over the table.

"Well, it's all good and fun, but now you're married, so I have to be a gentleman," Jake says as he raises his arms over his head, lowering the right one across Scotty's shoulders and the left one across mine. "Sorry, I just need to stretch my arms for a minute. It's a little tight in this booth."

"No problem. So why haven't you ever found the perfect girl to marry?" I ask.

"Not for lack of trying," Jake says laughing.

"What do you mean?"

"I feel like I've dated every single woman in L.A., including the Valley." He raises one eyebrow and smiles. "I just haven't found the one yet. Who knows, maybe I never will."

"Well, maybe you're better off," I say.

"There you go again, referring to marriage negatively. What is going on?"

With the alcohol lowering my inhibitions, I open up and tell him the whole story about Darren. He is silent through the entire thing, supplying nods and "hmms" when appropriate. When I finish, he just stares at me. I realize I don't regret telling him; I'm actually interested to hear what he has to say. But just then, the dinner arrives, and Scotty starts talking to Jake about a surfing trip they have planned for next week. I dig into the most delicious black cod and tiger prawns I've ever had and catch up with Kiki and Arden while trying to ignore Jake's body pressing against my own.

chapter eighteen

There comes a point during dinner when I feel like I've stepped out of my body and am watching the scene from afar. I see happy, laughing, smiling people. An abundance of plates gleaming with delectable food. Gestures and expressions of love and friendship. It is the type of scene that I would normally walk by and be envious of. But here I am, right in the middle of it, one of the happy, laughing, smiling people, eating that delicious food, receiving those warm gestures of love and friendship. I am soaking it in. I am present for it. I am simply being.

Dinner passes with more rounds of drinks and more conversations about ski trips we all took, parties we all remember, the children we all were. Jake doesn't mention the bombshell I dropped. At one point, he turns to me and for a second grasps my hands in his own and starts to tell me something, but stops. I sense that he is sad for me, but there are too many people around us and too much noise to know for sure.

Toward the end of dinner, I excuse myself to the bathroom. I feel like I'm floating through the restaurant. I've got a perfect buzz—the type where I'm still entirely aware of what I'm doing, but I have no fears, no shame, no inhibitions. The type of buzz that allows me to look in the mirror in the bathroom and see a really pretty, young, happy woman smiling back.

As I exit the bathroom, Jake is there waiting for me leaning against the wall.

"Grace, I need to talk to you," he says.

"Okay," I say, my smile fading.

He takes a deep breath and looks around to make sure we're alone. "I've been thinking a lot about what you told me, and I think a man who disrespected you by cheating on you might not be the right man for you."

"It's all just very confusing. It's not entirely black and white," I say quietly.

"I realize that. I just want you to know I'm here for you if you need a friend. I care about you," he says and a tiny laugh escapes.

"What's so funny?" I ask.

"It's just that it's been a long time since I've cared for a woman. And somehow, I find myself really caring for you. I really should never have let you go in high school, Gracie. I think we could have been something together. I just needed a little extra time to grow up," Jake says, reaching for my hands.

We stand there in the corridor near the bathrooms, holding hands, staring into each other's eyes, completely deaf to the noise coming from the restaurant. I'm not thinking. I'm just being. I've surrendered. The commotion in my stomach swallows any words I would even think to say.

"I would be crazy to lose you twice," he says, staring into my eyes. In one motion, he releases his right hand from mine and lifts it up to touch my cheek as he brings his left hand up to cradle the back of my head. And as he leans in and starts to bring his lips toward mine, my stomach clenches, and I close my eyes accepting what is about to happen.

His lips feel so soft as they press against mine. I feel my body surrender and my mind go blank as his lips slowly part and mine respond intuitively. It's slow at first. Hesitant. Then he kisses me a little more deeply, more passionately. My body, my mouth, respond, searching for, finding, a connection. He leans more closely into me, and I feel us fit together tightly. I hear a tiny moan escape from Jake—or was that from me?—and suddenly I'm back on earth. Outside the bathroom. Kissing Jake.

"I can't do this," I hear a voice quite similar to mine say slowly. I look at Jake and rush back to the table, taking the seat next to Arden on the end.

My heart is pounding, and I try to process what just happened. I think about the time Cameron's husband Jack told me he'd once been in a position to cheat at a medical conference, but that he was just sober enough to stay away. I realize that's what happened to me tonight, kind of. I was just sober enough. But I did kiss him. But it was only for a few seconds. Does that even count? Am I just like Darren? True, I was just sober enough to stop. But I did let something happen.

When Jake returns a few minutes later, my side of the table stands up to let him back into the booth. He whispers, "Sorry" into my ear as he passes me and slides back to his seat. I stay next to Arden. I don't want to go back to my seat and have to have any discussion with Jake about what just happened. Not now. Not here.

"I would like to make a toast," I say, clinking Arden's coffee spoon against her water glass. Dinner is winding down, and there are some things I want to say before another five or ten years go by. I'm a little shaken up by what just happened between Jake and me, but I continue. "I am so happy I was able to join you all here tonight to celebrate Scotty and Abigail. Scotty, we've been through so much together, through so many years. But I've never seen you so happy, and I know that's because you've found true love with Abigail. I'm thrilled for the two of you that you get to embark on this new life, this new love, together. Marriage is not always easy, and we often do things that hurt the one we love the most. But it's a point of always keeping, always trying to keep, the one you love in your mind when you do anything," I look at Jake, "that allows you to honor your spouse and keep your marriage true. I know the two of you will have a very successful, very loving, very true marriage. I also want to thank you all for being such wonderful friends to me over the years. I'm gonna cry," I say.

"Hold it together, Gracie!" Kiki says, laughing.

"It's okay, Grace," Jake says, handing me a napkin across the table.

"We all are who we are today for a lot of different reasons. The type of family we grew up in, the type of parents we had, all sorts of things. But so much of who we all are is because of our friends. There's something precious about old friends. I just want you all to know how much I cherish each of you and our individual and shared histories. I know I'm getting a little sentimental, but living so far away also makes me distant from these feelings, so when I'm home, they come up. Anyway, I'm not even making sense anymore. I just want you all to know I love you."

Arden turns to me and gives me a hug, while the rest of the table erupts in shouts of "Awww" and "Gracie!" I sneak a look at Jake, but he's already back in conversation with Scotty. I'm not angry at him for what he did. Not even a little. I'm flattered that he wanted to kiss me. Ecstatic even. Like in Darren's email when he wrote, "It felt good to have an attractive woman flirt with me and to have her want me." I get it. No matter how old you get, no matter how comfortable in your relationship, it still feels good to know you're attractive to another person. Especially one you're attracted to in return. The central point rests on what you do next.

"Welcome Home Mommy!!!" the signs taped to the mudroom door read. Henry's newly perfected bubble letters combined with James's green (he's in a green phase) scribbles welcome me to a dark and quiet, but not empty, home. I feel like I've been gone for weeks, and the house feels different. As if while I was gone, another family moved in with their belongings, their scent, their rhythms. There are lacrosse sticks and new cleats strewn across the mudroom floor, and new jerseys stuffed into their cubbies, evidence of Darren's trip to the sporting goods store with the boys. My boys' belongings, new to me, precious and familiar now to them. I quietly set my bags down and decide not to turn the lights on in the kitchen. The Darren-clean, as we call it, which takes great effort from him and receives vocalized appreciation with silent derision from me, can be dealt with in the morning.

I walk up the back staircase to peek into the boys' rooms. This ritual, my nightly rounds, is usually just an end-cap to the day, like brushing my teeth and removing the decorative pillows from my bed, one more thing I *just* do before I go to sleep. It always brings me great happiness to see my boys sleeping peacefully. And it's not just about their inability to ask me for one more baseball pitch, one more book, one more glass of water. It's seeing them safe, and knowing that it was me who was the one mostly responsible for returning them unharmed to their beds for yet another night. That I was the one who successfully managed to mother them appropriately for yet another day in this seemingly endless journey of parenting. But doing the nightly rounds, well, nightly, steals a bit of sweetness from the routine and makes it, well, routine. Having been away from the boys for two nights, I am excited tonight to do my rounds.

I open Henry's door and turn the light on while pushing the dimmer switch all the way down. He's sleeping with Matt Christopher's *Lacrosse Face-Off* open on his chest. Apparently, while I was away exploring the world of infidelity in L.A., my family was taking up lacrosse. I close the book, put it on his nightstand, kiss him on his forehead, and leave, switching off the light as I go. There is a light coming through the door to James's room, and I find him asleep gripping his new lacrosse stick, his favorite stuffed animal discarded to the foot of his bed. I have an urge, which I indulge, to take off my shoes and curl up next to James in his bed. I stroke his hair and inhale his innocent boy smell. I realize I'm easing my way back into connecting with my family with a kiss for Henry, a cuddle with James. Hopefully, by the time I reach my bedroom, where my husband will be in bed waiting for me, (his text when I landed letting me know the door was unlocked and he was still awake), I will feel comfortable enough back in my duty as mother to resume the role of wife.

Dinner last night ended anti-climactically. My aborted kiss with Jake, the big dramatic climax of the weekend, gave way to a boring-by-comparison end of Act Two. Jake gave me a few searching glances across the dinner table that I interpreted to mean either that he was sorry that he went in for the kill or that he was sorry that the vulnerable cub's overprotective mother lion appeared at the most inopportune moment. I returned those glances with my own, trying to convey with a squint of the eyes and a hint of a smile that what he did was okay, that I'm okay. That if I weren't so tethered to my station in New York, despite the fact that I'm mostly happy I am thus tethered, then I would have further explored that outside-the-bathroom-door kiss. I would have even followed it up with a request to leave the restaurant that instant so I could spend the next few blissful hours doing things with him that would hopefully leave us both breathless and in love. But, being a man, Jake was probably baffled by my telepathic communiqué and most likely just thought I had something in my eyes.

We all hugged and chatted around the valet parking station outside, saying our goodbyes, laughing, making optimistic plans for a sequel, while I tried to nonchalantly inch closer to Jake so I could have a quick word.

"No need to be sorry," I said, replying at last to the quick apology he had delivered when he returned to the table after I left him by the bathroom. "It's okay. I'm okay," I said, deciding it was best to leave out the part where, had things been different in my life, I would have taken that kiss along with whatever was behind doors one, two, *and* three.

"I know I shouldn't have done that," he said quietly. "I just don't want to have any regrets in my life."

"I think I'm going to go back to Darren," I said, for the first time even believing it myself.

"I think that's great," Jake said smiling, staring into my eyes.

"I hope you're right." I said, and I was able to hold his gaze without feeling myself blush, realizing that the anticipation of the zip line careening through the forest is much more exciting than the actual ride itself. I disembark at the end of the line and realize I'm stronger for having experienced it and ready to get on with the rest of my life.

"It was really nice seeing you, Gracie."

"It was really nice seeing you, Jake." I said and gave him a kiss on the cheek and a long hug.

Then Scotty grabbed me and started in with the Scotty hugs and sentiments, and before I knew it, Arden and I were back in Kiki's car, Madonna's "Over And Over" giving way to "Love Don't Live Here Anymore."

My mom and sister woke me up at ten o'clock on Sunday morning, piling on my bed with large cappuccinos my sister brought from The Coffee Bean and a tray stacked high with warm *Barefoot Contessa* strawberry scones that she must have woken up early that morning to make. They asked me about the night, and I told them all about dinner, Arden's presentation to Abigail of the who-loved-whom of our set, and what Scotty was planning for his wedding. I left out all mentions of Jake, especially the part where I almost cheated on my husband, still trying to convince myself—at times, unsuccessfully—that I didn't really cheat. That I didn't even come close. We talked and ate and before I knew it, I was in the shower, packing up, and then driving down the 405 with my mom to LAX to catch my flight back to JFK.

I had a glass of wine on the flight, curled up in a blanket, and listened to the soundtrack from *Once* over and over again. The melodies were haunting but my mind was, for the first time in a while, crystal clear. I led myself back through Darren's and my relationship, from when we first met to the early days of falling in love, through our carefree days without kids as we built our careers in the city, through those exciting and utterly exhausting days of having babies, to our easing into suburban life. I didn't go as far as the night he told me he cheated. I lingered in the feelings and atmosphere of life before The Bandit. Like loitering in the bridal room right before the wedding, knowing that outside that door waited something a bit scary and as soon as you entered that place, your life would never be the same. And though the experience of my wedding and the thought of Darren unceremoniously banging

The Bandit are, clearly, two entirely different animals, they both changed things forever.

In my mind, I wanted to just be Grace and Darren again. The Darren without the cheater asterisk by his name. Pure Grace and Darren. The couple who could still trust each other, whose business trips weren't second-guessed. I luxuriated in the memories of the looks he used to give me, the conversations we used to have, the sex that would go on all weekend long. I spent a lot of time on that flight perilously near the edge of Darren's indiscretion but not going there. I needed to remind myself why it was worth it to go back to him. So that if I ended up going through with my decision to *actually* go back to him, I would be excited to jump back into, or maybe, more appropriately, *fall* back into that place of my marriage before I knew about The Bandit.

And I decided that I didn't even come close to doing what he did. Yes, I flirted with Jake. Yes, I entertained thoughts in my mind of being with Jake. And, yes, I, kissed him. But I stopped it right away. Well, almost right away. I couldn't get rid of a sinking feeling in my stomach that I had done something wrong. But, I stopped it. And that means everything. I chalked up the small feelings of doubt to my overanalytical brain.

After all that, I made a decision. A moment of clarity as the flight attendant handed me my snack box filled with dried fruit, crackers, cheese spread, and sliced salami. After the last couple weeks of confusion and indecision and humiliation and all manner of what if, I realized that one unfortunate night did not my marriage make. I would not simplify what he did by calling it a mistake, but in essence that's really what it was. A really nasty mistake. And I saw personally, with Jake, how easy it was to make a mistake like that. I also realized that I have to give Darren a little credit for telling me about it. I certainly wasn't going to tell him about Jake. Maybe we both needed a little pick-me-up, a little shot of espresso to get us through the rest of the marriage.

"Hey there," Darren says, as I enter our bedroom. "Welcome home."

I walk over to his side of the bed, sit on the edge, and bury my head in his neck, wrapping my arms around his back and starting to cry. Darren hugs me back, but when my crying gets heavier, he pulls away.

"Hey, hey, what's wrong?" he asks me, gently wiping tears from my cheeks.

"I'm just happy to be home and happy to be with you, and I don't want us to be apart," I say, sobbing harder as I bury myself in Darren's neck again.

"Oh, Gracie. I'm so happy to hear you say that."

I pull away and look him straight in the eyes, "Just don't *ever* do that again."

"I won't," he says, hugging me. "I won't. I love you so much."

"I know," I say sadly.

"You still can't say it?" he asks.

I look at him. His eyes are smiling at me. I feel like I'm seeing him for the first time. "We still have a lot of work to do to get through this," I say. "But for the first time since you told me, I can say with certainty that I'm willing to do that work. I don't want the alternative."

After a while of lying together quietly, I go into the bathroom to wash up and then return to bed.

"So how was your trip?" Darren asks, grinning at me and lying on his side. I can tell he is relieved that we're moving on, that I've let him back in. Something light in his personality has been absent since he told me, actually since he cheated on me, and I'm happy to see the old Darren back.

"It was great, actually. I had a lot of fun with my mom and sister and such a nice time out with my friends last night." I tell him more about the weekend and the dinner, leaving out any mention of Jake, his appearance at lunch and dinner completely deleted from the story.

"And what made you decide to forgive me?"

"I didn't say I forgave you," I say sarcastically with a half smile.

"Okay, fair enough. Let me rephrase. What made you decide to allow me to retain the position of your lucky husband?" he asks, returning the half smile.

"I don't know. It was a lot of things, I guess. I just realized that I can allow what you did to be just small enough not to ruin us. I decided to not let your mistake—which I do believe didn't mean anything however much it hurts—destroy us. All that's good about you and me, our history, our relationship, our family, is so much bigger than that night. It may not be bigger than one more night though, so don't get any ideas!" I say punching him lightly in the arm.

"No ideas. None."

"It's like a crack in a really great vase. The crack is there and it's not going away, but you can kind of turn the vase around and after a while you might even forget the crack is there. And it's worth trying to forget about the crack, because the vase is so beautiful."

Darren kisses me gently, hesitantly.

"And," I continue, not one to be of few words when it comes to explaining how I feel, "I also appreciate very much the fact that you told me. You could have kept it secret. If you hadn't told me, I think it would have shown that you didn't think it was a big deal, that you could live with it. By telling me, I almost think you showed more respect to me. That our marriage was worth the honesty."

"That's why I told you," he says, holding both of my hands in his. "I don't understand how men do those things and keep it a secret. I don't know how they live with themselves. I was dishonest in what I did, and I realized the only way I could attempt to make that up to you was by being honest and telling you. But when I did tell you, I wasn't so sure I had made the right decision. Now that I see how this whole process has made us stronger, I know I needed to have told you. I'm glad I did. No secrets, Grace. I promise, no secrets."

"Me neither," I say. "No secrets."

Darren pulls me in and kisses me, still holding my hands. My stomach lurches. At first, I think it's because Darren's kiss is so pure. It reminds me of the way he used to kiss me when we kissed to kiss, before kisses became just one prerequisite in a night's journey to sex. But then I realize that my stomach is lurching because of Jake. How can I give all this weight to honesty and tell Darren no secrets when I did what I did in L.A. with Jake? No, I didn't have sex with Jake, I barely even kissed him. But I wanted to. And I engaged in secretive emails with him. And flirted with him. And did all manner of things that I would have been furious at Darren for doing. "Our marriage was worth the honesty," I replay Darren saying as his kiss gets deeper, more urgent. *No secrets, Grace? Really?*

"I have to tell you something," I say, pulling away from his embrace. I can't believe I'm about to do this, but something has overtaken my brain and I just start talking. "No secrets, right?"

"Right," Darren says, looking a bit worried. "What's going on, Grace?"

I sit up against the backboard and begin. "About the time when you told me about the cocktail waitress, I got an email from an old friend *(no secrets)*, well, actually, a guy I used to have a crush on in high school named Jake. Over the past couple weeks, we've been emailing back and forth, and it's been a little flirty. It wasn't like I was interested in him or anything, it was just because we were old friends and we used to like each other and all that. He was at the dinner Saturday night." I realize I'm sweating and Darren has repositioned himself so that he's sitting up now, too. I'm staring straight ahead. He's staring straight at me.

"Did you tell him about us?" Darren asks, his brow furrowing deeply.

"Well, yeah, I told him," I say, trying to sound calm, but actually sounding a bit defensive. "We're friends."

"If you're such good friends, why don't I know him? Did you tell Kiki and Arden?"

"Well, no. I didn't get a chance."

"Okay, so you don't tell your best friends, but you tell some guy named Jake? Jake? Really, Grace?" Darren asks, sounding mad.

"It wasn't like that, Darren," I say, and I start to cry because I can't believe how badly this is going and how much Darren is misunderstanding what happened.

"Did you sleep with him?" he asks, now standing on the floor next to his side of the bed.

"No! I didn't sleep with him," I say angrily.

"Did you do anything with him?"

"I could have," I say, getting angrier because he's the one who slept with a fucking cocktail waitress. "He started to kiss me, but I stopped him. And, unlike you, I kept my pants on, too."

"So you kissed him?" Darren asks angrily.

"No!"

"But you just said he started to kiss you, so clearly there was a kiss!"

"No. (*No secrets.*) Well, yes, for like a second, but then I realized what I was doing and I stopped him," I say, starting to feel desperate.

"Were you alone with him?"

"No."

"Then when did he try to kiss you?" Darren asks, his hands gesturing wildly, his face turning red. "At the dinner table with all your friends?"

"No. It was outside the bathroom," I say, as the story gets ripped out of proportion.

"He went to the bathroom with you?" Darren asks incredulously.

"No! Stop. Darren, please stop. Let me tell you what happened," I implore. He sits down again in the bed.

"I can't believe you were with some guy," he says, shaking his head.

"I wasn't with some guy. All I did was talk to a friend," I say calmly. Coldly.

"If all you did was talk to a friend, why are you making such a big deal about telling me?" he asks bitterly, looking at me for the first time since I started.

"I don't know," I say, curling my legs up and putting a pillow over my lap.

"You do know, Grace."

"I guess because I realize that I hid it from you. That I didn't want you to know I was talking flirtatiously to a man. That I didn't want you to know that even though I stopped the kiss, I did let it happen for a second," I say, deciding that I have nothing to lose now. I have to be honest. No secrets.

"When that friend of yours, I forget her name, had that relationship with that guy on Facebook, you told me that you thought that a married woman having an emotional relationship with another man was worse than a married man having a sexual relationship with another woman. Isn't that what you just did?" he asks, on his feet again.

"Absolutely not. This was in no way a relationship!"

"I can't believe you did this, Grace. I can't believe you can be so fucking hypocritical. That you could say the things you've said to me as we try to figure out what I did and at the same time you're doing the same fucking thing yourself. What? This Jake decided he didn't want a forty-year-old woman with two kids so that's what made you decide to come running back to me?"

"Darren! Stop!" I say firmly. "You are completely twisting my words and blowing this out of proportion." Darren quickly walks to his closet and starts collecting things. "What are you doing?" I ask, slightly panicked.

"I'm going into the city."

"Now?"

"I have an early meeting tomorrow anyway. I'll sleep at a hotel."

"Seriously? Don't go, we need to discuss this."

Darren looks at me with an expression I've never seen on him before. I realize it's disgust. The face you give a vagrant who flashes you on a subway. The face you give a frat boy in a bar who floats a highly offensive pick-up line. The face you give your wife when you believe she might be capable of something even worse than you are.

chapter nineteen

Perspective is important. When Danielle died, I was too young to put it in perspective realistically. My sister was dead, my parents were destroyed, all sense of normalcy in my life was completely eradicated. That being said, if I did have the ability to properly put that event in perspective when it happened, I probably would have synthesized it exactly as I did later. There are few things worse than losing a sister in a tragic car accident.

Now, as I brush my teeth, I try to put what happened with Darren and me last night—what has been happening with Darren and me over the past thirteen days—in perspective. And what I come up with is still a pretty lousy situation, but one, I argue with myself silently in the mirror, that could be a lot worse. Despite the lurching in my stomach and the haunting memory of Darren's disgusted face last night, I do believe, somewhere in the recesses of my brain, that we're going to be okay.

I do not regret telling Darren about Jake. I do not regret my interaction with Jake. I do not, surprisingly, regret any of it. Last night after Darren left, during the hours when I ached and searched for the sleep that evaded me, I came to the conclusion that the Jake stuff, including my admission of it to Darren, had to happen for Darren and me to be okay eventually. And if I really dig deep, I can even convince myself that the cocktail waitress had to happen for Darren and me to be really okay. Sometimes a marriage needs to be put into a cocktail shaker with sharp pieces of ice, sour limes, and some cheap licuor (in not-too-sensible black heels) in order to be mixed up and come out on the other end whole. Add some sweet apologies to the drink and some top-shelf makeup sex, and you've got yourself a keeper.

I know many people might tell me I should never have told him, that I could have kept that little gem to myself, that he never would have found out, that we gained nothing by my admission. But at that moment, amidst all the talk of honesty, it seemed like the right thing to do. I just had no idea he'd react the way he did. And if we're going to move forward in a healthy, honest relationship, then I needed, for my own conscience, to have told him. So fuck everyone else and their opinions.

Darren likes to think of himself as a bit of a rebel. Once in a while he'll even bust out his black motorcycle jacket from college or his old cowboy boots and fancy himself a real hip dude. He likes to think that he keeps me guessing, that I find him a bit unpredictable, footloose, and fancy-free. In reality, Darren is more like a chameleon in a tank at the zoo: he may change his appearance once in a while, but you know you'll always find him lounging under the same rock when you come home, waiting for a meal. I know Darren needs to be away from me to understand what I've done and get over the bruised ego. I don't blame him. But I also know that he will forgive me. That he will come home. That eventually the leather jacket and cowboy boots will find their way back to a corner of the closet so he can curl up on the couch with me in his Under Armour sweats and business school T-shirt once again.

And because I know fundamentally that we're going to be okay, I'm not allowing myself to be too upset about what has been going on. I finally feel free of the anger I feel toward Darren, because where I am now is in a place of proper perspective. My family is alive and healthy, and, truthfully, that is all that really matters. When you've been presented with a loved one's death in your life, like I was with Danielle, most other things tend to pale.

So as I get dressed and prepare to get the boys off to the bus, I smile, knowing that my family is intact, my marriage will survive, and the world will go on. It just might take a few days to get Darren to agree.

"Good morning, sunshine," I sing as I open the shades in Henry's room.

"Mommy! You're back!" he says in a sleepy voice, and the "Mommy," from a boy who switched to "Mom" a few months ago, does not go unnoticed by me.

"You knew I'd come back," I say laughing, thinking of *Owl Babies*.

"How was your trip?" he asks sitting up, rubbing his eyes.

"It was really great, Hen, thanks for asking," I say, picking up more dirty clothes from his floor than could possibly have been worn in one weekend. I'm pleasantly surprised I'm not annoyed that his clothes aren't in the hamper. I guess the time away really did recharge my batteries. All about perspective.

"Okay, buddy. Get dressed, brush your teeth, and come down. Daddy said you guys earned those chocolate-chip pancakes so I better get cookin'," I say.

"Hooray! Chocolate-chip pancakes! Pancakes in my tummy/very, very yummy/love my dear ol' mummy!" he raps his way to the bathroom.

I sit on the side of James's bed and wake him up.

"Did Henry just say chocolate-chip pancakes?" he asks me, opening his eyes wide.

"He did. Would you like some?" I ask.

He nods and reaches his arms out to hug me.

"I missed you," I say, my eyes starting to well up. "I missed our family."

"Our family missed you, too, Mommy," he says, hugging me tightly.

"Okay," I say, taking a deep breath, shaking myself off, and rising from his embrace. "School day," I say loudly for both boys to hear. "Get dressed and come downstairs, *rápido, rápido!*"

After the boys are satisfyingly full of chocolate-chip pancakes, I get them out the door and onto the bus. I call Darren on his cell. No answer. I leave a voicemail. I call Cameron to find out about Maine, see how she's doing, and fill her in on the latest chapter in the Darren-Grace saga. No answer. I leave her a voicemail, too. After a quick run to the supermarket to restock the house, I spend the next few hours unpacking, cleaning the house, and settling in. I realize that since I officially didn't get the job at *Well in Westchester*, I officially have nothing to do. I grab a cup of coffee and sit down with a pad and paper to start making a list of all my options when the phone rings and I see it's Cameron's cell.

"Hey," I say cheerfully, curling my legs underneath me on the sofa. "How was Maine?"

"Oh, Grace," Cameron says sadly.

"That bad? What happened?" I ask.

"No, Maine was fine," she says in a small voice. "Excellent, actually. But—" she stops and takes a breath. "I can't even believe I'm going to tell you what I'm about to tell you." Her voice sounds contorted.

"What?" I ask, suddenly unsure of where this conversation is going, my stomach immediately starting to turn.

"Oh, Grace."

"What, Cam? Tell me. What's going on? Where are you? It sounds like you're on a street in the city."

"I am." Another deep breath. "Okay. I went to my OB this morning just to get everything checked out and see if there are any tests he recommends. He was examining me, and . . ." she stops. I hear a crackle in her voice and then she continues, more in her Dr. Stevens voice than her Cameron voice. "He felt a lump in my left breast."

"Oh, Cam," I say, exhaling, finally.

"Yeah, he said it's probably not a big deal but he didn't want to take any chances so he suggested I schedule a mammogram. Meanwhile, I'm a little freaked out because 'not a big deal' could be a big deal and why should I wait around and wonder about it? So I called Shannon Kramer, remember my friend from med school? Anyway, she's a radiologist at Mount Sinai. She took my call right away and told me to come in and that she'd fit me in. So, I walked over there, and long story short, the mammogram showed a spiculated mass. She then ordered an ultrasound and that showed a nodule with irregular borders, which is basically doctor-speak for breast cancer. So, I might have breast cancer." She sounds resigned. And deeply sad. "She's doing a needle biopsy this afternoon on me, and she said she'd try to get the results for me tomorrow."

"Oh my God, Cam. Are you okay?" I didn't know what to say.

"Well, I don't know," and the contorted voice comes back. "I am okay right now because I feel totally fine. How could I have cancer in my body when I feel totally fine? But I'm a doctor so I know that, yes, I could have cancer in my body and feel totally fine. I also know that it's pretty likely from the tests that I have breast cancer. Shannon didn't sugarcoat anything. She told me she didn't like the way the scans looked. So I know I should be completely objective about this, because I should be approaching it from a clinical perspective, but then I feel completely outraged because how can this be happening to me? Grace, I had a fucking miscarriage last week, and today I'm being diagnosed with breast cancer? Really?"

Cameron is crying now and I can picture her gesturing wildly with her hands, which is something she does once in a while. Always when things are really bad. Cameron is also not one to cry. Suddenly I'm panicked, but I realize that if she's not holding it together, I need to.

"Oh, Cam. Okay. I'm coming down there. I'll go to your appointment with you. I can't imagine how scared you must be right now."

"I'm not scared, Grace," she interrupts angrily. "I'm fucking pissed. I'm pissed that I can't have a baby, and I'm pissed that I have cancer. This is so fucking unreal."

"I know, Cam," I try to sound calm. I'm pacing my family room, trying to hold back tears.

"No, Grace. You don't know," she says with a tone in her voice. She takes a deep breath. "I'm sorry. I don't know why I'm taking this out on you," she says, crying quietly.

"It's okay, Cameron," I say, and it is. "I know I can't understand how you're feeling, but I want to come and be with you. You don't have to do this test alone."

"It's okay," she says calmly. "Jack is coming. In fact, I see him walking down the street right now. I'm gonna go, Grace. I'll call you when the test is over. I'm so sorry I got angry at you."

"It's okay. Please call me. I'm worried about you, and I want to know what's going on. Promise me you'll call me."

"I will. I promise," she says and hangs up.

All of a sudden, tears are streaming from my eyes and my breathing quickens. I can't believe this is happening. Cameron is right: a miscarriage and possibly—she may be certain it's breast cancer, but I'm not going there until there's a definitive diagnosis—cancer in one week. It's unimaginable. I don't know what to do with myself. I'm tempted to go to Mount Sinai and be with her during the test, but I also don't want to impose. And Jack is there. I can't imagine what must be going through Cameron's mind. Actually, I can.

Whenever I would tell Cameron about my theory that because my life has been pretty excellent and, because of that, I fear some horrible thing will happen to me, she laughs at me. My realistic, cynical, decidedly unsentimental friend thinks that's a bag of baloney. She believes that what happens, happens, and it's not worth worrying about the unknown or borrowing trouble. It comes soon enough. So I *can* imagine what's going through her mind. Probably something like, "This sucks, but I'll deal with it." I just know the initial shock has completely thrown her. But, true to Cameron's form, she'll probably find out her diagnosis, and if she does have cancer, she'll deal with it. Although I can't be sure that she'll deal with cancer the way she deals with everything else. It is, after all, cancer.

It blows my mind how many people our age are getting sick. It used to be that I'd hear of my parents' friends getting cancer, and it was sad and all, but they were in their 70s and 80s, and that's just what happens. But thirty- and forty-year-olds? That's an entirely different story. And wondering how and why she got it is useless at this point. What matters is that my best friend might have cancer, and I will be by her side throughout the entire thing. I'm petrified. My mind, of course, goes straight to the worst-case scenario, but I shudder and don't let myself go all the way there. I'm completely stunned by what just happened. And I want to talk to Darren.

Unfortunately, he doesn't want to talk to me as evidenced by two unreturned phone calls and three unanswered emails I left him. I basically said the same thing in all of them: that he has no right to be mad at me. So I decide to try again. But this time I change my strategy and acknowledge his feelings, so we can try to move on.

Dear Darren,

I'm having a hard time understanding why you're so angry at me, and I think if you really understood what happened—that *nothing* happened—you wouldn't be so mad. So, I want to get a few things straight.

First, I never set out to have any sort of relationship with Jake. He contacted me as a friend. Unfortunately, it was right after you told me about your indiscretion, so I was vulnerable and angry. The attention he paid me felt good. Since you had made me feel so badly, his kindness was salve on an open wound. And then I just continued justifying my actions because it was a sort of payback to you for what you did to me. Second, I never gave Jake any impression that I was interested in having any sort of relationship with him. Third, I am not planning on interacting with him in the future. Our marriage is more important to me than reconnecting with someone from my distant past.

What I need you to understand most is that I'm not sure I would have been able to get to where I am with you right now—wanting to make our marriage work—if it hadn't been for what I experienced with Jake. You told me in the long email you wrote me while I was in L.A. that it felt good to have an attractive woman want you. Well, I guess I felt the same way. But what I realized is that I didn't want that person, just like you didn't want the cocktail waitress. I want *you*, Darren. I want our marriage. I want our family. It's basically finding out that, though that grass over there might have looked a bit greener from where I was standing, once I got up close, it was a pretty lousy substitute for my own lawn. Whatever *you* may think, and again, for the record, *I* think you totally overreacted, I didn't actively set out to punish you by talking to Jake and seeing him in L.A. (which, again for the record, was in a big group; we didn't go out alone). I really did go there for Scotty's party, to see my mom and sister, and to have some time to

think. But I think it could have been
the thing that saved our marriage. I'm
still very angry at you for what you
did, but I think now we can understand
each other better, understand ourselves
better, and use that knowledge to move
into the next stage of our marriage. And
I feel confident that having been
through what we've been through, it
will, I hope, prevent anything like this
from ever happening again. Let's start
being us again.

There's something else I want to discuss
with you but I would rather do it on the
phone, so can you please call me when
you have a chance? I love you.

I press "send."

I didn't want to tell him about Cameron in the email because I
felt wrong typing it. I need to talk to him though. I sit there for a
few minutes wondering what to do next. My inbox chimes. It's
from Darren.

Grace,

I realize this may seem all hunky-dory
and eye-for-an-eye to you, but I don't
see it that way. It may be a double
standard, but I'm just having a hard
time thinking that what you did was
okay. You know what I did didn't mean
anything to me. But you have a personal
relationship with this guy, and that is
just not okay with me. I am having a

> really hard time understanding how you
> could have done that to me, how you can
> think that your kiss wasn't a big deal,
> and how you can act like wrong plus
> wrong equals living happily ever after.
> It's not that simple.

I am speechless. I am staring at my computer, and I am frozen and speechless. And I don't know why I completely misjudged how Darren would react to this. I try to put myself into his shoes. Was what I did equal to or even worse than what he did? Am I simplifying it and telling him we both did something wrong, so let's just forget it now and move on? No. And no. But his ego seems to have been annihilated, and from what I understand about men, that is torture. Holy shit. Here I was thinking that all I had to do to move on with my marriage was to tell my husband that I forgave him. I can't believe how messed up this has all become.

My email chimes again and it's Cameron.

> Hey Grace. So sorry I blew up at you. In
> waiting room with Jack. This is so
> surreal. I can't believe this is
> actually happening to me. I know you, so
> I know you're freaking out right now.
> But please don't. We will deal with
> this, whatever it is. I promise. Will be
> in touch later. Cam

I write Cameron back and tell her I'm here for her. For everything. I feel like I have just been pulverized by a huge wave. I am fighting the powerful water to get upright and push to the surface for air. My marriage. My best friend. It's all too much. The tears unleash, and I am sobbing uncontrollably. And there's only one thing that I know will make me feel better: sleep. I go upstairs and set my alarm for right before the bus will come. It takes me a while to stop my brain from all the thinking, but eventually the exhaustion prevails, and I fall asleep. Just before I do, I think again about perspective. Right now, my life, in perspective, sucks.

chapter twenty

"Thanks for coming, Grace," Jack says as he opens the front door. "I wish I could stay home with her, but I'm in surgery all day."

"Of course, Jack. I wouldn't have it any other way. I just can't believe this is all happening."

"I know. But, we'll hope for the best with the biopsy results, and we'll deal with whatever it is," he says. He attempts a smile, but I know it's for my benefit.

"How does Cameron seem?" I ask.

"Pretty lousy physically, but you know Cameron, she can manage through anything."

"Yes, I do know Cameron. But this is all too much for anyone," I say, as I notice his eyes welling up. "Okay, you go. I've got her. I'll touch base with you later to let you know what's going on."

"Thanks, Grace," he says as he gives me a hug and rushes out.

"Hey, Grace," Jack stops and turns around, suddenly remembering something.

"Yeah?"

"I talked to Darren last night. He told me what's going on," Jack says carefully.

"I'm sorry he did that," I say. "You have enough on your plate to deal with right now."

"It's okay. I asked him how you guys were. I needed to be distracted with someone else's problems for a while," he laughs.

I return the smile. "It's all pretty much a disaster now. I thought he would realize pretty quickly that what I did doesn't come close to what he did and that, in fact, it was all a complete reaction to what he did. But he's taking it really hard."

"Remember when I told you about what happened to me at the medical conference?"

"Yeah," I say, recalling how he had just been sober enough to cut off a potential infidelity.

"Well, I didn't tell you the absolute truth because I was too ashamed. But I'm going to tell you now."

"Okay," I say, not sure about what's coming next.

"I actually did start to kiss the woman. But like you, from what Darren told me, I stopped it right away. I still felt badly enough about it to tell Cameron. And I was surprised that she blew it off, but that's Cameron and thankfully, she didn't think it was a big deal."

I'm stunned that Cameron never told me.

"I begged her to never tell you. I didn't want you and Darren to think less of me. But I told him about it last night. And I told him that I thought that what you did does not equal what he did."

"Wow, Jack. I don't know what to say."

"He certainly didn't like my taking your side. But I think hearing it from me made him think about it a little differently. And to be honest, with all that's going on with Cameron and how fucking scared I am about it all, I think it's pretty ridiculous that you guys should spend one more day being mad at each other. We have to hang on tight and cherish what we have. Because in the blink of an eye, it can all be taken away," Jack says and starts to cry.

I give him a big hug. I can't imagine how hard this must be for him. But I'm so appreciative for what he told me. For what he told Darren.

"Did you tell Darren about what's going on with Cameron?" I ask.

"I didn't get the chance," Jack says. "We were talking about you guys, and then he got a call from work and had to go."

"I tried to tell him yesterday and asked him to call me, but he wouldn't. I'll call him again later."

When I get to Cameron's room, she's in bed watching TV and laughing.

"What's so funny?" I ask.

"Have you ever seen these shows where these brides-to-be go to Kleinfeld's to buy a wedding dress, and little do they know, but the salespeople who are the reality stars are totally talking shit about them behind their back. It's hilarious."

"How are you feeling?"

"I'm sore, but I'm fine. I don't really need to be in bed, but I just feel shut down. I don't know what's going on, but I think this is what normal people would call a physical and emotional breakdown," Cameron says as she puts the TV on mute and sits up in her bed.

I open the bag I brought with coffee and muffins, and spread it out on her bedside table.

"Thanks, Grace," Cameron says. "You really are a good friend."

"You would do the same for me," I say.

"Yeah, but I wouldn't be nearly as patient," she laughs.

"How was the procedure?" I ask, taking a sip of my coffee and making my way over to Jack's side of the bed.

"It was kinda horrifying. I don't think I was numb enough, so I felt pressure. It felt like a crochet hook going into my breast. Not fun. But it was relatively quick, and now it's over, so it's not worth thinking about."

"Well, I'm just sorry that you have to go through all this."

"Me, too. But I'm not having any sort of pity party. Plus, I don't, at this point, have anything yet to feel pitiful about. For all I know, I could be cancer-free. So I might as well enjoy it until I get the phone call from Shannon."

"What time did she say she'd call with the results?" I ask.

"Late morning."

"Okay. Soon."

"Yeah. It can take up to a week for people to get biopsy results back. Shannon really went to bat for me."

"I'm glad you don't have to go through the nightmare of waiting," I say.

"Me, too. So, anyway," Cameron says with a shake of her body—a release, of sorts, of cancer talk. "What's going on with you? I don't even know what happened in L.A.," Cameron says, smiling and taking a bite of a banana chocolate-chip muffin, her favorite.

"Oh, L.A.," I say with an exhale. "I don't even know where to start." Jack had told me as we were saying goodbye this morning that he didn't tell Cameron what he had discussed with Darren, so I knew she knew nothing.

As Cameron nibbles on her muffin and drinks her coffee, I tell her the entire story, starting with the not-so-sensational parts about my mom and sister, and ending with the all-too-sensational parts about Jake, the kiss, and my confession to Darren. While I do, I stare straight ahead at the television watching women try on dresses for what they assume will be the happiest day of their lives.

"Jesus, Grace."

"I know, it's a disaster."

"Seriously," Cameron says, and I sense a bit of acrimony in her voice.

"I know, but I can't have you disappointed in me, too."

"I'm not disappointed in you. But I feel like you are trying to sabotage your marriage. Are you?" Cameron asks.

"No. Absolutely not," I say, taking a sip of my coffee and rearranging myself on Jack's side of the bed.

"Then what the hell did you do that for? And then why the hell did you tell Darren about it?"

"I don't know. It just kind of happened. I'm not going to say I didn't allow it to happen, but it all just took on a life of its own, and it happened. And I told him because I have this innate need to be honest with people, and that's really not such a bad thing. But now I have to deal with the nasty mess I've left behind."

"Has Jake been in touch with you?" Cameron asks, trying to pick the crumbs off her shirt and duvet.

"No, and if he does email me, I'm just going to say that I don't think we can be friends."

"Wow," Cameron says. "This is big. What was Darren's reaction?"

"Well, he left. After I told him on Sunday night when I got home, he left. He went to the city, and I haven't seen him since. I told the boys he's on a business trip. I sent him a long email yesterday, but he pretty much said that what I did is worse than what he did, which is absolute shit, and he's not sure he can ever forgive me," I say quietly, the unrelenting tears starting to find their way back to my eyes.

"Jesus, Grace. What do you think is going to happen?" Cameron asks.

"Well," I say sadly, trying to staunch the tidal wave of tears, "I originally thought that Darren just needed some time to process everything, and then he would realize that we're going to be okay, but now I'm not so sure. I can't believe this is all happening," I say, shaking my head.

"I just think—" Cameron stops when the phone rings. She reaches to pick it up.

"Hello," she says and looks at me nervously. From then, I only hear her side of the conversation: "Hi Shannon. . . . A little sore, but I'm okay, thanks. . . . And? Oh, okay. Is there someone you would recommend? . . . Okay, that would be helpful. . . . I know. Thanks, Shannon. . . . Okay, bye."

I turn to look at Cameron and she's holding the phone, staring straight ahead with a stunned look on her face. All of a sudden, she hangs up the phone, straightens up in bed, and turns to me.

"So, yes, I have breast cancer. Specifically, I have invasive ductal carcinoma in my left breast and lobular carcinoma in situ, which means that there's an increased risk of cancer developing in my right breast in the future. I have to have surgery, and then based upon the pathology, they'll be able to figure out what comes next in terms of postoperative treatment with chemotherapy and maybe radiation," Dr. Stevens says in a very detached, clinical voice.

"Oh my God, Cam."

"Don't worry, Grace. It'll be okay. They caught it early, and I'm going to be okay. Really, I am," she says definitively. I can't tell if she's trying to convince herself of that or if she knows more about breast cancer statistics than I thought she did, being a pediatrician and all.

So I decide to go along with her positive attitude and leave my worrying and freaking out for when I'm alone.

"So what happens now?" I ask, deciding to be more matter-of-fact, because I know that's what Cameron is comfortable with.

"Well, I have to find a breast surgeon to do the procedure. Shannon recommended someone at Sloan-Kettering who she says is the best. I'll ask around and see if there's anyone else I should meet with too, just to get another opinion. I'm assuming they'll just need to do a lumpectomy, but since they found the lobular carcinoma in situ, it may indicate a double mastectomy. That's what I have to find out from the surgeons."

"Okay, is there anything I can do to help?" I ask calmly, trying not to sound patronizing.

"No, and you know what, Grace?" Cameron asks, looking determinedly into my eyes.

"What?"

"I'm really lucky."

"Okay," I say, unsure where she's going with this.

"I'm lucky because I live in New York, one of the best places in the world for medical care and for cancer care. I have the connections and the resources to find the best doctors and get the best treatment. That is so empowering. It completely eliminates the stress of having no idea what to do next. I could be some scared woman in a small town in North Dakota who gets this diagnosis and has nowhere to turn. Can you imagine how overwhelming that must be? Instead, not only did I get my biopsy results the next day, I can make one phone call and have an appointment tomorrow with a leading breast surgeon at Sloan-Kettering. I'm really lucky, Grace."

"You're right, Cam, you are lucky. And I know that you're going to do what you have to do and find the right people and get yourself better."

"I am. That's exactly what I'm going to do."

"But aren't—" I hesitate.

"What, Grace? Say it."

I turn to her and my eyes betray my fear. "Aren't you scared, at all?"

"Oh, Grace," she says looking into my eyes and then she hugs me. "Of course I'm scared. But I do scared very differently from you. You do scared all crying and sad and retreating and needing love. I'm not judging, I'm just saying. And that's fine. That's your scared, and you don't know how to do it any other way. And sometimes I think that way of doing scared would be more comforting because other people help you get through it. But you know me. I do scared like a battalion on the front lines: a plan, a rush of adrenaline, and then lots of ass-kicking," Cameron says, making karate chops with her hands.

I laugh.

"Yes, if it makes you feel better, then yes, I'm absolutely, ridiculously, fucking scared, but I'm not going to let it paralyze me. I'm just going to do what I have to do and get on with it. I am not seeing this as a death sentence at all. I know this is beatable. So I need you to not see it that way either. Deal?" she asks, turning toward me and putting her hand out.

"Deal," I say, shaking her hand and drying my eyes. I smile at my friend who does scared really well and give her a hug.

"Now, I need to make some calls and schedule some appointments, but I'm not done with you and this Darren shit show, so don't go anywhere."

While Cameron goes into her study to get on her computer and make some calls, I open her windows, make her bed, clean up the muffin crumbs, and thank my lucky stars for this strong woman who is my best friend. I hear my phone ring, so I rush to find it in my purse before it stops ringing. It's Darren.

"Hey," he says in a detached voice.

"Thanks for calling me. I really need to talk to you."

"What's up?" I hear him typing. He's not paying attention to me, so I just spill it.

"Cameron has breast cancer," I say in a lowered voice. Cameron is downstairs, but I don't want her to hear me.

"What?" The typing stops. I know I have his full attention.

"She went to the OB yesterday for a routine exam, and he felt a lump. She had a mammogram yesterday and then a needle biopsy. She just got the results. It's cancer."

"Shit."

"I know."

"How is she doing?"

"She's being very Cameron. I'm at her house right now, and she's on the phone making appointments with breast surgeons. She's acting very gung ho and normal, so I don't know if she's in denial or if she's really that strong. I would normally say she's really that strong, but this is cancer, Darren."

"I know. Well, I guess we need to let her handle it in her own way. I can't believe what a bad run of it she's having."

"I know. It's horrible."

"Do you think it's okay if I send her an email and let her know I know?"

"Yes, I think that would be really nice. I'm sure she'd appreciate it."

"Okay, I'll do that."

"Do you have time to talk about some stuff with me right now?"

"Not really, and I'm not really ready to talk to you anyway. I need to figure some things out in my head, and I've just been really busy at work, so I haven't had much downtime. I'm actually calling because I have on my schedule that you need me to be home early so you can meet your father in the city for dinner. Do you still need me to do that?"

"Yes, thank you. I have one of the high-school girls from the neighborhood coming over after school, but if you could get home by 6:30 or so, that would be great. And I know the boys would love to see you."

"Okay."

"Darren—" I start.

"I gotta go, Grace."

And then I realize he has hung up.

I take the 4:42 train to Grand Central. My train gets in at 5:26, a half hour before I'm supposed to meet my dad at the Oyster Bar, his favorite restaurant in New York and a convenient one at that, being on the bottom floor of Grand Central. I walk up to the balcony of the terminal and go to The Campbell Apartment, one of my favorite bars in New York City, for a glass of wine and some quiet contemplation.

The Campbell Apartment was the private office of John W. Campbell, who was a tycoon in the 1920s. It is a spectacular space with soaring ceilings, a huge leaded-glass window, and enough historic Grand Central architectural details for me to admire in one sitting. The bartender gives me the wine with a sly smile, motions to the other end of the bar, and tells me the man sitting there has bought the wine for me. I look to see who my benefactor is, a little annoyed that I'm now going to have to deal with some stranger's overtures and wondering why the guy didn't just make the extra effort to notice that I have a wedding ring on, the universal sign for, 'No need to waste your time and money on me, friend.' I see an attractive older man with slicked-back, graying hair impeccably dressed in a dark suit, a white shirt, and a decidedly Hermès ice-blue tie. He raises his glass, and I do the same, and then he smiles and gets up from his seat.

"It's my father," I say to the bartender, not wanting him to think I'm that easy. Or into old guys.

"Uh huh," he says and gives me a look that means he's heard that one way too many times.

"Hey, Gracie," my dad says to me, giving me a kiss on the forehead.

"Hey, Dad. Thanks for the drink. Funny meeting you here."

"I was early, and I remember you mentioned this place to me last time we ate at the Oyster Bar, so I figured I'd give it a try. And you were right. It's magnificent."

"Well, I'm happy to see you. How has your trip been going?"

"Fine, just fine."

My dad and I sit amongst the splendor of The Campbell Apartment, enjoying our drinks, and talking about the case he's working on.

"Do you remember the first time I bought you a drink?" I ask, nudging my dad in the shoulder.

"I certainly do. It wasn't in quite as rarefied a place as this," he says, laughing.

"No, not quite," I say, laughing along.

"A beer on tap from Smokey Joe's, I believe," he says.

"That would be the place. But in my day we called it Smoke's, Dad."

"Right, Smoke's," he says of the dive at Penn, my dad's alma mater as well as mine. He had been in New York for work one week and took the train to Philly to visit me for an afternoon. After a walk through campus, I decided that we should go to Smoke's so I could buy him a beer. I remember feeling so grown up. I wasn't even 21, but my fake ID worked fine at Smoke's, and my dad didn't mind. I know he was proud of me that day, that he stopped seeing me as a little girl and was starting to look at me as a woman. And I could tell by the way he said goodbye that night that, in his own way, he felt sentimental about his baby being all grown up.

"Well, shall we?" my dad asks as he hands money to the bartender, who winks at me.

"We shall," I say, sneering at the bartender.

My dad has been coming to the Oyster Bar forever. A venerable New York institution, the restaurant opened in 1913 but fell into disrepair until it reopened in the 70s as the much-lauded, beautifully designed restaurant it is today. I am smitten with the vaulted Guastavino tile ceilings as much as I am smitten with the gorgeous astronomical ceiling in the terminal's main concourse. The dining room is crowded and filled with an interesting mix of tourists, commuters, and native New York Oyster Bar devotees. After we order—oysters Rockefeller and a tuna steak for my dad, and a shrimp cocktail and grilled salmon for me—I tell him about Cameron.

"Oh, Gracie, that's just terrible," my dad says with a grimace, setting his butter knife and roll back down on the plate.

"I know. But she says the statistics are in her favor, and she's going to go all Cameron on cancer and get rid of it."

"Well, I hope that she's going to be okay."

"I know. I can't imagine losing someone else close to me."

"I can't imagine it either," he says, looking into my eyes, knowing that I'm talking about Danielle just as much as he's thinking about her. For someone so tough as nails in the courtroom and so seemingly emotionally simple, I know my dad is deeply distraught to this day over the death of his daughter. He smiles at me and we make a silent truce to change the subject.

"How's Darren's business going? The market is doing quite well these days."

"Well, yeah, Darren's doing well. Very busy."

"I'm sorry I didn't get a chance to see him."

"It's just hard with sitters and all, so I thought it would be easier if he stayed home with the boys. Next time, though. Hopefully, you'll come in for longer, and you can come up and see the boys."

"That would be nice, Gracie."

I stare down at my plate and fidget a bit as I decide whether to tell my dad about my and Darren's problems.

"What is it?" my dad asks, sensing my internal debate.

"I don't know if Eva already told you, but Darren and I are having some problems."

'She didn't. What's up?" he asks, taking my hand across the table.

"Well," and suddenly I'm embarrassed sharing something so personal with my dad. "Believe it or not, he cheated on me."

"Oh, Gracie."

"Yeah, he was at a conference over the summer and it's a long, drawn-out story, but the bottom line is he had been drinking a lot with his friends, and somehow the cocktail waitress ended up in his bed."

"Ouch."

"Exactly. It's been really tough. He only told me a couple weeks ago."

"And how do you feel about the whole thing?"

"Well, that's an interesting question. I have gone through all the predictable feelings: anger, sadness, humiliation, you name it, I've felt it. But right now, I feel mostly like I don't want to let it ruin my marriage. I don't want to give that random woman who serves martinis in a hotel bar in Chicago the power to destroy what Darren and I have created together. I love him, Dad. It's been really hard." I decide to leave out the pivotal Jake part of the story, despite the fact that it was actually the turning point in my journey to forgiveness, because I don't want my dad to be disappointed in me.

"I'm sure it has been," he says, and he evades my eyes.

"What do you think?"

"Oh," he says with a bit of a chuckle that sounds more like a grunt than a laugh, "I'm not a big fan of people cheating on their spouses, but I know it happens all the time. It's real hard to understand when the cheater says he, or she, didn't mean anything by it, but I think I've realized over the years, that it might actually be true," he says, again looking somewhere over my right shoulder.

His lack of eye contact confuses me. Reed Roseman the cut-throat defense attorney has made a career out of eye contact, persistent, penetrating eye contact. It's only when he's uncomfortable that he looks away. Why is he uncomfortable? I suddenly have the nagging suspicion that he's cheating on Amanda. Or maybe that gold-digging, botoxed bitch is cheating on him. To be honest, I secretly hope he is cheating on her, because I never liked her. I pray they had a prenup. Thankfully, my dad looks at me and continues.

"But I do hope you two can work it out because of the boys. It's not easy being a single mother, Gracie. I know you girls would have been better off living with your mother *and* me. I'm not claiming any awards for being a good father, but I know that having two parents is always better than one."

Now I reach over and grab *his* hand across the table. "You and Mom did the best you could. And I think Eva and I turned out pretty well," I say, smiling.

"Exceedingly well," he says, and we start our first courses that the waiter has just brought.

"These shrimp are huge!" I say.

"Enjoy," he says, offering me an oyster. "Are you still volunteering at the boys' school?" he asks.

As we eat, I tell him about my adventures in reentering the workforce.

"Well, did you fight for the job when that Nicole told you she was offering it to someone else?" he asks, eye contact in full penetration mode.

"No. I guess I just accepted that she had chosen someone else."

"You've got to fight for yourself, Gracie. I know you'll be surprised to hear this because professionally I am very aggressive, but I haven't been too great at fighting for myself in my personal life over the years, and I see a little of that in you," he says, gesturing with an empty oyster shell.

Again, my thoughts go straight to his and Amanda's relationship, and I wonder what's going on.

"What do you mean?" I ask innocently. "I do fight for myself. I honk like crazy when a car swerves in front of me on the highway, and I do a lot of exaggerated weight-shifting and loud *tsk-tsking* when someone cuts in front of me in a line."

"That's not what I mean," he says, laughing. "I just don't want you to spend your life letting people get away with not choosing you."

And now I'm thoroughly confused. "You mean that Darren's cheating showed he wasn't choosing me and not getting the job showed she wasn't choosing me?"

"Yes, both in a way. But I understand why you don't fight for yourself. You're kindhearted and you don't want to be confrontational. You just need to advocate for yourself, too. You need to make sure that your needs are being met, not just those of everyone around you."

I sit back, and take a sip of my wine and think for a moment about what my dad is saying. I'm a little confused, baffled actually, by what he means about this relating to his own life. But he does have a point about how it relates to mine. And it ties into what my mom and Eva were trying to tell me in L.A. I've always been concerned about how things are *supposed* to go and what I'm *supposed* to do at the expense of really figuring out what I *want* and going full-throttle in that direction. Although, in my little fling with Jake, I did the latter, and look where that got me.

What I think my family is trying to tell me is that I should stop being so careful and just go for it, whatever "it" may be at that particular moment. I should "go" for my marriage and make Darren realize that we need to be together. I should "go" for a job and wholeheartedly find something that's going to fulfill me intellectually. I should "go" for making sure that my life is filled mostly with want to's and get to's instead of have to's and must do's.

We spend the rest of the dinner talking about NPR and L.A. restaurants and other neutral subjects. My main takeaway from our dinner is that I'm pleasantly surprised by how much easier our relationship is becoming now that I'm an adult. I think my dad is uneasy with people needing him. I'm assuming, although I've never learned the exact reasons for their disconnect, that's the reason that he and my mom broke up. Maybe she was too intense emotionally. And I think, as a kid, I must have been, too.

Now that I'm an adult and my needs are being met by my own nuclear family, I think it makes my dad feel like he's a bit off the hook. Still doesn't explain how he deals with Amanda and what's going on there. But I guess most of her self-esteem needs are dealt with by a certain plastics doctor in L.A. On the train ride home, I think about Darren and whether he'll be waiting up for me in our bed or asleep in the guest room.

He's waiting by the door, anxious to get back to the city. Anxious to get as far away from me as possible.

chapter twenty-one

"I'd like to make a toast," Cameron says, lifting her glass of Prosecco.

I smile and lift my glass.

"I'd like to make a toast to two pretty big things: friendship and life. To friendship," she says, smiling and looking me straight in the eye. "For the past three weeks, you have been the most magnificent friend. You have been there for me every step of the way, and I am so grateful to you for that. To life. My life is about to change in a big way on Wednesday. Well, I guess it already has changed. But starting with my surgery, I am going to embark on a journey that I know will impact me forever. So I'd like to toast to a successful surgery, an easy recovery, a manageable treatment regimen, and good times around the corner."

"Cheers," I say, clinking her glass and savoring the delicious sparkling wine.

"I really can't believe the surgery is finally here. I just want this cancer out of me already," Cameron says assuredly.

"I can only imagine," I say as the waiter sets down roasted beet salad for Cameron and deviled eggs for me.

We're at BG Restaurant on the seventh floor of Bergdorf Goodman. This is our favorite place to have lunch in the city, mostly because of its breathtaking views of Central Park, but also because of the ridiculously chic design by Kelly Wearstler. We were lucky enough to land one of the tables with the pale-blue leather egg chairs. In the past we've come here to celebrate birthdays, job promotions, and other milestones in our lives. Today, we're here to celebrate, maybe commemorate is a more appropriate word, Cameron's double mastectomy that will take place in exactly two days.

"I realize it's strange that I wanted to come here for a sort of celebration lunch," Cameron says, shrugging her shoulders and looking around at the hustle and bustle of waiters, society ladies, and overcompensating tourists.

"I actually think it's perfect," I say, trying to gracefully eat one of my delicious deviled eggs. I order them every time I come here. I know I should branch out and try something new, but I dream of these. Really.

"I just feel like I should elevate this occasion in my life. Now, I know *that* sounds strange. But I almost feel like I should respect it, give it some reverence. It's huge, and if I just go into this huge life event and pretend that it's not huge then I somehow let it win. I'm not trying to make light of the seriousness of this whole thing, because I *am* nervous as hell. I just need to not make it all so heavy."

"I get it," I say. "You feel like you need to acknowledge the prominence it has taken in your life, and what better way to tell cancer to, pardon me, fuck off, than to give it a going-away party at Bergdorf Goodman?" I ask giddily.

"Well, I'll drink to that!" Cameron says, and we toast.

I smile at Cameron and reflect on all we've been through over the past few weeks. If everything happens for a reason (and someday maybe we'll learn the reason that Cameron got breast cancer), I know why I didn't get the job from Nicole. If I had, I would have been working instead of being there for my best friend during one of the most, maybe *the* most, unstable periods in her life.

After Cameron met with several breast surgeons, she selected a brilliant young female doctor at Sloan-Kettering. Based upon their discussions, Cameron opted for a double mastectomy. There technically isn't any cancer in her right breast now; however, the diagnosis of "lobular carcinoma in situ" means that she is at increased risk of new cancer developing there in the future. Cameron decided she didn't want to take any chances or have to go through this all again, so she is going with the double.

Once Cameron had made her surgery date, we came up with a list of everything she needed to do to prepare: meet with the plastic surgeon about reconstruction, figure out what to do with her pediatric practice in her absence, meet with a fertility doctor about freezing her eggs, buy zip-up sweatshirts and pajamas because she won't be able to lift her arms after the surgery, etc.

"I don't know why I feel so light," Cameron says. "This is very strange. But one thing I've learned from all this is you can't predict how you're going to react or feel or behave when trauma is presented in your life. So I'll embrace feeling light. It's certainly better than feeling depressed. Thank God I'm not depressed."

"I think you're right. We all fear the worst. Okay, I'll rephrase that. *I* fear the worst. But quite possibly, when the worst comes it brings with it a little bit of relief because the worst has finally come. Does that make any sense?" I ask.

"Only because I know you," Cameron laughs.

"Okay, whatever, you know what I mean. I am so proud of you, though, Cam. You have taken this whole thing in stride, you've done what you've had to do, and you're confronting this breast cancer like you've confronted everything else in your life: you are looking it straight in the eye, and you're confident you're going to kick its ass."

"Thanks, Grace," Cameron says. "That being said, I'm ready to get this surgery over with. I feel like the anticipation of it has been consuming my life. And then I'll be able to deal with what comes next. But the good part is that I've given myself the opportunity over the past few weeks to feel as well as I can so that I have the capacity to be this confident. I'm so happy I went back to work, even if my schedule was a bit sporadic. And I'm so happy that I've been eating so well and doing so much yoga. I think it has all just given me a really good foundation."

"I think you're absolutely right," I say. "You're a true model for what to do in a situation like this."

"How are you doing with the whole Darren thing?" Cameron asks me carefully. I can tell she's relieved to change the subject.

I exhale dramatically. "It's so bad, Cam. It's been exactly three weeks since I came back from L.A., and it boggles my mind to think he's been staying at one of those apartments his firm has in the city this whole time. Thankfully, he comes home several times a week to see the boys and put them to bed; but then he drives back to the city. They have no idea he doesn't sleep at home. They just think he's been traveling a lot for work."

"Jeez," Cameron says.

"Sometimes I feel really confident that he just needs to go through this phase and punish me for what I did, or what he believes I did, and then he'll come back and we'll be okay. And other times, I completely give up hope and convince myself that I ruined everything, and that he's going to serve me with divorce papers any day."

"Oh, Grace. I really can't believe how crazy it has all gotten between the two of you. And I'm sorry I haven't been keeping up on it all. I've been a little distracted," she says softly.

"Of course, Cameron. And you know I haven't wanted to bother you with any of it anyway. I've mostly been just trying to not focus on it, which is a big joke, to try to stay positive. But I've never been very good at that. I feel like I've tried everything in my quest to get him back and to convince him that I didn't do anything wrong. And I'm growing impatient at trying to be understanding of why he's angry, when, in all honesty, I think his anger is unfair and a big barrel of crap. I should be the one pissed at him for trying to equate what we did. In the meantime, he doesn't answer my emails or return my calls. He's completely shut me out."

"I'm so sorry you guys are going through all this. I really hope it comes out well on the other side," Cameron says.

"Thanks. Me, too." I try to move Darren to the back of my mind so I can focus on Cameron.

The waiter brings us each a Gotham Salad, which is basically a Cobb, and we talk about what needs to happen before the surgery on Wednesday morning.

Over tea and raspberry sorbet, I get serious with Cameron.

"You know, I've been thinking a lot about some of the conversations we've had over the past few weeks, and I just want you to know how eye-opening they've been for me."

"In what way?" Cameron asks, licking the sorbet off her spoon and diving in for more.

"Well, remember that time we were talking about how your diagnosis opened our eyes to thinking about how we prioritize our lives and what we fill our days with? Whether we should live our lives differently?" I ask.

"I do," she says.

"You reminded me of how I used to be so happy-go-lucky and carefree. And I know having kids changed that landscape and I had to act more responsibly and all, but your saying that really resonated with me," I say, dipping my spoon into my sorbet.

"How?" Cameron asks, taking a sip of her tea.

I sit back in my chair and look out the window. "I need to reclaim some of my old self. I need to lighten up a bit and stop focusing on expenditure of time always being for the sake of impressive accomplishment. Sometimes I should just spend my time doing something I want to do and not feel guilty if it doesn't result in something."

"Do you think you're gonna change?" she asks me, tilting her head quizzically.

"I'm certainly gonna try."

"That's great, Grace."

"It's just that between what my family has been telling me and what you've been trying to tell me for the past few weeks—"

"And past twenty years," Cameron interrupts.

"Yes, that, too. And between what is happening with you and what is happening with my marriage, it's all just really banged me over the head and made me think about how I just need to enjoy my life."

"Hallelujah!" Cameron says, lifting her spoon in the air.

"I'm serious," I say, smiling.

"I'm serious, too," she says.

"I don't know why it's taken me so long to figure this out, but we're all going to get sick, have marital problems, or have some other shitty thing happen in our lives. So during the gaps when that crappy stuff isn't happening, we need to take advantage of the peace and quiet to do what we love, to be vibrant with the people we love, to celebrate the good things in life, to not rush all the time, to know that we're doing exactly what we're supposed to be doing, to stop . . . wait for it, wait for it . . . to stop worrying about not doing things the right way and just do them, goddamn it, the way that feels good!" I say, my voice rising at the end and inviting looks from fellow egg chair diners.

"Oh, Grace! We've broken through!" Cameron cheers. "We've broken through!"

"I think, possibly, we have."

"The most important thing for you to remember is that you can't sit around waiting all day for your kids, or some boss, or your husband, or anyone to tell you you're great. You have to know it, Grace. You have to know you're great. Because you are."

After lunch, Cameron walks uptown to tie up loose ends at her office for a few hours, and I head south to Grand Central. During my walk and on the train home, I think about all that has taken place since the first day of school five weeks ago, and it seems utterly ridiculous, more like a soap opera script than my life: husband cheats on wife, wife gets rejection from two jobs, wife's best friend has miscarriage, wife reconnects with old flame, wife tells husband, husband storms out, wife's best friend gets breast cancer. All we're missing is amnesia, a secret love child, and murder. Unfortunately, it *is* my life.

But, looking on the bright side, I also know that the past five weeks have been filled with enough obstacles to effectively change my perspective on life. And that's a really valuable thing.

I've given up trying to figure out what's going through Darren's head and what I should do next. Everything I've ever thought I've known about him I'm not so sure of anymore. I never suspected he would react like he did. I go over it all the time, questioning if he's right and I'm wrong. I keep convincing myself that the right thing to do is give him space and time, and then just see what happens.

"Hey, Grace! I feel like I haven't seen you in such a long time!" Lorna practically shouts at me with one of her dramatic head tilts as I make my way to the bus stop that afternoon. She's wearing a ridiculous sailor getup, and it's all I can do to not look at her and laugh.

"A couple weeks ago the boys asked if they could just go from the bus into the house without my waiting for them, so I'm letting them do that. I think it gives them a sense of independence. Plus, I watch from the window, so I know they're okay," I say, turning my head down the street to look for the bus. I tried to time it today so I wouldn't have to talk to Lorna, but, damn, the bus is late.

"Oh," she says, as if I just told her I'm letting them prostitute themselves downtown at midnight. "I would never let the triplets walk home alone. Even though we are only six houses away. There are just too many reports of abductions these days. You know?" Lorna asks, wiping grass clippings off her navy espadrilles.

"I heard that a child is more likely to get struck by lightning than to be abducted, but you have to do what you're comfortable with," I say sweetly.

"Well, you can never be too careful, now, can you? Especially when it comes to our most precious commodities. So," she clucks, "I've been meaning to ask how your new job is going."

"Unfortunately, some things didn't work out as I had planned," I say, craning my neck, "But that's okay. Everything happens for a reason."

"Maybe that reason, Grace, is because you're supposed to be the third-grade class chair for the winter book fair. We still haven't filled the spot, and it's yours if you want it," she says, blinking heavily and smiling broadly.

"So sorry, Lorna, but I've got a lot of other things going on right now, and I just don't think it's good timing."

"Oh? Other things?" Lorna asks with a bit too much interest. The gossip-gathering muscle in her jaw pulsing wildly.

Just then the bus pulls up, and I am saved from having to make up something just to get the damn woman to back off.

"Mommy, why are you waiting here for us?" James asks with disappointment in his voice. "Remember, we're big boys and we can go inside by ourselves now?"

"Yes, I do remember, but once in a while I like to come out here and greet you guys in person."

"Okay," James says and hands me his backpack. Henry does the same.

"What are we doing this afternoon?" Henry asks.

"Hmmm. No plans. Did you have anything in mind?" I ask.

"Ice cream?" Henry smiles, showing all his teeth.

"Ice cream?" James chimes in.

"I think ice cream is a great idea," I say. "And then, what do you say we go over to Hooper's Farm and pick us some pumpkins?"

"Can we carve them when we get home?" Henry asks.

"Of course!" I say, excited about the afternoon. Since Darren's disappearance—what I've taken to calling it—I have slacked off a bit in the dinner category. The boys are happier with the less elaborate meals, and I'm happier not having to put in all the time and energy making dinner.

"Jack L. got pumpkins yesterday, he told me. He said he tried to get his babysitter to take him all last week, but she said that his mom wanted to take him on the weekend when she didn't have work," Henry tells me as we open the door to dump the backpacks.

"I'm so glad you don't work," James says.

"Yeah, James? Why?" I ask him, kneeling down in front of him and placing my hands on his shoulders.

"So we can get pumpkins on Mondays," he says sweetly.

I've been trying to be less intense about my should-I-or-should-I-not-work mental dilemma. And I've been trying to slow down, see the beauty in the everyday, and appreciate the mundane. Recently, I've lain in bed thinking about what if it had been me who got the cancer diagnosis. What if I were too sick to make their breakfast, to welcome them off the bus with treats at the end of the day, to drive them to soccer practice? All the things that I've often complained about having to do because they're so tedious, so thankless, so time-consuming. Because they rob me of the time I want to spend on Something Else. These are suddenly the things I have to see the gold in. I have to shift my thinking from "have to's" to "get to's." Unfortunately, sometimes a cancer diagnosis is required to make that clear.

Seeing the gold in, say, making school lunches isn't always easy. Philosophically acknowledging the mundane as a gift doesn't always make cutting off crusts fun. But I'm trying to build that muscle. At least I'm mindful of it. And that's far beyond where I was a few weeks ago.

I still think about getting a job, though I'm glad I don't have one right now, so I can be with Cameron. But, when she's doing better and back at work, that urge to escape the totality of being a mom, to find something fulfilling to do with my days, will return. But, I'm now certain that I want a job that gives me flexibility so I can tend to my best friend after a cancer diagnosis and so I can buy pumpkins on Mondays.

chapter twenty-two

When I walk into the waiting room at Sloan-Kettering Wednesday morning, Jack is already there.

"Hey," I say, giving him a hug and setting down the large coffees I got for us. "How did all the check-in and pre-op stuff go this morning?"

"As well as can be expected," he says. "She seemed a little preoccupied and distracted, but I think she was just psyching herself out mentally, trying to prepare for the battle, as she kept referring to it," he says with a nervous laugh.

"How are you holding up?" I ask, looking around the nondescript, standard-order hospital waiting room. According to Cameron, Jack has been a mess. He hasn't taken this news well at all, not that I blame him. And she says that although he's been trying to put on a brave face in front of her, she can see right through it and sometimes hears him crying when he thinks she's asleep.

"I'm okay, I guess," he says, his hands in his pocket, his shoulders shrugged. And then he breaks. "I'm just so scared, Grace. I don't know what I would do if I lost her."

"Hey, hey. She's gonna be fine. Come here," I say and give him a long hug.

"Hey." We pull away and see Darren in the doorway. He goes up to Jack and gives him a hug. "Sorry, man. I know this must be so rough."

"Thanks, Darren," Jack says as he sits down and takes a sip of the coffee.

"You okay?" Darren asks me.

I look at him and shake my head no. I can't speak. I'm suddenly overcome with emotion: relief that Darren is speaking to me and looking at me so tenderly, and fear about what's about to happen with Cameron. I try to hold back the tears, but they are too strong for me this time. He looks at me and smiles hesitantly, but I can't tell what his eyes are trying to tell me. And then he hugs me. For a very long time. My heart is racing, and the tears are unremitting. And he keeps hugging me. Tightly.

When he releases me, he whispers, "It's gonna be okay."

I can't help but wonder what he means by "it."

It's just the three of us in the waiting room. A slow day for cancer, apparently. Cameron's parents are driving down from Maine, and they're scheduled to arrive this evening. They'll stick around for a few days to help Cameron once she gets home from the hospital. I try to talk to Jack, but he just answers my questions with yes or no answers, and then looks back down at his iPad. So I take the hint and realize he doesn't feel up to talking. Darren sits in the corner of the room speaking quietly on a conference call. I've brought things to read, but I can't focus. The television in the room is set to MSNBC. We can't find a remote to change the channel, and it's mounted too high to reach the controls. I could go in search of someone for help, but instead I just close my eyes and think.

The surgeon promised to come in here after the surgery to update us on how it went. She told Jack this morning that she'll need two hours and that the plastic surgeon will need two more to insert the tissue expanders, the first step in reconstruction. I figure there are three possible outcomes to this surgery. The optimistic and in-denial part of me hopes the doctor will come in and say, "You'll never believe it! It was just a big misunderstanding. We found nothing. It must have been dust on the ultrasound machine and a mix-up in the lab. She's fine!" The pessimistic, doomsday side of me considers the doctor might come in and say, "It's worse than we thought. The poor girl's body is riddled with tumors. There's nothing more we can do." When the surgeon finally comes in the waiting room, she says something in the middle.

"The surgery went really well, and she did great. There appeared to be some signs of spread to the sentinel lymph node, so I removed more of the axillary nodes to make sure I got it all out. All in all, I'm really pleased."

"Great," Jack says, relieved.

"The plastic surgeon is in with her now. He'll come in here in a couple hours, and then you'll be able to see her when she's in recovery."

"Thank you, Doctor," Jack says, shaking her hand firmly. "Thank you so much."

"You're welcome," she says with a smile and turns to leave.

Jack and I look at each other and smile. I ask him if he wants anything from the cafeteria, and he says no. I tell him I'm going to get a coffee or something, and Darren, who had gotten off his call just before the doctor came in, offers to join me.

As we walk down the hall toward the elevator, I feel like I'm walking next to a stranger. I don't know what to say. So I decide not to say anything at all and let him start.

"Do you feel a little better now?" he asks, as we stop at the elevator bank, and he pushes the down button.

"Yes, a lot," I say, tears stinging my eyes as I stare at the closed elevator doors.

An elevator opens, and we get in. It's crowded, so we don't talk. When we get off, we walk side by side silently until we get in line at the cafeteria.

"I don't want to lose you, Gracie," Darren says softly as we slide our trays slowly along the metal counter.

I look at him. I'm a bit stunned. I didn't expect this from him.

He stops and turns to me. "I've been thinking a lot, about so many things. About us. About what each of us did. About Cameron. About what's actually important. I've tried to analyze this situation from every angle. And the more I think about it and the more time that passes from the night you told me, the more I realize that, yes, I did overreact. I certainly don't like that you were, as you said, flirting with another man, but I understand how it could have happened. I see how what I did to you could have led you to do what you did. And you didn't let anything physical happen beyond that start of a kiss, and that's more than I can say for myself. I was an asshole, Gracie, on so many levels. And I'm sorry."

I'm speechless. I look into his eyes and smile.

"I'm so glad to hear you say that, Darren," I say, as I realize the other people in line are quietly stepping around us.

"I've tried to imagine my life going forward in all different scenarios. And what I've come up with is that I don't want to move forward in a life that doesn't include you and that doesn't include our family together," he says, as we start moving again. Darren takes an apple that's resting in a little paper tray and continues, "I'm sorry I put you through what I did these last few weeks."

"Apology accepted," I say quietly, the joy and relief bubbling inside of me like almost-boiling coffee in a percolator.

"Let's just make a deal, though, that we'll save all our flirting and kissing and feelings for each other from now on," he says, smiling at me.

"Deal," I say, smiling right back.

We pile our trays with fruit, muffins, and coffee; get in the cashier line; and then make our way back up to Jack in the waiting room, the ride up the elevator being monumentally more pleasant than the one we had taken down just fifteen minutes earlier.

"Wow, what happened to you two down there?" Jack asks, as he notices we're smiling and holding hands.

"Just a little perspective, that's all," Darren says, pulling me closer to him.

"Well, I'm glad that some good is coming out of all of this," Jack says as he gives us a look and turns back to the heated game of Scrabble on his iPad.

epilogue

February

"How does it feel?" my mom asks amusedly as I come into the kitchen and make my way toward the coffee pot.

"Feels great, actually," I say, inhaling the steam from my mug and sitting down next to her at the table.

"Well, it just makes me feel really old," she says with a half frown as she gets up from her chair and gives me a hug. "Happy birthday, Gracie," she says and kisses me on the forehead.

"Thanks, Mom. I'm really so glad you're here."

"I'm happy you wanted me to come," she says with a tinge of sadness in her voice.

"I really needed you here with me."

"I know you've been through so much lately, Gracie. I imagine celebrating will be bittersweet," she says.

"Happy birthday!" a voice sings coming down the back stairs.

"Thank you," I say, smiling at my sister.

The three of us sit at my kitchen table, looking out the windows at the bright and cloudless February morning, the bare trees, the cold blue sky. When my alarm rang this morning at 6:30, Darren gave me a kiss and told me to sleep in, that he would get the boys off to school. So, with a smile, I fell back into a deep, blissful sleep.

"Anyone want to join me for a run?" I ask.

"It's freezing outside," Eva replies. "I don't exercise when it's freezing."

"It's energizing!" I say.

"I brought a Pilates tape, if anyone wants to join me," my mom says, already dressed in a spandex ensemble that Jane Fonda would envy.

"What time do we have to be ready?" Eva asks.

"We'll leave at 11:15. The restaurant is about twenty-five minutes away. Lunch is planned for noon, but I need some time to arrange the place cards and the centerpieces, and take care of a few other things."

"I'm really looking forward to this party, Gracie," my mom says.

"I am, too. And I'm so glad the party is on my actual birthday. It makes it that much more special."

"You really are going to have a fabulous day," Eva says.

"So, remind me, what happens after the party?" my mom asks.

"You guys will drive my car back here and get the boys off the bus. I've already typed out very good directions, and I'll set my navigation system as well so you won't have any issues finding your way," I say.

"Always so organized, that baby sister of mine," Eva says with a little punch to my shoulder. And then she sticks her finger in her open mouth and pretends to gag.

"Ha, funny," I say. "But seriously, thank you so much again for babysitting tonight. I know the boys are really excited about it.

Darren has a full day of meetings today, but he's gonna meet me tonight for dinner around seven. And then we'll be back home around nine or so tomorrow morning," I say, draining my cup before I head upstairs to put my running clothes on. I joined a running group right after the new year and we meet up at different spots three mornings a week. And I started doing Rye Boot Camp by the Beach and SoulCycle as well. It's amazing how my body has already changed so much from the regular exercise, and I feel like my head has never been clearer.

I leave the house as my mom and Eva cook breakfast and dance in my kitchen to Mariah Carey blasting out of my sister's iPod. I laugh to myself, and a wave of love goes through me. I am really so happy that they both made the effort to fly out here to be with me for my fortieth. There was a point when I wasn't so sure I wanted my mom to come. At the beginning of January, she called and dropped a bomb on me.

"Gracie, I made a New Year's resolution to be honest with everyone in my life."

"Great, Mom. But don't you do that already?" I asked, regretting having picked up the phone. I was in a hurry.

"Yes, most of the time, I do," she said, a bit flustered. "But I haven't always, and I haven't always been honest with you."

"Okay." I said, drawing the word out, unsure of what my mom was going to tell me. I really didn't think I would be able to handle another major thing in my life. I heard her take a deep breath.

"Okay, here goes," she started. "I'm just gonna blurt it out. I cheated on your father."

"What?" I asked. "What are you talking about?" I had been getting dressed to go to a birthday lunch for one of the moms at the boys' school. I sat down on my bed.

"The reason we got divorced was not because we couldn't communicate well. The real reason was that I cheated. There, I said it. Ah. Thank God."

"Jesus, Mom. I, I don't even know what to do with this information right now," I said, putting the phone on speaker for a minute so I could have both hands free to cradle my head in.

"I know, Gracie. I realize this is a really big deal and a lot of information for you to digest all at once, but I'm so glad you finally know. Not telling *you* has always been a huge internal conflict for me," she said, a decided tone of relief in her voice.

"Not telling *me*? You mean, Eva knows?" I asked in disbelief.

"Yes," she answered quietly. "She's known for a few years."

"Why did you tell her and not me?"

"Oh, Gracie. You're just more sensitive than Eva. I wasn't sure how you'd take it. Plus, it just came out one night when we were out for dinner together. I don't even remember how it came up."

"Did Dad ever find out?" I asked, as suddenly a million questions came into my head like: Who was the guy? Was it just once or did you have a relationship with him? How did you tell Dad? My mom and I talked for the next half hour and she answered my questions (a business partner of my dad's; just once while my dad was away on business; his partner felt too guilty and told my dad himself, then my dad pushed him out of the firm, and now he does trusts and estates in Boca). Despite my being very late to the lunch, I found out that my dad was devastated and that together they had decided to keep it from us girls because they didn't want us to resent my mom for breaking up the family. Looking at it from a forty-year-old woman's perspective, I think they made the right decision. Despite the fact that I felt completely betrayed.

But, it explained a lot. It explained why my parents got divorced in the first place (their "real" reason never made much sense to me, considering they actually seemed well suited to each other most of the time). It explained why my mom was so gung ho from the beginning about Darren and me getting back together, and why she tried to convince me that an affair doesn't need to end a marriage. It explained our conversation back in September at Il Cielo. And it explained why my dad was so cagey when we had dinner at the Oyster Bar.

I got off the phone that day entirely confused, and I spent a lot of time over the next week or so thinking back to my childhood and looking at everything through this new lens. Some things about how my mom and dad related to each other after the divorce made more sense, knowing that my mom had cheated on him. And I also started seeing my mom differently. After her admission to me, I was really angry at her. But slowly, I decided that I wanted to move forward.

Mostly, I realized that I had to let the whole thing go because my other option is to not have a relationship with my mother, and that is not an option for me. Knowing that she did that also humanized her a bit more for me, and allowed me to see her as just another woman who made mistakes in her life and is now trying to make up for them the best way she can. And I appreciate her for that. We went through a period of not talking. When I called her a few weeks ago to invite her to come to my party, she cried. I know she worried that she might have lost me.

"Hi Grace! Happy birthday!" Callie says, running up to me and giving me a hug. "I'm so happy to be here!" she says.

"I'm so happy, too," I say, taking the beautifully wrapped gift she hands me and setting it down on one of the side tables.

"I think you're really gonna like forty," she says.

"I think you're right," I say. "I've been meaning to tell you that I'm so glad we've reestablished our relationship over the past couple months. I love that I've totally gotten into yoga, but I think the best part of it all has been reconnecting with you during our Friday after-yoga coffee dates."

"Aww, Grace. I feel the exact same way," Callie says as she sets down her bag and takes a glass of wine off the waiter's tray.

"Hi, ladies."

"Hey, Nicole," Callie and I say.

"This place is beautiful!" Nicole says. "I've been to yoga here and to the little cafe, but I've never been in the main restaurant. What an amazing room," she says, looking around the private dining room at the Bedford Post Inn where my fortieth birthday luncheon has officially begun.

The Bedford Post Inn is a gorgeous place that Richard Gere (yes, that Richard Gere) and his wife Carey Lowell opened in northern Westchester County. There's an eight-room inn with really beautiful and cozy rooms, a yoga loft, a casual cafe in the renovated barn, and a more formal dining room, all set on a magnificent property dating back to the late 1800s. After the lunch, I'm going to go upstairs to the lovely room I checked into when I arrived here this morning to relax in the bath, read a book, and wait for Darren. We have dinner reservations in the formal dining room, and then we're going to spend the night. I couldn't be more excited.

"It's just a little something," Nicole says, handing me a gift.

"Thank you," I say, as I give her a hug.

"Callie, I'm glad you're standing here because you are the reason I met Grace," Nicole says. "And I think this is a fitting occasion to let you know, Grace, that we have decided to officially make *Wee Well in Westchester* a permanent part of our site. And, if you'll accept, I'd like to make you an official member of our staff instead of just a freelancer," Nicole says, beaming at me.

Back in December, Nicole called me out of the blue and told me that the new email product was doing really well and they had decided to do a series of emails and short-form pieces on the site for families, called *Wee Well in Westchester*. She immediately thought of me, and I immediately agreed to the freelance opportunity. I spend about five hours a week researching yoga classes for kids, natural allergy relief practitioners, cafes with healthy kids' offerings, etc. The *Wee* division has been mostly ad hoc, but I had heard rumblings around the office that it might become a more permanent part of the company with more resources and a dedicated staff. Well, it appears that dedicated staff is now me. It's the perfect opportunity.

"Really?" I ask.

"Really," she says.

"Well, then, Nicole. Yes, I accept," I say, and I feel like I'm going to burst with happiness. "But," I start, suddenly not so sure of something.

"Don't worry. It isn't a full-time position, and I'm able to be very flexible with your hours so you can be at the bus for the boys."

"Wow. Thank you so much. I really appreciate that, Nicole. That sounds perfect," I say.

"Okay, enough of that, there are lots of people here who want a piece of you, so go have fun. We'll have plenty of time to talk about your new job next week."

"Excellent," I say as I watch Nicole and Callie sit down on one of the sofas at the end of the room.

The private dining room is exquisite. There is a long wooden farm table that takes up most of the space. At one end of the room is a wall of windows looking out on the beautiful grounds, certainly more beautiful in the summer with the lush greenery and colorful flowers, but almost equally beautiful today with the snow-covered stone walls and evergreens. At the other end of the room is a seating area with two cozy couches, a low table, and a crackling wood-burning fireplace. I've always longed for a summer birthday, but today is perfect and I wouldn't have it any other way.

"Hey there, Grace. Happy birthday."

"Hey, Ainsley. I'm so glad you could come," I say, giving her a hug.

"Well, I was able to reschedule all my appointments for today, so it all worked out fine," she says in her gorgeous drawl. "I absolutely love your dress," she says, holding my hands and twirling me around. "You look gorgeous!"

"Thank you," I say. "As do you!" I'm wearing a winter white leather tight-fitting dress with cap sleeves. I feel amazing, and apparently, I look it, too.

"It means a lot to me that you're here and that you're in my life. It's amazing how far we've come as friends in such a short period of time," I say.

"Well, I'm so glad you're in a good place. The timing of this party couldn't have been better."

"I agree," I say. Ainsley goes to say hi to a few women whom we both know from the kids' school.

Darren and I have been going to counseling with Ainsley since October when he moved back home. We go every other week together, and I go by myself the weeks in between. I wasn't sure at first if I should use Ainsley as a therapist, considering she's a mom in our school. But I found her so calming, and I didn't really have a friendship with her that would make it awkward, so I decided to try her out. Darren and I clicked with her immediately, and she really helped us deal with our situation. She was able to be purely professional with me in our therapy sessions, but now that I'm feeling ready to wrap up the therapy, I'm excited to be able to become better friends with Ainsley without having to maintain careful boundaries.

I look around the room and take a mental note to see if everyone has arrived. I wanted to keep the party small and meaningful so I kept the guest list pretty short. There's my mom and sister, Callie and Nicole, Ainsley, the three women from the boys' school, and my college friends Lucy, who lives in New Jersey, and Aimee, who lives in Manhattan. Kiki and Arden considered flying out, but instead, the three of us are going to meet at a spa in Arizona and celebrate our birthdays together. My stomach turns a bit, and I decide it's time to start lunch.

Everyone sits down and the waiters serve the first course, a delicious salad made with local greenhouse lettuces, herbs, and flowers with a Champagne vinaigrette dressing. I am taking a sip of my wine when I see the door open.

"I'm so sorry I'm late."

I get up and walk toward the door.

"Don't worry at all. I knew you'd be late. I'm just so glad you're here," I say and give my best friend a huge hug.

"It's a good thing they took me on time for chemo," she whispers as she puts her bag down in the empty chair next to mine. My mom gets up from the chair on my other side and gives Cameron a hug. Cameron is beaming as she makes her way around the table to greet everyone.

Cameron has come a long way since her surgery back in October, but it hasn't been completely smooth sailing. I am almost giddy seeing her now, so in control, so healthy looking, so, well, Cameron. The recovery from the double mastectomy was awful.

Cameron had to rest for about three weeks, and she got antsy and impatient after about the first. I kept her entertained with chick flicks and gossip magazines. One of the worst parts was when she had to get her drainage tubes removed. She said it was horrifying, and it felt like they were pulling snakes out of her body.

The pathology report that came back a week after her surgery showed that the tumor measured 1.8 cm—large enough to warrant chemotherapy but not too large to be alarming. There was one focus of metastatic disease in the sentinel lymph node, but the fourteen additional lymph nodes removed showed no signs of cancer. They also found something small in the right breast, so Cameron was so relieved that she had opted for the double mastectomy. If she hadn't, she would have had to do this all again. She started her six-month regimen of chemotherapy in November and, luckily, she won't need radiation. She goes to the plastic surgeon every week or two to get her expanders pumped up with saline to prepare for the permanent implant reconstruction that will start early this summer.

Cameron has been experiencing all the expected side effects: hair loss, nausea, fatigue, and bloating, and the doctor said that as she continues there will be additional ones, like numbness and tingling in her fingertips and toes. But she's soldiering through, relieved to have the cancer out of her body, and willing to do what she needs to do to make sure it doesn't come back.

At first, Cameron thought she would be unemotional and clinical about losing her hair; that as soon as it started falling out she would go all Commando Cameron on it and just shave her head. But when it actually started happening, it was all just too much. She became tearful and upset; the gravity of all that was happening to her proving more debilitating—as I expected it to be—than empowering—as she expected it to be. She said that when she looked in the mirror, she felt like it made her look "sick." She's slowly becoming accustomed to her wig and scarves, and, I give her credit, really makes the most of it. Or at least pretends to.

The best news is that Cameron and Jack met with an adoption agency, and they're ready to start the process of adopting a baby. They feel energized that they have been given another chance at their lives and are excited to welcome a baby into their family. It might take a while, but they're willing to wait.

My friendship with Cameron has strengthened, too. After being friends for twenty-two years, I didn't think that was possible. But we feel like we've just been through a war together, and we've bonded considerably. She has been so supportive of me, as well, as I took on the freelance writing job with *Wee Well in Westchester* and as I worked things out with Darren. I had some dark days where I worried terribly about Cameron and how she was going to come through this, but I don't worry anymore. Mostly because she's gotten better, but also because I've learned a bit about going through bad times and how worrying about every little thing is a monumental waste of energy. It's impossible to entirely destroy every trace of worrying from my DNA, it's wrapped up in those little strands pretty tightly, but with practice, I'm seeing quite an improvement.

During lunch, a choice between grilled chicken paillard and wild mushroom risotto (I choose the risotto), I ask my guests to go around the table and introduce themselves and how they know me. I know it's a little corny, and I try to be sympathetic to people who don't love public speaking, but there are only twelve of us at the table so I hope it doesn't cause too much anxiety for anyone.

There are lots of laughs and jokes as my friends and family tell funny stories from my past, and everyone gets to know each other. Some of my friends give short speeches about our relationship and why they treasure our friendship. I always find it shocking to hear what other people think of me. It's strange to realize that the persona I think I project to the world is sometimes completely different from what is perceived. It's only through my friends' words that I realize they think I'm fun, ridiculously smart (their words, not mine), a great mom, that I've got great potential as a writer, and that, as Callie says, I've got it all together. And although I'm trying to care much less what people think of me, knowing that this is what *these* people—some of the people I respect most in the world—think of me makes me beam. When everyone has finished speaking, and we all are full and satisfied, I clink my wine glass and stand.

"I want to thank you all so much for coming. It's so important to celebrate the good things in life, so I'm exuberantly happy and thankful that you're all here today for my celebration. We've all been witness recently, some a little closer than others, to what I'll just call deep sadness and seemingly insurmountable obstacles, and it makes it even more important to grab the happy occasions by the horns and ride that bull till you just can't hold on any longer. So that's why I'm having this party.

"I guess it's customary on any milestone birthday to reflect a bit on where you currently are in your life. And I'm actually happy to be turning forty finally. I no longer have little babies, so I'm sleeping through the night. I've developed the self-esteem and requisite wisdom to know what to worry about and what to laugh at; what's worth the tears; what's worth the calories; what's worth the call to the school or doctor; when I should care what other people think and when I should fly my own flag; what's worth saying yes to and what's worth saying, 'Let me think about that'; what I should put one hundred percent effort into and what will be just fine with seventy-five percent; who my true friends are; and why, above all else, I'm so damn lucky. For me, most of that really did take forty years to figure out. Some of those things I figured out a little early, and some of it I'm still working on and will undoubtedly continue to do so.

"As Cameron has been saying to me lately, I've hit my stride, and honestly I'm really, really happy. And there are some people whom I want to acknowledge and thank for essentially being there for me every step of the way, for supporting that journey and enabling that happiness. To my beautiful mom and sister. I'm so unbelievably touched and thrilled that you made the effort and the trip to come here for this. It wouldn't have been the same without you. We've been through a lot together: good times and bad. But we went through them together, and we've come out pretty damn well.

"Eva, you've always been there for me, and I am so thankful for that. You continually crack me up with all your Hollywood stories, you know I love your *Barefoot Contessa* repertoire, and you are my favorite person to go tooling around L.A. with.

"Mom, now that I'm all grown up and have had my own life experiences and my own family, I am so appreciative and aware of the sacrifices you made for Eva, Danielle, and me in the early days. It couldn't have been easy. You have always been there for me as a constant cheerleader, stalwart supporter, proud mommy, available confidante, amazing grandmother, and wise sage. You always implored me to do what makes me happy. Thanks, Mom. I am. And I thank you from the bottom of my heart for that. For helping me grow up.

"And I also want to thank all of you. My friends. My authentic, smart, honest, beautiful, accomplished, motivated, loving, and dear friends. Every single one of you at this table has been there for me at some point or another, for something or another, to cry with or to share good news with or go out with or have drinks with or share the milestones of our lives with. You've all put up with me. There is something about girlfriends. They provide something no mother, no sister, and no husband ever could. I've been so lucky to find each of you, and I thank you all for showing me the meaning of true friendship.

"So thank you for allowing me to indulge myself with this reflection on my life. It's not often we are given the opportunity to do something like this. I just ask for one more moment of indulgence. Over the past six months, I've gone through a lot. And each of those situations has made me stronger, has made me look at life differently, and in turn has made me start to live my life differently. I know life is a journey for all of us. Sometimes, as we all know, the path is straight and unencumbered. Those times are pleasant, easy, predictable, and manageable. But sometimes, the path is filled with twists and turns, impasses, cliffs, and other difficult, and even scary, obstacles. It's during those times that we are tested. That we are required to act with grace. And it's once we leave those obstacles behind that we learn that the next time we confront them, we can get through them.

"I have learned so much in the last six months about myself and about life, and I am so excited to have the opportunity to start living my life differently. I want to tell you all, partly because you are the people closest to me but mostly so that you'll hold me to it, that I am going to be making a few changes in my life. I am going to work toward becoming the healthiest and happiest I can be, I'm not going to complain about things I can change, and I'm not going to get stuck on things I keep getting stuck on. I'm going to make my life extraordinary. From now on, if there's something I don't like, I'm going to change it, even if I have to take baby steps to make that happen. I'm going to manifest for myself the life that I know I deserve, and I hope you will join me and do the same.

"Thank you for helping me celebrate my birthday. Thank you for being there for me. Thank you for helping me lead a happy life. I love you all."

The whole room erupts in smiles and applause, and I feel so happy. Then all of a sudden, everyone starts to sing happy birthday, and I notice them looking toward the doorway behind me. I turn to see my birthday cake, candles blazing on top, being carried in on a shiny silver platter by a handsome, tall guy with dark hair and ridiculously blue eyes.

"Happy birthday, my love," Darren says, as he sets down the birthday cake in front of me.

And as I bask in the warmth of the candles and the love of my husband, my friends, and my family, I close my eyes, smile, and make a wish. On grace.

acknowledgments

I know most authors save the best for last in their acknowledgments, but I want to thank first the four people who not only mean the most to me but who were the most supportive while I wrote and published *On Grace*. To my three smart, excellent, adorable, and adored boys: Jason, Will, and Judson. Thank you for cheering me on when I felt both encouraged and discouraged. And thanks for the cupcake celebrations. I promise there will be more. With extra frosting.

To my wonderful husband of almost two decades, Rick, I'm so sorry that the readers of this book will always look at you funny and wonder if you Darren'd me. To them, I say: He did not. To you I say: Thank you for being my true partner in life. You could not have been more supportive, loving, encouraging, and realistic in this whole process.

Thank you to my dearest friends and first readers: Sharon Cooper, Karen Cousin, Bets Miller, Sally Paridis, Allison Wohl, and Cathy Yaffa. Truer friends do not exist. And to the loads of other friends who were so enthusiastic about the early manuscript and/or encouraged and helped me along the way: Rene Benedetto,

Mark Bezos, Franci Blassberg, Laurie Boockvar, Sarah Davis, Jana Edelbaum, Jordanna Fraiberg, Stacey Gendelman, Julie Gerstenblatt, Shellan Isackson, Jenny Jacquette, Kate Kies, Sandi Kornblum, Penny Kosinski, Alyson Lane, Beth Lipman, Maura Mandell, Jenn Mann, Lou Marinaccio, Allison Mignone, Jessica Mindich, Annabel Monaghan, Elizabeth Moyer, Megan Mulry, Jennifer Ostfield, Melinda Pressler, Eric Rahe, Alison Dickinson Rao, Richard Rosenzweig, Angela Santomero, Melissa Shapiro, David Shorrock, Robynne Smith, Rachel Strum, John Thomas, Tara Turnbull, Nancy Weiser, Suzy Welch, Beatriz Williams, Britney Williams, Emily Wolk, Jackie Wyman, Jillian Rice Zriebec, and Lauren Zucker.

Thank you, Kristin Harmel, the talented and kind bestselling author of numerous fantastic novels, for challenging and improving my writing and supporting my process. You are a true mentor and cheerleader.

Thank you, thank you, thank you, Crystal Patriarche and Heidi Hurst of SparkPress, a BookSparks imprint, for your wonderful enthusiasm, support, encouragement, professional guidance, and, most especially, for seeing something in me and this work. I am so excited to be on this journey with you! Thank you Wayne Elizabeth Parrish for your excellent and thorough editing skills. A huge thanks to the talented Julie Metz for the beautiful cover of Grace. And special thanks to Caitlin Alexander, Andrew Brown, and Kate King for starting me off.

I received a great deal of guidance on breast cancer treatment from both a doctor's and patient's perspective from my friends Dr. Julie Monroe and Melissa Boxer. Thank you both for your wise, thorough, and compassionate input. If there are any medical inconsistencies in Cameron's story, they are all mine.

I have a big and wonderful family who has always lovingly supported me in everything I do. Thank you Nancy and Ira Norris, David and Marsha Orman, Terry Orman Gevisser, Mike and Leslie Norris, Greg and Joanne Norris, Joy and Robert Schnall, Jodi Quintiere, and Lisa Smukler.

Dad, thank you for the writing gene! I appreciate all the time you put into the early editing of *On Grace,* all the love you tirelessly show me, and all the pride I know you have in me.

Mom, you're my #1 fan and the person who has invested more of her time and love in me than anyone else on the planet. Thank you for your constant and unconditional love.

And thank you, readers, for spending your time and money on *On Grace.* I hope I made you smile.

about the author

Susie Orman Schnall was raised in Los Angeles and graduated from the University of Pennsylvania. She lives in New York with her husband and their three boys. To learn more, visit her website, www.susieschnall.com and connect on social media at:

www.facebook.com/SusieOrmanSchnall
www.twitter.com/susieschnall
www.pinterest.com/susieschnall

About SparkPress

SparkPress is an independent boutique publisher delivering high quality, entertaining, and engaging content that enhances readers' lives, with a special focus on female-driven work. We are proud of our catalog of both fiction and non-fiction titles, featuring authors who represent a wide array of genres, as well as our established, industry-wide reputation for innovative, creative, results-driven success in working with authors. SparkPress, a BookSparks imprint, is a division of SparkPoint Studio, LLC.

To learn more, visit us at www.sparkpointstudio.com.